TOMMY BABCOCK

by Rich Whitney Turner

FOR CUI-WEI

June 28, 1940

FLASH

By D. H. Quinn

Philadelphia (UP)–Police today rushed to the Warwick Hotel after gunshots were reported in the hotel rooms of Republican Presidential Nominee Wendell Willkie, who only hours before had been selected to carry the GOP standard.

Unconfirmed reports have an ambulance en route to the scene and a physician in attendance.

Willkie received the nod on the sixth ballot after delegates failed to choose either frontrunner Robert Taft or Thomas E. Dewey on initial ballots.

Chants of "We Want Willkie" thundered through the convention hall until the convention adjourned at 1:30 a.m. with Willkie the victor.

February 1940

𝕷𝖔𝖘 𝕬𝖓𝖌𝖊𝖑𝖊𝖘 𝕿𝖎𝖒𝖊𝖘

ANTI-NAZI GERMAN SLAIN IN SAN JUAN CAPISTRANO

San Juan Capistrano– The body of an anti-Nazi leader, whose courageous stand against the Third Reich had him marked for death was
discovered in an alley one block from the San Juan Capistrano Mission
last night.

Jonas Fischbach, the legendary German democrat who kept one step
ahead of Nazi

September 1939

DAILY MIRROR

NATION PRAYS FOR SILENCED STAR

Hold for art

Washington—As the mysterious woman the press knows only as "The Angel of Mercy" sits by his bedside, the actor who redefined the image of the movie "tough guy" holds his secrets in a coma. She reportedly discovered him lying in the road outside her apartment a week ago.

CHAPTER ONE

November 1938

You may remember me. For an all too brief period, I was on the movie screen in your town. You probably filed me under "boy dancer," or if I was really lucky, "boy singer." But if you've missed seeing me at your theatre, you probably paired me with my sister, Ginny. Everybody else did.

Yes I'm Tommy Babcock. If you're a fan, you know that Ginny and I started out on Broadway in the 20s and arrived like gangbusters in Hollywood in '31. Our first film, *Buenos Aires Rhapsody*, sold a lot of tickets. The critics and the studio agreed we were boffo, so they put our names above the title for *Christmas in the Rockies* and *Dangerous Lady*. Every movie had a bigger box office, so we pushed out three pictures a year and you wanted more. Then came our public appearance tour in England in 1937 and everything fell apart. Well, to be more specific, it fell apart for me. Ginny landed a British guy with a lot of bucks. I got a return ticket to L. A. and a co-starring role with a Saint Bernard.

Okay, save the tears because I saved my money. Except for acquiring a 400-acre ranch in a place called Encino, I made some good financial moves. And I've got enough money coming in every month to keep the ranch afloat and some horses fed. But it isn't the same as being in pictures.

The phone rang as I was mixing myself a Manhattan. It was the overseas operator with Ginny on the other end.

"How's the weather?" she said.

"Better than where you are," I replied, relaxing into my Stickley Morris chair.

"How would you like to come over here for Christmas and help us welcome 1939?" she asked.

"Sure. Leaving a place where the sun always shines, for one where it's a stranger makes a lot of sense," I said.

"You have to come," she said. "Jimmy wants you to help with something important, so it would be really great for all of us if you joined us."

"What is it that's so important?" I asked.

"He won't tell me, but he'll tell you when you get here. He says he can't discuss it on the phone. You've got a first class cabin on the Queen Mary leaving New York Friday. By the way, don't say nice things about him on your way over. He's very serious about this, in fact act as if you're angry I left the act," she said.

"Tell your husband he's whistling up a drainpipe."

"I love you, little brother," she said.

"Me too, your highness, or whatever you're supposed to be called, but that doesn't mean I'm coming" I said.

"What happened at Columbia?" she asked.

"Harry told me I couldn't carry a picture without you. When you were on the screen, he said, nobody noticed me, because everybody looked at you. He said I had something below the surface that put people on edge, and the audience notices it now that you skipped town and made me a single. Harry said he felt it in his butt."

"Harry and his butt," she said, her exasperated tone arriving intact over 6,000 miles. "He was trying to bait you. I made sure you had two years on that contract, with or without me." She was quiet for a moment before asking an all too familiar question. "Did you stay calm and wait for him to lose his head of steam?"

"He told me I would share third billing on the next picture with this wonder dog, which they brought into the room. I like animals, as you know, but this female Saint Bernard really took a shine to me and proceeded to use her entire body to declare her affection. I tried to take it as a compliment, but it took about three minutes for me to establish who the boss was before she'd behave," I said. "I'm never wearing Royall Lyme around a Saint Bernard again."

Ginny was laughing, as she said, "The details of billing were all worked out in the contract. Did you tell him that?

"No. I told him I didn't want to work for an asshole and quit."

"That was really smart," she said sarcastically. Then she said, "Now I feel bad. Diplomacy was never your strong suit."

"You didn't have Saint Bernard slobber all over your pants, Sis. Anyway, you're my sister, not my mother. I'm 36-years-old, with more than enough money to get by. Even without Hollywood, we would always have had enough."

"You're just like Grandpa. He could go from sitting with his hands folded to a right jab faster than any man in New England. The difference is that he owned his own company and didn't have to please anyone."

"I'm enjoying myself now. If you were riding Seabiscuit you couldn't win against my new thoroughbred," I said.

"I'm a lady now. I don't make a lot of noise, or shoot craps 'till dawn, or ride a horse into the ground anymore just to beat my brother," she said.

I didn't say anything and for awhile there was silence on her end of the line. She broke it by saying, "I'll call you tomorrow this time and we will talk about the trip. I really miss you."

"Tell your husband you took a stab at it but I'm not coming." She hung up the phone.

I walked over to the Victrola and put on Bunny Berigan's *I Can't Get Started* and listened to him get those impossible sounds out of his trumpet. Everybody in show business knew the guy was an alcoholic fighting his demons, but he made the trumpet sound like it was blown by the Angel Gabriel. I picked the needle off the record and wondered what to do next.

My life was boring without Ginny. I thought of the time we drove Barrymore's roadster into Bill Field's pool with John passed out in the back seat. Or the time she'd convinced me she'd run away to Mexico with Cary Grant, which led me to Juarez, a bout of Montezuma's revenge and a weekend with Marisol, the Latvian flamenco dancer. Picking up one of the barbells I kept around the house, I did two sets of 12 bicep curls and followed with work on my triceps. Now I was a bored guy with muscles.

I looked around the ranch house that I'd filled with all the Stickley furniture I could get my hands on and decided I needed a new obsession. There were more Frank Lloyd Wright pieces out there to go with these, but I would have to bide my time and wait for them. The guys in Pasadena needed reasons to sell what they had. That mission oak furniture, with its stark lines that harkened back to the 19th century, spoke of a practical America that tied me to my grandfather and kept me centered. My admiration for the simplicity of its lines probably confirmed Harry's butt's assessment of my potential as an actor. At least the entertainment industry wasn't tied to the front of Harry. Then Columbia's movies could only be shown in Tijuana.

Deciding to wake up early to ride my new, slightly crazy, thoroughbred, I started up the stairs to dreamland. Before I hit the landing, though, the phone rang again. It was Jack, a friend who'd produced *Christmas in the Rockies* and four of our other hits.

"Jack, Wie gehts?" I said. My grandmother taught German to Ginny and me before we'd learned how to climb out of a highchair.

"I'll never speak German again," he said, his voice a whisper.

"Your voice sounds bad. Drive down and we'll talk," I said. "Stay over and we'll both get drunk."

"No. I can't go anywhere. I'm waiting to see if the children survived."

"What children are you talking about?"

"My brother is dead. My sister-in-law is dead, and my niece and nephew have disappeared.

"I'm sorry, Jack, I forgot for a minute about your brother and his kids. I've certainly heard enough about them over the years," I said, feeling embarrassed. It was as if I'd just flunked Friendship 101.

"I'm getting in the car and heading over the hill. I'll be there soon," I said.

I walked outside and looked at the clear sky over the San Fernando Valley. There were lights on in Burbank to the East and some lights on Ventura Boulevard, but on this side of the Santa Monica Mountains it was mostly dark. I knew when Sepulveda Boulevard hit Mulholland Drive; I'd look down and see thousands of lights in

Hollywood. Which reminded me I'd better dress up for the other side, so I went back in the house and buttoned up an Arrow Shirt and put on a Hickey Freeman single breasted silk shantung suit, just in case the Cadillac broke down or I ran into a newspaper photographer. Even in an emergency you couldn't look like a bum.

I drove out of Encino, using Sepulveda until I reached Sunset. I took a left and drove east on Sunset until I reached the imposing gates of Bel Air. My La Salle Convertible quickly covered the twisting roads to Jack's home, a 6,000 square foot white house with front pillars that made you thirsty for juleps and had you listening for Negroes singing spirituals.

I parked on the circular driveway and noticed every light was lit on the first floor. I found him in his library with a bottle of Haig and Haig Pinch scotch and a large seltzer bottle. The room was floor to ceiling leather books and boasted a giant globe made with semi-precious stones, marble, and slices from other rocks I couldn't identify. I was sure that Jack had never touched anything in the room except the desk, the leather club chairs and the large RCA radio.

As I expected, he looked angry, probably taking a crying break. He had a five o'clock shadow that had a five o'clock shadow. In the sleeveless undershirt and suspenders he looked more like a gangster than a big time producer. In actuality, was there really any difference?

Jack was the only man I'd trust with a secret. We understood each other; the bonding taking years, evolving over bottles at Hillcrest Country Club, in this study, and in Palm Springs. Sometimes he'd tire of civilization and drive over to Encino where we'd talk into the night. An immigrant Jew, he'd fought his way up in the garment district in New York before coming to Los Angeles, pushing his way into the motion picture business. I was a song and dance man whose relatives tapped their way across the Atlantic on the Mayflower, but we were kindred spirits. He kept saying that underneath we were the same. I took that as a compliment. I pictured the first Thanksgiving; "Hey Squanto, leave some Gefilte Fish for the rest of us."

This was a time when it was best to be quiet, so I just sat there, maybe for half an hour. I had walked into a funeral and one of the family members was waiting to speak.

"I couldn't get a visa for them," Jack said. "I tried everything, but a sign seems to be hanging in the State Department that says 'No More Jews.'

"You know he was the one person I really, truly loved. My nephew and niece were going to get everything I had. Those four people were my family. I never think about my ex-wives, but every night before I went to bed, I thought about Robert and his family moving into this goddamned mansion with me.

"Robert always was a fighter. He ran the family jewelry store in Frankfurt, right off the Zeil, and he was unafraid. Robert never took shit. If the shagetz yelled 'Juden raus,' he'd give those low classes Arschloch a look that would turn them to stone. So, the Nazis had this big party called 'Kristalnacht.' All over Germany the people took to the streets looking for Jewish shops to destroy.

My brother tried to stop the schwein from getting into the store. The leader shot him and the rest fired round after round through the plate glass windows until the glass fell on the sidewalk, leaving everyone, including my sister-in-law, Judith, dead. None of my cousins can find Karl and Liesel," he said. "They've vanished.

"The Nazis take Jews and others they don't like to camps called Konzentrationslager, with high barbed wire fences and watchtowers. When people go into a KZ, they're en route to death," he said. "I thought I knew about all the terrible things in the world, but I was wrong. This time the pogrom is too well organized to be stopped, and it will destroy Europe. Jews have always been in danger, but Hitler has pigs whose full-time job involves finding new ways to kill my people.

"If those two kids are dead, the Nazis are going to pay," he said, snapping his suspenders and lighting a Cuban cigar. If Hitler had come into the room at the same time I did, he'd already have been beaten to death.

Jack was fifty, but looked forty, with a rugged look women seemed to go for, even women who didn't want to be in pictures. A major actress called his appeal animal magnetism, and told me she'd been in love with him while he was between wives, I forget which ones.

"Do you have any idea where they might have been taken?" I said.

"Their friend who contacted me mentioned Dachau, near Munich," he said. "They've been taking Jews there since '33. Of course, the Nazis don't come over to the Jews and say, 'Excuse me, we're taking these kids to Dachau.'"

My presence here was more important than any questions, so I gave up on conversation. I took a Cuban cigar from the inlaid wood box that always sat on the edge of the desk, lit it, and poured myself some Pinch straight up. I looked up as tears started to roll down Jack's face and I put my hand on his shoulder. Jack was not a guy you hugged.

It went that way for the first couple of hours. One hour he was ready to kill and the other he cried, not exactly weepy, but you could see the tears drop silently from his eyes.

When the sad part of the cycle seemed to stop, I told Jack I'd been invited to England.

"Why the fuck would you go to that terrible climate in the middle of winter? See Ginny in the summer, after your next picture," he said.

"I'm not going. But it doesn't matter, because there won't be a next picture. You probably knew Columbia was going to release me before they told me," I said.

"I'm not talking about another silly tap and sing picture. I'm talking about something else," he said.

"What else can I do?" I said.

"You can show the real Tommy Babcock, the Tommy Babcock that belted the guy who called me a kike last February in *Musso and Frank's,*" he said.

"That cost money. It's hard to believe that one guy falling over could cause so much damage to a bar," I said.

"In pictures you can show what I see when you take off the Broadway smile and let me know how angry you are," he said.

"Spencer Tracy did Dr. Jekyll and Mr. Hyde," I said.

"Let people see how you really feel," he said, before his attention returned to the kids.

"There has to be a way to get those children here," he said.

"I believe you have the ability to get about anything done," I said. "However, Americans are mostly Christian and don't want any more Jews coming to *their* country. The government's not going to openly help you because they are in enough trouble already for being pro-English. Maybe the congressmen that you and the other esteemed Yids have purchased will step up to the plate or maybe we'll have to find something we can trade for them."

"Put on your thinking cap. You're the one with the photographic memory who'd rather read books than sleep," he said.

"I'd actually rather sleep than read books, but I can't seem to hit the road to dreamland with any regularity. I don't think anybody Jimmy knows in England could get the kids out, but when I talk to Ginny on the phone I'll have her ask him. I'll also call Wendell Willkie?"

"Why would you call Willkie?" Jack asked.

"Because he's a man of his word and a lot of powerful people ad-mire him. If anybody has the clout to do this, he does," I said.

"You can try anything you think of. You know you're my best friend," Jack said, trying to keep his emotions in check.

"In this town everyone wants to be your friend," I said.

"Yeah, but you're the only one who'd take me in if I lost it all," he said

We talked until four. While I closed my eyes and let my mind drift, Jack fell asleep. I decided to let him be. A nap in a chair was better than not sleeping at all. I went upstairs to one of the bed-rooms, hoping the sheep were ready for a census.

I had the feeling I was awake, yet trapped in a nightmare. There I was in a little town in Bavaria, where the sun was shining, and the Volk were dancing in the town square. All of a sudden, the sky turned dark, and the dancers turned into Dracula and other movie characters played by Lon Chaney Jr. Men with rifles shouted "Juden, Juden," and pointed their guns at me. "I'm not a Jew," I shouted. "When did I become a Jew?" I decided to run for my life. Before they pulled the triggers, I awoke, with the California sun streaming in through the bedroom window. The pajamas I'd found in one of the guest rooms were wet with sweat as if I had a fever. I walked out by the pool and sat on a chaise lounge until the fear left my body. I couldn't sit there forever, so I decided to drive back to Encino, call Ginny, and pack for a winter cruise across the North Atlantic.

CHAPTER TWO

The next morning I put my trunk in the back of the wood paneled ranch wagon and headed for the train station. As Francisco, my taciturn ranch manager, drove out toward the highway, I took a mental picture of the Washington navel orange trees that stretched for acres and that, thank God, paid the property tax. The days were fine, but not as fine as they would be in spring when the trees bloomed and the San Fernando Valley swam in their scent.

We headed up through Cahuenga Pass, while I counted the number of Camels left in the pack. I made a note to pick up a couple of cartons in the station and a lot of cartons in New York for the rest of the trip. Europeans smoked shitty cigarettes.

If Francisco hadn't been such a good manager, I would have fired him a long time ago. He never offered information. You had to ask specific questions that were narrowly focused. He was honest; I was sure of that, but I had to read up on citrus cultivation, grafting and irrigation to know what to even ask about. I made friends with other farmers to understand prevailing wage rates in late depression California. If I hadn't grown up on horseback and around livestock, the entire ranch experience would've driven me nuts.

Francisco didn't treat me like a star when I was with a studio, so I figured he wasn't about to start now. His replies came in grunts, or occasionally in Spanish, although he knew that I knew he'd graduated from L. A. High and had a hell of a lot less accent than Caesar Romero. Knowing I was acting like a sap, I still told Francisco about the call from Ginny and about Jack's situation. He didn't say anything, so I lit a cigar, let smoke waft in his direction and hoped he felt the Dutch Masters had farted in his face.

I attached a black moustache to my upper lip as we traveled the last few miles to the old SP train station. The *Times* said that in a few months all the passenger trains in LA. would be arriving at and departing from the Union Station we'd been promised for over a decade.

Pulling up to the side of the station, Francisco carried the steamer trunk while I pulled a Borsalino down over my forehead and headed to an entrance favored by celebrities to avoid crowds and the press. Pretty soon, I figured, I wouldn't have any fans left to avoid.

CHAPTER THREE

The train got into New York early Friday morning, so after buying smokes, toothpaste and a lot of books, I headed up the gangplank and into Cunard's flagship. After a shower, I poured myself a shot of Glenlivet, and read the newspaper as the single malt loosened my traveling muscles. The Herald-Tribune was decidedly negative about the situation in Europe. To the editors, Hitler astride the continent had all the appeal of a buzzard circling carrion. It seemed I could not be going across the pond at a worse time.

I brought only one trunk, since I knew my sister and she knew my measurements. Tailors on Savile Row were working right now to greet my arrival with clothes right for an English winter. The duds I packed would see me across the Atlantic. Of course I always traveled with dinner clothes, which my fans consider my uniform. The thought of dancing reminded me of my exercises. A dancer had to stay fit, even if he didn't have an upcoming engagement. Staying in shape was as important as brushing my teeth or shaving, so I began with stretches and followed with 100 pushups. I attached a rod across the bathroom doorway and chinned myself 20 times, followed by a lot of abdominal lifts.

A knock on the door preceded a uniformed kid bearing a note on a tray. Tipping the boy, I picked up an envelope that said "John Alan Merryvale." The card invited me to a party in his rooms. It didn't take much thinking to make me go and drink some of his family's scotch for free, so I showered, put some Pinaud on my hair and splashed on some 4711, before slipping into a Brooks Brothers Polo Collar shirt and one of their repp ties. I put on a cashmere blazer with grey flannel slacks that had just the right break at the shoe and decided the effect was all right. My tailor had warned me I should never wear a Polo collar at night but I figured nothing was worse than mating with a St. Bernard.

Merryvale's cabin, as you might have guessed, was the finest on board. There was caviar, foie gras and ice sculptures in the shape of swans. Amongst the Dom Perignon and Pouilly Fuisse stood proud bottles of Glen Alan 18, which along with the other booze his father owned and imported, acknowledged the source of Merryvale's dough.

"Tommy, you bright eyed bon vivant, now the party can begin," he said, louder than was necessary. He always insisted on kissing me on the cheek, which I didn't like, but for some reason tolerated. I thought I spied mascara on his lashes. His breath smelled like a combination of peppermint and....

I stepped back and said, "What's the news from Cole these days?"

"Coley is Coley, ever the same. He's asked many times if I've seen you."

"Cole used to pretend I could sing, I miss having someone around like that," I said.

There was no way I would ever refer to Cole Porter as "Coley," noticing that only men with that tunesmith's other interest found it stylish.

"Oh, come on. I know that a lot of people think you sing divinely." John, without asking, filled up a large highball glass with Glen Alan 18.

"I had thought about drinking, not being embalmed," I said, not refusing the glass. "I hear you have a rare 21, but I haven't been able to find it in L.A."

"I'll send a bottle to your cabin," he said. "Now meet the other guests."

I was introduced to people with titles, people with money, and two young chorus boys who had something else that interested John.

"Ausgezeichnet, Sehr erfreut," said a ramrod straight, middle aged man with silver hair whom I recognized as Johan Von Taunus. I replied in German, shaking his hand.

"I saw the play 'Universe,'" I said. "It was in English, but I was very impressed."

"You are too kind. It took me two years to put an American production together. I am gratified that someone thought it was worth the effort," he responded. "The translation seemed to be well received in New York."

Von Taunus created plays where actors were forced to search deep within themselves. The plays dealt with complicated subjects that touched on the universality of the human condition. Each play was a parable that moved beyond the physical location (Paris, Berlin, etc.) to a place all of us might end up, especially if we were plagued with guilt or felt a failure. I'm not the only one who thought he was a genius.

"Are you heading home?" I asked.

"Yes, I miss Germany. It is time I returned," he said.

"Even with all that is going on?" I said

"Ah, yes. Germany is still Germany to me. Besides, the press has distorted what is happening. Except for the racial laws I do not approve of, everything is fine in the Fatherland. If you feel like a trip, after England, please come and stay in Kronberg with me."

"I appreciate the invitation. The sooner I put a visit with my brother-in-law behind me, the better. If I'm able to get off that island, I'll contact you."

"How do your countrymen feel about the situation in Europe?" he asked.

"Most everyone just wants to stay out of it," I said. "Everyone feels we made a mistake marching over there the last time. Dying for the English or the French isn't something that appeals to anyone.

Von Taunus handed me his calling card and said, "It would be a great honor to have someone of your stature visit me."

If the folks in England wouldn't think I was a washed up song and dance man, I supposed that in Germany they would think me an actor of Olympian proportions. "If there is any way I can fit it in, I would be delighted," I said.

During the next few days, I saw a lot of Johannes von Taunus. I complained a lot to him about how Jimmy had taken Ginny out of the act and how angry I was. I expressed distaste for the British as a people, made much of my German heritage and promised to give his invitation to visit a chance to percolate in my brain. Von Taunus continued to express his distaste with Hitler's racial policies.

Merryvale provided a constant party with more and more people dropping by every day. I assumed he had another cabin, because he and the boys would disappear for awhile, but the party kept going. It actually was a fun voyage, unless you went out on deck. Some days, I even found the cold North Atlantic bracing, although it helped me appreciate Encino. During the trip, I pledged to myself I'd never live north of Santa Barbara County.

When we disembarked we were fast friends and I promised to call Von Taunus as soon as I could. We said goodbye as I spotted Ginny's Chauffeur, standing like a member of the Coldstream Guards, holding a sign that said "Tommy."

CHAPTER FOUR

After a few hours and some watercress sandwiches, supplemented with good cheeses and a bottle of Château Lafitte Rothschild, Ginny's Chauffeur had the Bentley close to home. Breakcliffe sat astride a ridge overlooking a valley cut over time by a river running towards the Irish Sea. The first time I saw the estate, I realized why some of my friends in Hollywood were driven from England by the class system. (Most of them were born in slums and learned their upper class accents in the theatre) The fact that one person owned something so beautiful wasn't the problem. Men in Montana had such views and a lot more land. However, the residents of that postcard town in that valley had to fawn over someone who had inherited that land from his father, who had inherited it.....But Jimmy was married to my sister, so I kept my democratic thoughts at bay.

The grounds of the Los Angeles Country Club, which barred me from membership because I was an actor, would have taken up one 100th of the acreage surrounding Jimmy's country home. Their main building would have been the gatekeeper's cottage. I made a note to remind the members the next time our elbows touched at a horse show. (At those times, I always used my "Squire Babcock" act, made up of 1/3 New England money and 2/3 Hollywood improvisation. I had the outlines of it put in my publicity material.) It would impress them because they all liked duck decoys and putting on winter tweeds when the temperature dropped to 65, as if they'd just returned from shooting grouse on their own estates.

My reception was all I had hoped for and I was glad to see my relationship with Jimmy remained the same despite the distance of time and geography. I gave him my word that I had cursed him across the North Atlantic and would continue to do so. That seemed to make him very happy. My sister smothered me with affection. Within the house I found all the warmth I'd been looking for under the California sun.

Ginny never weighs more than 115, so her five foot, seven inch frame is easy to lift and she knows how to hold herself to make it less challenging for me. What the camera can't capture, especially in black and white, is her skin with its look of porcelain suffused with pink highlights. Her hair is black, so the stark contrast draws more attention to her beauty. It's said that Carole Lombard once smacked Gable for looking at her too intently, for too long. Unfortunately, even our last picture was in black and white, although the next one was to be in color. So our fans never got to see what I'm looking at right now.

There is a famous scene in "Tahoe Tap Dance" that has her looking up at Gilbert Garcia after her head had been down on a table. Her eyes were large as saucers, so when the camera captured tears in those spectacular orbs, it's said that audiences gasped at her beauty. She looks like a cross between Vivian Leigh (who I'd met with Larry Olivier) and Madeleine Carroll. Her face has a radiance the camera could never fully encompass. Her neck reminded some critics of a swan, while Jimmy Stewart once said he'd swim the Atlantic for the opportunity to dance with her. When you view our films, think about how much you're missing. I stood there and marveled at her, before speaking.

"Hello, Toots. I brought all the recent Goodman, Crosby and Artie Shaw's...."

"It's good for us to be together again," she said, stopping me in mid sentence and holding me close.

Jimmy begged off because he had to meet with the estate manager in the farm office. We walked into a sitting room and after she closed the door, she held onto my left arm as she put her head against my shoulder. "You probably don't think I miss you very much, but I do. Jimmy is wonderful, but the world doesn't seem right when I can't see you every day."

I looked to see tears running down her cheek. I pulled a handkerchief out of my coat pocket and blotted her tears. "It's worse when you don't have anyone," I said. "I'd go out on dates with actresses and wannabe actresses and feel empty. I'd leave the ranch and find that none of the items I should have brought were with me."

"You haven't done anything crazy I need to worry about, besides what happened with Harry, have you?" she said.

"Don't worry, Mammy, "I said, getting down on one knee like Jolson in a minstrel show. "As you get on in years, mammy, I know you can't handle too much drama." I began to sing, "My old Mammy is looking like my Grammy since she left Alabammy for Old England. Her hands are cold and clammy since she left Alabammy for Old England."

"Stop it. That was really bad," she said, laughing. "I want the complete truth. Isn't there any girl you like?"

"There is a girl I can't stop thinking about, but you won't like the story," I said.

"Why don't you tell me about her and let me decide," she said.

"We met on *Hello Hong Kong, Hello,* a film I made after you skipped town that surprisingly ended up in the black. When I saw her, I knew Feng Feng met every standard of beauty I had."

"Her name is Feng Feng? Does she call you Dumb Dumb?"

"Ginny, I think I'm sorry I told you anything," I said, really angry. "That's enough," I said, desperate to change the subject. "I don't like talking about it anyway."

"Okay," she said, looking chastened.

"The orange crop this year will pay the taxes and I saved most of the money they'd been paying me for the last couple of years.

If you're a star, you don't have to pay for very much if you're will-ing to listen and sign autographs. I even get citrus plants at half price."

"You were always good with money," she said. "Over the last eight years I let you invest for me and I can't believe how much there is."

"You don't ever need to be worried that you're stuck here in Dog-patch if something happens, although you look pretty happy with the cooking," I said, patting her belly.

"Up until a few weeks ago I was at my dancing weight. Then a lot happened," she said. "I'll tell you about it later."

"How does everyone feel about the situation across the channel?"

"No one wants to think about it. They believe Chamberlain will get us through this. It's very frustrating and worrisome. Would you consider living here for awhile?" she said.

"Sure. We could pretend Revere never rode and Betsy never stitched a flag. You've got someone to take care of you and I need to figure out what to do next. Dad called and said he was going to sell the department store and asked if that was okay. We both knew I couldn't sit still long enough to run a store." I started to laugh and said, "Jimmy Stewart told me a couple of months ago that his fa-ther was still holding on to the hardware store back home so Jimmy would have something to do after acting finished. We had a laugh over it, but nobody's parents think acting is a real job. Dad said we were going to end up with a lot of cash after the sale. I told him the percentage you and I have been earning on our savings. He wants me to work with his banker in New York when I return."

"You would live in New York?"

"God, no. I would just take the train back there every quarter to talk about what to do with the money. Dad said half will be in their name and we'll each receive a quarter of the proceeds. When I told him you and I had plenty of money, then he really wanted to give it to us. He probably never expected us to actually save the money we made in Hollywood."

"I love them and miss them, but you and I have been our family for a very long time. It's you I need around me." She started crying again, this time with more tears per minute, if that's a measure, like acre feet of irrigation water.

"I never thought you'd get in this kind of shape. It always seemed it would be me who wouldn't take the separation well. Of course, I never would have cried," I said. "Jimmy doesn't know you feel this way, does he?"

"No," she said.

"Don't ever let him know you feel like this," I said. "No guy would ever understand. It's kind of like a kick in the teeth."

"Listen, you big lug, you had Jack for a friend, but you can't trust women in Hollywood, so I always counted on you as my rock. You just never realized it," she said, holding more tightly onto my arm.

"In England brothers and sisters can be very close, so I don't think Jimmy would get as upset as you seem to think he would."

"Don't bet on it."

"If you can get your arms around my waist, give me a big hug," she said. When I held her I suddenly realized why she was acting so strangely. Ginny had always watched her weight, no matter what. It was almost a religion for her. She was going to be a mother in somebody else's country.

CHAPTER FIVE

After dinner, Ginny said she felt tired, so Jimmy and I adjourned to the library for some postprandial libation, or as they say where I come from, more drinks.

"A lot of people here think Winston is just an old man who still has outrageous ambitions," Jimmy said of Churchill. "Some of that rings true; he can be a pompous egomaniac, but he understands what's going on in Germany better than anyone else. I'm one of the fellows who think he's absolutely right. There is an evil man in Berlin who won't stop until he has control of every nation in Europe. Hitler will have to invade us to make sure he gets to keep those countries, so we're up against it," he said,

I always wondered why the Brits never thought they were part of "Europe," but I decided this was not the time to ask. "Are you sure it's gonna come to that," I asked.

"As sure as I know that our child will be a credit to both the Babcocks and my family," he said.

"I'm gonna be an uncle?" I said. Sure, I already knew, but happiness was warming every part of me. I hadn't done anything to keep the Babcocks an ongoing entity, but Ginny had stepped up to the plate and hit a homer.

"Ginny said I could tell you. We just found out last week," Jimmy said. "We're keeping it quiet until it's been two more months."

"Thought of some names?"

"Winston Thomas, if it's a boy, and Emma, if it's a girl," Jimmy said.

"Well I guess you do believe in him." I responded.

"Let me tell you more about an idea I have and then, after the New Year, we might drive down to Chartwell."

"Okay," I said, more bewildered than enlightened. *The World Crisis* was one of the best books I've read."

"Another? "Jimmy asked, reaching for the decanter.

"They say you must drink a bottle of port in the same evening you open it, so I'm willing to do my part," I said, waiting for more information about Jimmy's "idea."

"What I wanted to talk to you about involves some dissembling on your part and the collection of information," he said.

"About what and where?'"

"We'd like to have you travel to Germany and tell us what you hear," Jimmy said.

"Why me?"

"Because you speak German and look like their Aryan ideal. Your movies were even more popular there than in the USA. Those movies were so nonpolitical they were never censored, so you were on the screens there longer than most American actors. You and Ginny still have a large following in Germany, and Germans believe that many Americans feel like they do. Remember, there are more Americans with German blood than from any other foreign country."

"You want me to join the Bund? That isn't even in the realm of possibility," I said.

"No, the German-American Bund is made up of lower class Americans your countrymen call 'crackpots.' You don't have to do anything so odious, just travel to Germany, look open to all sorts of ideas and find out what you can. Those of us who believe Churchill is right will fund a first class lifestyle for you on the continent. It will be your greatest role," he said.

"I may seem impulsive to you, but that doesn't mean I'm gonna do everything I'm asked. I bet Ginny doesn't know what you've got planned."

"And you can't tell her," he said.

"That's what I figured. If she knew, she'd leave you. You may think I'm kidding, but I'm not. If something happened to me, she'd never forgive you, so take that into consideration before you send me on a mission."

That comment seemed to make him uncomfortable. "Well, we still have more Port, so tell me some stories about Hollywood. Even the landed nobility like gossip," he said, lighting another Cuban cigar.

CHAPTER SIX

All the new information I'd taken in since I arrived left me nervous about navigating the rocks and shoals of Ginny's marriage and dealing with Jimmy's plans. The train and the ship left me with a need to move about, so the next day I jumped into Ginny's MG and drove to Ambleside. This area of Cumberland was cold and bleak in the winter, but Lake Windermere had an attraction in any season. As I drove roads leading towards the coast, I thought about dinner last night and tried to clear my head of the Port, while absorbing Jimmy's offer. It was an offer that hit me like bathtub gin in a Chicago speakeasy. I knew it might be the right thing to do. It also might, for a while, turn off that ceaseless inner motor. There often was a runaway railroad train inside that threatened to tear me apart if I couldn't keep moving. Sometimes all the pushups or miles I'd run couldn't stop it and I wouldn't know what to do next. Explorers are oftentimes described as heroes, but I believed men went in search of new lands because they couldn't handle staying where they were. The men who remained in St. Louis were probably more comfortable in their own skins than Lewis, Clark, and the others who'd followed the Missouri to its source or crossed the Sierras in November. Meriwether Lewis was so haunted by those demons he stabbed himself to death.

The chill in the air was lessened by the first brandy that slid down my throat at "The Solitary Reaper" pub in Ambleside. The tavern was on the smallish size, with an attached dining room with seven tables. I leaned up against the bar and smiled at the powerfully built man next to me, who seemed to be in his late forties.

The brown haired man raised his almost empty glass, which prompted me to order him another pint of Theakston's. This way I could enjoy watching the publican pump and pump in such a labor intensive display of true service. In America no one would go to such an effort to pull some watery post Volstead suds out of a barrel.

"Thank you for the bitter," he said, his face breaking out into a wide smile. "Haven't we met before?" he asked.

"No, I've only been here once before, and that was in June two years ago," I said.

"Well, I think you look familiar, all the same."

"That's good. It makes me feel less like a visitor," I said, having dealt with this more times than I can remember.

"You sound like you're from America? Americans are all right with me. I'd still be in the trenches in France if you boys hadn't come along," he said.

"I was just heading for the boat when they ended it," I said.

"You got lucky, thank God," he said, a sad look crossing his formerly happy face. "In my village, I was one of the few who came

"It clearly is like some kind of illness and it moves through the males of our family like a poisonous river," she said.

"By the way, most people in your countries, however many of those there might be today, don't want to go to war," I said, recounting my conversation at the Ambleside pub

"Winston doesn't seem to understand how strongly people feel about that. What do they think in America?"

"Anyone who came out and said we had to save England and France again would be signing his own political death warrant," I said.

Ginny looked over and focused those blue eyes on me, the eyes American men had been captivated by, once their eyes left her legs."

"I know what's going on and I don't like it." She always tried this approach, which let me know she didn't know very much about what Jimmy and I had been talking about.

When someone's used this trick on you since you were four, you eventually catch on. I wonder if Jimmy had figured it out yet.

"He's so infatuated with Churchill that he's losing his perspective," she said. "I think Winston is right, but he comes off as the ultimate egoist and, for a lot of reasons, people don't trust him. They say they don't know whether one day he'll be on one side or, suddenly move to the other. He's become a pariah and Jimmy's like the people who follow Amy Semple McPherson."

"I guess you don't like Churchill much," I said.

"Oh no, that's not the case at all. I love being in his company, because he's smart and funny and quite overpowering. If you could imagine a charming, witty, intelligent, Louis B. Mayer, than you'd understand what he's like," she said.

"Wow," I said. "The next description will be of a smart, forward looking, flexible and funny Herbert Hoover, or a quiet, sweet, unassuming Huey Long. Who writes your dialogue these days, your eminence?"

"If Jimmy gets you involved with Churchill and his schemes, his baby will be born in California," she said.

"You can't get kippers in California," I said.

"All the more reasons to go," she said, looking as noble as she did in the *Dancing Duchess.*

"I'm not telling you anything," I said, reaching for the beer a servant had brought in.

"Winston is a terrible name for a boy," I said. "Can you talk him out of it?"

"I had to fight to name the girl Emma."

"You've turned into a patsy," I said, looking disgusted.

"You never won with me and he won't either. If you don't do something stupid, I'm going to call him Thomas," she said a triumphant look on her face.

"I forgot to tell you the *Mirror* conducted a poll to pick out the most popular number from all our films."

"You don't even need to tell me which song won. It was the hokiest number we ever performed, the song I never get asked about in England," Ginny said.

"But it's the song everybody mentions in the good old USA," I responded. "In fact, some people say it helps get them through the depression and stops them from worrying about what's going on in Europe."

"It's not doing much for me," she said.

"Remember how it went. I was the famous producer walking down the main street in that little Vermont village…"

"No," she said, "any song but that one."

"I remember that you were pruning that rose trellis and fell on top of me."

"I didn't fall on you."

"I asked your name."

"My name's Hope."

"Of course, (I began to sing) there's always Hope in America, in a land that's ever free."

(Her voice was better than ever.) "And there's Strength in America. I'll help you and you'll help me."

"From Plymouth Rock to Bunker Hill we forged a bond that's strong.

"In 'Frisco and Chicago we became a mighty throng.

"From Miss Liberty to the Golden Gate the light came shining through.

"We're Americans together, and it all began with you."

"Yes, there's Hope in America."

The kitchen help and the gardeners were clapping as we took our bows. The look on Ginny's face told me she missed the sound of two hands clapping much more than I'd figured. I knew then that the *Adorable Aristocrat* had only a few more months to run and even the star hadn't realized she was going to close the show.

CHAPTER EIGHT

Jack always got up early so I had the operator place a call to him at 11 p m. British time. He was just about to leave for the studio.

"How are you holding up," I said, pouring myself a glass of The Macallan to go with my Stilton cheese and biscuits.

"I've been better. I've run out of leads. The children have disappeared inside Dachau and no one knows anything about what goes on in there." His voice was strong but had a edgy quality to it that I wasn't used to hearing.

"I may be taking a trip to Germany," I said. "Would you like any Cuckoo Clocks? How about a Nazi Bride? You haven't had one of those yet."

"If you remember, kill Hitler for me while you're there. You can disembowel Goebbels while you're at it."

"You're dating the diction coach with the big ones again, aren't you? Whenever you use a new word I can tell you're with her again. How come you never married her?"

"I didn't, because she never made me marry her. She's too nice a person to force me into it and she doesn't realize that's the only reason men get married. So once in a while, I buy her a car. I even bought her a house once. She's always surprised and grateful. I suppose I should have married her."

"She's the only one I ever liked," I said, "and you gave her the bum's rush."

"I didn't trust anyone that nice. Freud, or one of those other crackpots from Vienna, said we're looking for our mothers and my mother was used by the Rabbi to show how people ended up when they didn't go to services. I tried to run away from home when I was three months old," he said, trying to get out of this discussion, probably because he was keeping a justice of the peace waiting somewhere. "I'm counting on you with Hitler."

"You only needed to ask. Remember, I'm descended from the people who survived those first winters in Plymouth Plantation. And because it's your request, I can guarantee that after so many years on top my people have learned how to dress while we're making the hit. You've hired a stylish assassin."

"I can't wait to read about how you took out Himmler with your backhand," Jack said, hanging up.

CHAPTER NINE

On the third of January, we took the train to the London residence, a magnificent Gothic structure Jimmy said proclaimed the strength and longevity of the line my niece or nephew would join. A few of the servants were driving down that day, bringing the rest of my clothes with them. We had duck for dinner, brandy after dinner and then, as the British say, toddled off to bed.

The next morning we had a big English breakfast, with kippers (which I refused to eat), potatoes, eggs, exotic fruit (the presence of which always surprised me) and a selection of sausages that normally would require an exceptionally long exercise session.

Jimmy said it was time to go, so we said goodbye to Ginny and went out and climbed into the back of the Daimler to head for Chartwell.

As we "motored" out of London to Kent, Jimmy said," Chartwell is so beautiful, but you won't be able to appreciate it as you would in the summer. Winston has put in many ponds and fountains and built the walls himself, with the help of a man named Harry Whitbread. He tells Winston what the workingman thinks as they put brick on top of brick. It's a truly lovely place that Winston pays for with books like 'The World Crisis.'"

"I guess you think I'll like him?" I said.

"There's a fine young man, Edward Heath, who is head of the Oxford Union, a group that wants us to face facts about Hitler. He recently was going down to ask Winston to speak to their group, so I told him the secret of dealing with Winston.

"He'll try to bully you, but if you don't let him, he'll respect you and change his tone,'" Jimmy said. "Because I've never seen you shy away from an opinion, or obsequiously kowtow to anyone, I don't think that will be a problem."

"In the photographs I've seen, he always looks so solid and confident," I said.

"That's how he looks, but sometimes that exterior hides something quite different, a kind of vulnerability that only a few people ever see. Since his speech on October fifth attacking Chamberlain and assailing Munich and all the other betrayals, many people he thought were his friends now ignore him. Women cross the road to avoid Clemmie, his wife, which makes him feel even worse. You won't see this, of course, but, believe me, it is there."

"I talked to a man the other day that will never get over the Somme. You'll never get him on board your train," I said.

"When we prepare for an invasion, he'll join up. The trenches were horrible, but no Englishman wants his offspring speaking German."

"You're very sure it will come to that?" I said.

"Most people underestimate Hitler, Winston never did. He's seen trouble coming since 1932," Jimmy said, frowning. "You know he believes we're going to need the Yanks again."

"Right at this moment you could raise a battalion of Jews from Brooklyn, but nobody else wants to go 'over there' ever again," I said "We want to get involved even less than my friend from Ambleside."

"You have all those great oceans around you," he said, with the greatest delicacy. "I hope very much that you'll never have to worry about California the way I'm concerned about Cumberland."

We sat back and rode in a most unusual silence the rest of the way until we reached Chartwell.

We looked at the impressive brick exterior; while Jimmy told us part of the building was constructed in 1086, twenty years after the Battle of Hastings. Other sections of the large country home dated from later centuries. The gardens and heated pool postdated Churchill's acquisition of it in the '20s.

So now I was going to meet a hero of the Boer War, who served as Lord of the Admiralty in The Great War, a post from which he ordered the sacrifice of so many men in the Dardanelle's. In truth,

I looked forward to meeting the author and speaker who frequently was boffo on his trip's to my (and his mother's) country. I've heard he was a performer who knew how to hold a crowd.

We were ushered into his study, where his broad smile welcomed us. He had a brandy in his hand. At his urging we sat and a servant placed half full snifters on the side tables. I wanted to say I hadn't had brandy in the morning since the last time I saw John Barrymore, but thought better of it.

"I do not frequent the cinema, but someone kindly brought down some equipment so I could see *Buenos Aires Rhapsody*, where I discovered Ginny was almost as lovely as she is today. I also noted that you seemed quite comfortable dancing down the Argentine," he said, smiling again.

"Thanks for taking the time to see it," I said, both surprised and worried that I was worth this attention.

"Jimmy is very complimentary and loquacious about you and your character, so I thought it was worthy of further study," he said. His skin was almost pink, and he filled his three-piece suit more than completely, which made him look like a baby in a business suit. At the same time he had the charisma that spells "big box office." In his world, he could carry a picture.

I smiled as he lit up a cigar.

"England and the rest of the free world are about to confront a force of Evil without parallel in Western History," he said. "I told

Parliament in October that we faced a great reckoning that was only beginning. I told them what happened in Munich was only the first sip, the first foretaste of a bitter cup which will be proffered to us year by year, unless by a supreme recovery of our moral health and martial vigor, we arise again and take our stand for freedom as in the olden time". Jimmy had told me Churchill used the same words in private conversation he used in public, but I was not prepared for the power of the words he had delivered to Parliament and once again used here.

"They did not listen and they've made pariahs of those who would urge them to stand up before they awake in the chains of tyranny. I am a voice crying in the wilderness, but soon they will see across Central Europe the mark of the beast," he continued. "I have sources who say we are close to that moment of truth, but my countrymen and their befuddled leaders look for any means of appeasement, refusing to understand the consequences of that supplication."

"We will be having lunch and some champagne shortly," he said. "Why don't you tell us what concerns the American people?"

"America, as you know, is very diverse. I'm afraid I can only tell you what they're saying in Hollywood and among orange growers. I can only guess at what they might be thinking in Alabama or Missouri, The one person everyone talks about is Roosevelt and people either love or hate him, there's no in-between."

"I knew him when he was Secretary of the Navy and I was First Lord and I think he's a determined, insightful chap." He took another draw on his cigar and said, "I am very fond of my orchard here at Chartwell, so tell me of these men who produce oranges in desert soil. Do you grow 'Clementine's?' I would love to tell my wife that you do."

"I don't, but I promise I will put some in. As to the conversations, everyone wonders if we're really out of the depression yet. They worry that they can't get what they want for their citrus. Republicans, who believe everything they read in the Los Angeles Times, own the larger orchards and have enough cash to continue. The Democrats, who own the smaller orchards, listen to the president on the radio, or on a friend's radio, and hope things will get better, so their kids can eat more than navel oranges for lunch the next day."

"Two great countries, one of which cannot survive without the support of its cousin, approaching Armageddon with its people's eyes shuttered in the false hope The Four Horsemen will bypass them and enslave other nations, whose statesmen also cling to that chimera," Winston said. "Now Sir, if you will, please tell me what your view is of this gathering storm."

"Without radio, Hitler would be nothing. The newsreels show a crazed German monster telling us he will eat us whole. He looks ridiculous, but like our Father Coughlin and Huey Long, radio is his tool. What sounds to me like a hyena in heat, probably sounds like the Messiah to the German people," I said. "I speak German and he frightens me as I sit in a movie theatre on Wilshire Boulevard in Los Angeles." These last words came out unbidden, as if in speaking I

was deciding what I thought. This, I realized, was the moral equivalent of signing enlistment papers. I was on an Australian troopship
headed for the Dardanelle's and that failed Great War campaign that
hung over Churchill's political life like the Sword of Damocles. My
impulsiveness, once again, had put me over a barrel.

"Then we should discuss your role in that project over lunch," he
said, beaming at his new acolyte.

CHAPTER TEN

Later that afternoon my brother-in-law and I sat in the back of the Daimler and went over plans for my trip. Jimmy, it seems, had already had his solicitors create bank accounts in my name in London and Frankfurt, arranged letters of introduction to Warburg executives in Hamburg and Frankfurt, as well as a letter of credit at the Adlon Hotel in Berlin.

"How did you know I'd agree to do this?" I said.

"Ginny once said you are what is called a 'sucker' for noble things. By the way, doesn't 'sucker' have a slightly odious sound to it?"

"You folks use the word 'intercourse' for talking, so I wouldn't throw stones."

"Also, my observations told me that if I put you, with no current scripts to read, in the presence of Winston, the outcome was pre-ordained. If you've stopped dancing, something needed to replace that activity. I thought spying might provide an outlet for all that energy," he said, grinning.

"So I've been hired for a new performance and Churchill is the producer. You know I still don't know what's true and isn't true about what's going on in Germany. I'm sure there are bad things happening, but until I see it for myself, I'm reserving judgment."

"That's understood. We want unbiased reports. You only need to pretend to be open to their arguments. You don't have to sign up for the SS. By the way, your sister has always said you were much better than the studios realized," he said, lighting a Dunhill.

"You only offered me one script," I said.

"Ginny says if you don't have something in which you are totally involved, you ride dangerous horses very fast or disappear into unmapped terrain."

"My grandfather was like that. If he hadn't had my grandmother, he would have jumped on the next train passing through and never stopped until he'd seen everything there was to see," I said.

"Well," he said, "take this journey for both of you."

CHAPTER ELEVEN

The Germany that greeted me as I crossed the Rhine seemed much like the same country I toured in '35, except that the station platforms bypassed by the Paris-Strasbourg-Frankfurt Express contained more uniformed men. Germans had always loved clothing trumpeting their vocation and rank, but now few were in street clothes. It looked as if someone had taken a country obsessed with order and security and turned it into a perverted Gilbert and Sullivan operetta with real guns. However, while the characters in Gilbert and Sullivan sing silly, whimsical lines, I could anticipate these tenors trilling, "We will take your homes. Set fire to your cities. And rape your women." As I looked closer, even the adolescents were all in uniforms. I pictured babies bursting into the world decked in brown, with miniature swastikas on their arms.

As we were passing one station, a woman, dressed in gray, and a beautiful, brown haired, little girl, were surrounded by men in brown shirts who were punching and kicking them as they fell to the ground. Everyone around was watching, with some apparently delighted by the action. As the train moved slowly past, the beating became frenzied. I stood up, pulled the cord and rushed for the exit. The train kept moving and the conductor was standing across from me shouting

"Setzen Sie sich! That meant I was supposed to sit down. My face must have had told him to back off because all of a sudden he decided he'd had his victory because the train hadn't stopped. I looked at him, said "Fuck you" and punched out the windows on either side of his face on the exit doors behind him. I went back to my seat, the image of the girl and young mother flooding me with anger at the Germans who stood and condoned this. I wondered how many of them called themselves "Christian." It sure didn't match up with the Christianity I'd been taught. I kept working at trying to kill the emotions that made me a civilized man. Up until then, I'd wondered if all the stories I'd been hearing from Jack, Jimmy and Churchill were exaggerated.

One man across the aisle said to me. "You have to understand. They were probably just Jews."

He didn't seem to like the look on my face either because he left to find another car.

I lit a Camel and remembered Ginny had given me a beautiful leather flask for Christmas that allegedly had 21-year-old blended scotch in it. She'd made sure it was in the outside pocket of my great-coat. I stood up, found it more easily than I thought, and took a big swig. The conductor returned with a bill for the windows. I assume some passengers who liked movie musicals had informed him who I was. This probably gave him a way to save face without having a Hollywood star arrested. I pulled out deutschmarks and gave him the cash. I looked down and saw my hands had stopped bleeding. My heart would take a little longer.

CHAPTER TWELVE

Von Taunus's chauffeur, Helmut, was standing there in a perfectly pressed uniform at the Bahnhof's track 22 as my train pulled in. The railway station was full of flags adorned with swastikas advertising the supremacy of the Nazi party over the German people in the same way banners trumpeted the virtues of Binding and Henninger over lesser local beers. I noticed Helmut's uniform was understated and sported Von Taunus's coat of arms on the jacket pocket. He arranged to have my trunk loaded in the boot of the Mercedes and drove me north and west through the suburb of Hoechst, with its bustling IG Farben complex, giving me a leisurely tour of Frankfurt and the surrounding area. The roads coursed like small creeks through towns where buildings accented by large visible beams had stood for centuries. The Great War had been fought on French soil, so Germany looked as it must have before Napoleon dominated Europe.

The road signs told me we were leaving Eschborn and entering Schwalbach. The chauffeur drove slowly through the woods, so I might appreciate the beauty of the forests of the state of Hessen. Helmut praised the virtues of Weissbier as we passed an orchard, with its carefully trimmed trees standing amongst the January snow like gnarled Teutonic sentries guarding Deutschland. I personally thought that making beer out of wheat was a dumb thing to do. It tasted terrible and should be used to make rolls to eat while you were drinking Pilsner or Lager beer. I heard Belgian sissies put fruit in their beer. No wonder they always got invaded first.

"Your German is very good," Helmut said, as we continued through the Schwalbacher Wald, a kind of manicured forest. "The only thing that is noticeable is that you use the expressions of my grandfather. For example you use Advocat for lawyer, when we now use Rechtsanwalt," he said.

"My grandmother left when she was eighteen, so I'm not surprised." "We have Mennonite and Amish farmers who speak like Goethe without the poetry." I said. "I'm sure you would find their German quite funny."

"But I am not laughing at you, Herr Babcock."

"I know. I'm not taking offense," I said, remembering how very precise and careful the German approach was to everything. "I will be careful not to use 'du,' with anyone. My grandmother always spoke to me in the familiar."

It was easy to see we had moved from the country into a richer community with impressive estates. One estate sported large high-strung horses called "warm bloods." One was circling a trainer who controlled her with a lunge line and a whip. It was a rare winter day; with the thermometer above zero Celsius and the ground thawed enough to be struck by the legs of an expensive horse. I couldn't understand how the Germans were supposed to be big warriors when they were known for riding in large halls, seldom going outside in the winter. As someone who had never ridden inside, except once in Madison Square Garden during a promotional tour, I found it hard to understand how anyone could resist riding through the forest here in any weather. Couldn't they take the cold? Was there something girly about them?

"You must ride with Herr Von Taunus during your stay," he said. "He is very will regarded in the world of Dressur"

Dressage is the closest a horse gets to ballet, where you get a man and a horse to dance together. When you get on top of a good horse and make him move the right way you can create a dance step that causes other horsemen to say holy mackerel, but what's best is the feeling of becoming one with that money eating, pampered head-liner trotting below you.

We arrived at the Von Taunus Schloss, which is German for castle, which could have provided headquarters and defense for a hundred knights.

Von Taunus greeted me and had a manservant show me to my room, where I took a bath in hot water especially prepared for my arrival. After taking a few minutes to shave and arrange my papers and documents, I walked down the large curving staircase to the main floor. Von Taunus came out of a room off the entrance hall, shook my hand and led me into one of the most beautiful libraries

I'd ever seen. The leather bound books in German, English and French filled bookshelves of Oak that had taken on a rich color over generations. On the only wall not covered with books, a painted German Eagle that you would see on public buildings, shared space with the Von Taunus crest. I gave Von Taunus a box of Cuban cigars and a servant brought wine and Calvados. The Apple wine, spiked with this apple brandy, was refreshing; although Von Taunus warned me not to tell other important Germans we had been drinking it, because it was perceived as a lower class habit. Much of the alcohol I'd consumed in the twenties had been made in bathtubs, so I felt no shame in this acquired taste.

"Would you like to ride my favorite Belgian tomorrow? She stands eighteen hands and raises her hooves higher than any horse at the Spanish Riding School," he said.

"It would be a pleasure. People look to Germany when they think of the best dressage," I said.

"I will ride with you."

"Thank you," I said, finding my German as comfortable to put on as an old sweater."

"Have you ever met Herr Lindbergh?" Von Taunus said.

"Yes, I met him once in Hollywood."

"He is a very private man, but a close friend of Germany. He understands how we were treated after the War and what we have suffered.

We do not wish to have anything more than what has always been ours. If you look at history, the Sudetenland in Czechoslovakia, Alsace and Lorraine in France, as well as Danzig, were always ours since the days of the Holy Roman Empire. Did you know that the people of Austria voted to join with us as one nation in 1919, but the French and British would not have it?

"It is not surprising that Hitler came to power. He has successfully mobilized Germans by reminding them," I said.

"He has given us back our dignity. There are some things I do not like about how he is solving our problems, but accepting some less significant things to bring the German nation together is something I applaud," he said. "Lindbergh was going to take a house in Berlin, but after incidents in October and misguided American reaction to it, he decided to winter in France."

"Oh, Kristalnacht. Yeah, that really changed attitudes toward Germany in America," I said. "I suppose it would be hard for Lindbergh to stay here after that."

"There are many who think he should be your next President," Von Taunus said.

"He is, perhaps, the most important living American hero," I said, not adding that those that Americans decide deserve top billing soon melt under the spotlights and end up playing the Ithaca, Rome and Cooperstown circuit in run down vaudeville houses or in tents they have to strike themselves.

"Well, unlike you, we haven't pulled out of the depression yet," I said.

"Isn't it amazing to see how dynamic Germany has become?" he said.

I nodded in the affirmative, but my mind, as it was prone to do, was wandering. I was glad of my Savile Row suits in this spacious but drafty castle. The tweed was necessary, not because it was bitterly cold, but because Von Taunus, just like English aristocrats, had not installed central heating. Feeling the warmth of the herringbone fabric, I still couldn't understand how it draped like tropical wool. I was almost driven to ask for British asylum. Any country that had such tailors had to be the center of Western culture. Perhaps, saving the tailors on Savile Row was as good a reason as any for me to be on this mission.

"The first movie of yours that I saw was *Latin Lady*," Von Taunus said. "It was quite good and I was totally dazzled by your sister. Like many others, I'm sure; I couldn't wait for your next picture to come out."

"When this ridiculous talk of war disappears and everything gets back to normal, you'll even get a chance to dance with her. You won't believe what it's like to see her in person and whirl her around the dance floor. I have to admit, though, that I've become more than a little anti-British because my arrogant brother-in-law took her from the movies," I said. "And this friend of his, Churchill, has the most pompous manner and treats people as if they're his servants."

"I'm sure that's true, but despite the Great War, Germans feel a kinship with the English. We found it hard to believe an Anglo-French alliance was possible then, or now," he said.

"My brother-in-law and I had a fight about Churchill over the holidays," I said. "His devotion to the man who killed so many in Gallipoli has me seriously questioning his judgment. He appears to be an arschlak," I said, hoping my grandmother couldn't look down and hear her grandson use the German equivalent of "asshole." "In America, we want a world where the Europeans are not at war, and especially not in one involving us," I said.

"We think it is wonderful that an individual of your stature is willing to listen to our point of view," Von Taunus said. "Perhaps we could suggest how you might help to make sure Americans and Germans never have to fight each other again. After all, there are more Americans of the German race than of any other in America.

"But enough of politics," he said. "Try the Calvados by itself. It's the one thing of which France can be proud. It is certainly very much better than their army," he laughed.

"It's fascinating how you and your sister seem so exceptionally close," Von Taunus said.

"We really are," I said. "She wanted me to stay there with her; at least until she has the baby, but I tried to explain to her that her husband really wouldn't understand."

"It's good you understood that," Von Taunus said.

"When it was the two of us, we really didn't need anyone else," I said. "My life just isn't the same."

"I might write a play about that," Von Taunus said

"Crackerjack idea," I said. "I want to play the brother."

CHAPTER THIRTEEN

There were a couple of evening parties in which I was treated like a distinguished visitor. For three days I concentrated on dressage, riding indoors on Von Taunus' Warmblut champion. On the fourth day, however, I decided it was time to fish or cut bait and took the train from the winter gardens of Kronberg to the Frankfurt railroad station, the Hauptbahnhof. Because I always slept so little, Churchill had given me some books to read before I went to Germany, which included *Mein Kampf* and *I Knew Hitler*. The insomnia was a blessing, because the city of Frankfurt was so imprinted on my mind I felt I'd gone to grade school near the Main River. Exiting out the station's ornate entrance, I grabbed a taxi to the Neue Stadt Oper. The white building had lighted columns and used empty space to convey its significance. I noticed they were performing Wagner. What else for the master race?

Frankfurt was a financial center, with investment decisions made every day about forward looking businesses such as I G Farben, Krupp and Porsche, but the city itself had a medieval look. Only stupid people who hadn't read *Mein Kampf*, the blueprint for the future that Hitler wrote in a jail cell in the '20s, could question where

Hitler was headed. The buildings I'd read about under construction in Berlin were advertisements about what a big shot he was. Frankfurt, on the other hand, was a criminal cover up. Buildings in the Romerplatz appeared to go back 600 years, but the façade of the City Hall, with its complicated construct of 11 separate buildings, had been rebuilt at the turn of the century. Structures tried to sell the story they'd been standing there since the Franks first crossed the Main, but many really dated from the 18th century or later. There was new architecture, such as the modern Farben headquarters, but most buildings pretended to be as old as time. Of course other European cities sent that same message, but here in the real Murder Inc.'s hideout there were too many secrets. Frankfurters implied Kristalnacht was just one little screw up. They sat in their new/old houses and pretended the Jews who'd made Frankfurt a banking powerhouse were somehow at their summer cottages, not in concentration camps. Think of Dante's Inferno hiding below the soil at Stonehenge.

I walked by the Dom, the great cathedral, and took another taxi to the Steinzug Markt along the Main River. The market was surprisingly busy for February, because the weather was 45 degrees Fahrenheit and the sky was clear, which didn't fit Grandma's normal description of German weather.

I bet Frankfurt residents must have felt cut off before Hitler marched into the Rhineland in 1936, not fully a part of the new Germany. Today I knew the city was really German. Nobody wearing a yarmulke tried to sell me any fish.

I walked away from the river to an apple wine bar and ordered a small pitcher while waiting for Ulrich von Geisel, a member of the German diplomatic corps. He was a silver haired man with a military bearing, whose finely tailored tweed suit and camel overcoat looked out of place in this workingman's restaurant.

"Mein Gott, you don't intend to drink that, do you," he said, aghast. "No individual with any breeding drinks that stuff." Von Taunus had hit the jackpot in predicting how his fellow bigwigs would respond to my new drink of choice.

"I actually like it," I said, refilling my glass.

He reluctantly took half a glass and ordered some soda water to cut it. It was obvious that his choice of an Apfelwein bar was a mistake; he had forgotten they didn't serve beer. I was starting to feel like a native.

"It was nice of you to meet with me," I said, smiling.

"I hope you weren't followed," he said. "But then, it could be an innocent meeting. After all, I served in London in the early thirties." He looked around and decided he was comfortable in proceeding.

"Things are not good in Germany," he said, pulling out a cigarette. I stopped him before he lit his own and offered him a Camel. He looked pleased, lit it, and inhaled rich Virginia tobacco. What were they rolling into German cigarettes these days?

"Everything looks prosperous to me," I said, knowing where he was jumping to, but furnishing a diving platform.

"Oh, yes. We have a new Germany where a person such as I can reap the harvest of Hitler's sowing," he said, irony filling his voice.

"It sounds strangely as if the Fuhrer does not meet your expectations," I said.

"The little corporal is a peasant with a death wish and I would not like to see him take Germany down with him," he said, sitting even straighter in his chair.

"You seem to be in a minority," I said.

"I am proud to be a German and would never work against the Fatherland, but Hitler will take us into the depths of hell before he's done. There are others who feel as I do," he said.

"Why hasn't someone done something already?" I said.

"No nation tells him he cannot have what he wants. The German people like feeling proud again," he said. "People will move at his first miscalculation. He is convinced England will never fight and that America is solely concerned with its own hemisphere, so he goes on taking anything he wants, the Rhineland, Austria, the Sudetenland. All the world leaders say, 'We wish you wouldn't do that, but it's all right with us if you must.'"

"There are people around Churchill who want to stop Hitler now," I said.

"No one listens to Churchill."

"Perhaps that will change. Maybe Chamberlain will realize he's being a blockhead," I said.

"Only if Hitler overreaches and is humbled will anyone make a move. We are not fools and we are good Germans," he said. "England needs to stand up to him or America must."

"At this point, your only hope is England. There are too many men in my country who remember the trenches or wonder why we came here the last time," I said.

"The people around Hitler seem to think that Lindbergh is the most important man in America and that he speaks for his country."

"Lindbergh is moving toward the fringe but people still admire him," I said. "He is not, however, the kind of man who could become President of our country."

"The Nazis hope Roosevelt does not remain in office and that someone who is absolutely against intervention becomes your next president," he said.

He looked at his Rolex and said, "I cannot stay longer. Remember that no one will move until there is imminent danger to the Fatherland through his leadership. We Germans are trained to respect authority, especially the army. They don't like him but they've taken an oath," he said, getting up and heading for the door. "I hope your stay in Deutschland is a pleasant one. Pease try our Rieslings and stay away from that awful crap."

After he left I poured what was left in the small pitcher into my glass and finished it before paying. I walked by the river, before crossing the bridge to Sachsenhausen, like any other tourist. As I rambled, an idea percolated. I looked for signs of gaiety in the streets and came up empty handed.

CHAPTER FOURTEEN

"Let me be honest with you," I told Von Taunus. "I'm in a career slump and I know somebody who will help me if I do him a favor. He's obnoxious, like all Jews, but he's put out a request for help in getting his niece and nephew back. He's a very powerful man and would owe me. I think it would help establish my credibility with the Jews in Hollywood if I could get these two children out of your country and into America," I said.

I could see Von Taunus was disappointed in my flagrant self dealing, but, in a way it made my efforts believable. All the Nazis were hypocrites so it didn't really seem surprising. I was just another skunk his class had to hold their noses and suffer in the new Germany.

"Would it be in the newspapers?" Von Taunus said. "It won't happen if the press might find out about it," he said.

"I'll make sure Greenberg only tells the Jews at the top of the power structure, the few men who control the studios. So much remains secret in Hollywood that shutting this story down would be easy. Money could be spent," I said.

"And you would be a hero, someone they could trust. I see," he said filling the bowl of his Meerschaum pipe.   "But how do you know you can get them into the United States?"

"I would take them to Cuba. I know some people there, and they could wait there until I could get them into the country," I said.

"I find it interesting that your country doesn't want Jews either," he said. "We could ship all of them to you if you'd take them. In my mind, it would be far more humane."

"You hold on to them," I said. "We don't want any more bolshies than we already have. Only the people who play fair should come to America."

"I see. Well, Canaris wanted me to recruit you, so I will have him get on the phone to Himmler and see what he can do. Himmler won't like any of them getting out of our hands, but he can tell them there will be two less to feed in our camps," he said. "You know, I don't quite approve of what we're doing to the Jews. It seems to be going overboard." He stopped himself and realized it might be best not to continue that thought.

I jumped into the conversation by saying, "You guys are the only ones with enough guts to take care of the problem. You should be proud. I salute you." My words came out suitably angry and I thanked Louise Graber and those acting lessons on the set. It was too bad somebody wasn't getting this on celluloid. It would get me an Oscar hands down.

"So, you can serve our cause and advance your career at the same time." He tried to hide his disgust.

He went off to use the phone while I prepared a telegram for my sister saying I wouldn't return to England and sliced the baloney about her husband being a dope who gave me the heebee jeebies.

CHAPTER FIFTEEN

Early the next morning two SS Obersturmfuhrer's (comparable to lieutenants in the American Army) came to the castle and picked me up. My steamer trunk was put in the boot of the car. Von Taunus seemed happy I was leaving, but his breeding had trained him to cover it up. He didn't go through some phony rigmarole, but instead was exceedingly polite. I knew he wasn't happy about discovering another fallen idol. They drove into Frankfurt to Lindenstrasse where they pulled up in front of a building displaying a large golden German eagle, with a swastika flag hanging on a pole jutting out from the second story.

This was just one of the many buildings around Germany that housed Heinrich Himmler's army of SS thugs. In this instance, the building was home to the Gestapo. Churchill told me Himmler had built a national police force and Army from a few hundred men, when he took it over in 1929, to a force of at least 300,000. I'd heard he'd built the Dachau concentration camp and presided over the persecution of the Jews.

I was ushered into an office which bore the title SS-Obersturmbannfuhrer. The stocky man, whose black uniform jacket boasted medals over the left breast, told me his name was Reinhardt and gestured towards a wooden chair at the front of his desk. (I guessed from what I saw on the train the medals showed how many Jewish women he'd beaten in a single quarter.) I assumed his desk was his instrument of power and that my rump was perched in a chair that had seen the beginning of the end for many Jews and political dissidents.

"There may be a chance we don't have records of the particular children you are looking for," he said, seemingly savoring the thought. "Many are given just numbers before they are resettled."

Somehow the word resettled sounded like another word for imprisoned, but I kept my emotions under lock and key.

"Well, it's important to me that we try to find out if you have them," I said in measured tones.

"Reichsfuhrer Himmler called me and told me that it is important for Germany to find them for you. What are the children's names?" he said.

"Karl and Liesel Gruenberg," I said. "They probably were taken on Kristalnacht."

"Liesel? My daughter is named Liesel. How does a Jew get the nerve to use a good German name like that?" he said, his anger strong and real.

"I have no idea why they are so brazen," I said. "We need people in our country such as you to show them where their place should be. In America they have risen to power in our economic structure, but no one has had the will to bring them down as you have in Germany."

"Our fuehrer is the greatest man the world has ever seen," he said. "He will make sure Germany is the most important nation in the world and it will be free of the animals that others mistakenly call human beings." He pulled his tunic down where it was riding up on his stomach and then cut a fart.

"I will have my men look through our records to see if we can find them. Perhaps you might wish to go to a restaurant and have some food and read the Allegemeine Zeitung while we work on it."

"Fine. When should I come back?" I said.

"You could come back about two o'clock," he said, seeing me to the door.

I had the feeling that freeing a Jewish girl, with the same name as his daughter stuck in his craw, but he didn't seem ready to disobey Himmler. That could put him in the same facility with the two children.

CHAPTER SIXTEEN

I went to my hotel just off the Hauptwache and lay on the bed. The disgust I felt came up like the bile that announced you'd gone one drink too far. I'm not sure the Oberststurmbannfuhrer had trusted me, but Himmler was the boss and he had blessed this transaction because I had German roots. And because I spoke German, they'd assumed my sympathies were with them. It was lucky for the British that my Grossmutter had passed in the twenties, because a simple check would have told them their ideas would have fallen on barren ground. My grandmother had taught me German because it was the language of Beethoven and Mozart, not the language of Wagner. There had been a spirit in Germany which ran in different currents from the idea of the ubermensch. Grandma told me how Beethoven decided not to dedicate a symphony, after all, to the disappointing Napoleon, once seen as a reformer, after he revealed himself to be a simple conqueror. My grandmother despised the Kaisers' Germany.

Her beautiful coloratura soprano voice had surprised and delighted her family and their neighbors. However, when it came time to use that God-given instrument on a stage, her family and society said no. So one night she crawled out of the second story window of her large home in Wiesbaden, walked to a town north of the city and sat there until daylight. She caught a boat up the Rhine to Holland, where she booked passage to America.

Her looks got her a voice teacher in New York, who reluctantly informed her that a career in opera could only flourish in Europe. Her voice, however, was perfect for a different venue, so she'd taken to the stage. During her first week in what then passed for show business, my grandfather was smitten. Two weeks after she first stood in the footlights, she became the wife of a man who built carriages. (I always wondered if it would have been so easy to get her away from Florenz Ziegfeld, instead of the timid theatre owner my grandfather faced that day.) For my Grossmutter, the narrowness of the German mind held no appeal. They had driven her away and she had never gone back. When I proved to be perfect mimic, she began teaching me German, careful not to pass on any of the attitudes associated with her native land's negativity.

I looked around the room, realizing once again that my mind had drifted and that drift (the only force that could stop the inner motor) had taken me away. "Well," I said to myself, "this is not the time."

I put on a sweater and a trench coat and left the room. It was drizzling when I first came out and then the drizzle turned to rain, but I had to keep moving. My hat could be replaced and Jimmy, and what the America Firsters would call his warmongering bogeymen, were paying for everything until I returned home to bring in the orange crop.

Von Taunus told me that while the SS (Schutzstaffel) was run by Heinrich Himmler; the Gestapo, the secret police, was under the thumb of Reinhard Heydrich. Heydrich reported to Himmler, as did the entire Gestapo, but he was ambitious and had plans of his own. And Hermann Goering, who had run the Gestapo's forerunner, the Prussian Secret Police, could still exert power. I didn't know whether this local man, Obersturmbannfuhrer Reinhardt, was really Himmler's man or not. I was walking on eggshells balanced on nails.

I thought about Jack's niece and nephew as the rain turned heavy and prayed they were alive. Feeling the energy accumulate, I picked up the pace when the rain intensified. It was getting colder, but I turned left when I hit the Main River.

After an hour's run I turned back downriver and moved even more quickly, my shoes turning into squishy leather containers of rain that made anguished sounds. At one o'clock I got back to my hotel and took a shower, after carefully putting my shoes near the radiator. They were made by Church in England, so I knew they'd recover, and, of course, I had more in my trunk. I thanked the Lord for heavy tweed as I put on a double breasted suit Ginny had ordered for me.

Filled with apprehension, I walked over to Schlesinger Strasse. In my mind, I saw Jack nervously waiting in Bel Air. I hoped he wouldn't marry someone new just to keep his mind off his troubles. If it had to be, I hoped it would be someone over thirty who loved to cook, hated shopping and had never considered a career in show business.

The Oberststurmbannfuhrer was sitting behind his desk. I wasn't asked to sit as he said, "It seems we don't have them. I told you that most of them are given numbers. There is no Liesel. I am sure of that. No Jew has that name. If we find one, or a Karl Gruenberg, we'll bring them up here so you can talk to them and discover if these are your Jews." It sounded as if I was looking for a lost dog and they were checking the pound. "Come back here next week at this time," he said, dismissing me. He had a sneer on his face that told me I would come next week and be told to return in a month.

The longer I stayed in Germany, the better chance I'd be smoked out. I was sure that the Oberststurmbannfuhrer was already taking steps to have Liesel and Karl killed, because she had the nerve to share a name with his daughter. The rain was ending, so I decided to go out and wait to see if the fat bastard left Gestapo headquarters. In a half an hour, he emerged, walking in the direction of the Hauptbanhof. For a man who looked like a prize porker he moved surprisingly swiftly. He walked five blocks before stopping in front of an apartment house. He looked up at a window and quickly entered the building. Staying a few steps behind, I followed, listening to his footsteps stomping up the stairs. I determined he had gone up two flights before ascending the stairs myself. When I reached the top landing, I watched him pound on an apartment door.

"Liebchen, meine Liebchen," he said, pounding harder. He grew angry and raised his voice, before remembering he'd been given a key. He reached into his pants, pulled out the key and unlocked the door. I knew what had to be done, came up quickly behind him, and smashed in his skull with the Luger I'd taken from a drawer in von Taunus' library. I quickly pulled him inside, closed the door, and laid him on the bed. Moving swiftly, I picked up a pillow and held it over his mouth and nose until I was sure he had stopped breathing. At first I was sickened by what I was doing. Maybe there could have been another way? I told myself. Then I looked down at him and the questions ended. This man had no feelings. My instincts told me this choice was the right one. Maybe I still hated myself for what I'd suddenly become, but I decided this transformation happened for a reason. I left the room, wiped off the doorknob and closed it with a handkerchief. Then I headed away from the stairway I had used to come up and found one in the back that I descended quickly, holding my hat down over my forehead, with the collar on my trench coat turned up against my face. I emerged into an alley crowded with trash cans and walked until it ended in a large thoroughfare. How had I come to kill a man? A close examination of this would have to wait for another time, but it was almost like the Beast within me had finally broken out. And it certainly wasn't within the rational New England compartment that I'd thought provided the walls that surrounded who I was. This was some throwback to the Thames River before London was built or Northern Africa right after we walked on two legs. I'd looked into his eyes and knew Jack's niece would die if I didn't act.

I walked west for three blocks before I thought I had put enough distance between myself and the crime. I was breathing hard, so I slowed down and slowly walked ten more blocks until I reached the Zeil, the main shopping street in Frankfurt.

I resolved to take a taxi to Sachsenhausen, drink Apfelwein and, later, find a restaurant featuring Entenbraten, roast duck. I had decided that mindless conversation with others, while alcohol flowed, would help me get through the rest of the day. Sachsenhausen was once known as a delightful place before Hitler seized the Rhineland, and it was trying to pretend it still had that spirit. When I say delightful, you have to understand I'm comparing it to the rest of Germany, a country where being morose and depressed was the 98.6 of Teutonic mental health. From what Grandma told me and what I saw on my tour here before, you should never let a German become the social director of an international event; the games would involve competitive suffering, and feature an angst festival. The only time most Germans will open up is when they've been drinking. For a short time the walls will drop and questions will be asked and answered. In America, when you go drinking with someone you don't know very well, a new friendship frequently carries over into the next day. In Germany, however, the walls reappear the next morning, as if the booze laden confidences and conversations never occurred.

I looked for an Apfelwein bar with a pine wreath hanging outside, indicating the establishment made its own wine. Der Fliegende Hollander looked as old as time itself, but must have arrived on the local scene after Wagner's Flying Dutchman hit the boards. You entered through one of two doors which swung out to reveal a cavernous room with a long bar running down the left hand side. Above the bar hung hundreds of grey Bembels, pitchers of varying size decorated with raised blue branches. Once filled with Apfelwein, they provided fuel for imagination and an entry into liberation.

I, of course, was immediately recognized by a group of women at a table, who were sitting with two SS men. I assumed these women worked in governmental offices because German females had been urged by the Fuhrer to stay home and get knocked up for the greater glory of the Reich. I hesitated to approach them, but an SS lieutenant stood up, crossed the room, and asked me to wet my whistle with them.

His name was Hans and he introduced me to the others, but the only name that stuck was Trudy, whose long brown hair framed a perfect face, although thinner than other Northern European women I'd previously found attractive. She gave me a smile more than welcoming, but I made sure to move my smile around the table, unaware of relationships. Being among the SS was a perfect spot for me at that moment, so I planned to give the men at the table more attention than the women.

"It is an honor for us to have a famous at our table," said Dietrich, an SS captain. I knew what was coming next. "It is too bad for us that you didn't bring your sister with you."

"It's not too bad for me," said Trudy

I knew then I didn't have to worry about Dietrich, and said, "She married an Englander and I plan to have nothing to do with him. Ginny will not be going places with me very soon."

"At least it was an Englander. They are much like us, unlike the Slavs and Italians. We like the British, except for that crackpot Churchill. He must never again have power in that country," said Hans.

"Does your sister look as good in person as she does on the screen?" Hans said.

"Better," I said, thinking "Halleluiah, I'm safe." I immediately gave another smile to Trudy, who seemed to have anticipated it, responding with a knowing look.

For a moment I wondered whether the Obersturmbannfuhrer's body had been discovered, before pushing him out of my mind. I needed to keep my wits about me. The waiter handed me a menu after I pulled him over and said I wanted to pay for the next round. I knew that in Germany my decision to buy a round would not be reciprocated, but hell, I was a big movie star and could afford it. A spirited discussion sprang up while I was talking to the waiter, so I took advantage of it. Apfelwein is already ten percent alcohol, but you could add calvados to a Bembel, so I ordered the largest pitcher and had him fill it with a lot of apple brandy, which is 70 proof. I also ordered a knockwurst, so I would have something to soak up the powerful liquid. Since the French make Calvados I decided I was helping Germans prepare for enslaving Paris. You needed to keep your wits about you when you invaded another country.

When the waiter returned and the group thanked me, I filled everyone's glass and said, "Zum Wohl," a German toast. Hans said "Prosit," a toast more suited to beer than wine, as I consumed the entire glass at one time. Not to be outdone by someone who is not a Frankfurter, they all followed suit, except for an older woman that remembered she had a husband who would not take kindly to her coming home drunk.

"What was in that?" Trudy said.

"I asked for a small shot of Calvados," I said. She gave me a look that said it wasn't necessary to get her drunk, but it wasn't the women I wanted to drink under the table. Once the SS, were on the way to WolkenKuckucksheim (Cloud Cuckoo Land), I would have an alibi without a time stamp.

"Do men drink like that in Hollywood?" Dietrich said.

"This really isn't considered very strong in America," I said, pointing at the Bembel.

"In Germany this is very strong," he replied. I knew that no one else would want to propose chugging such a mind altering amount, so I sat back and nursed my drink. I was counting on Hessen pride to keep the wine flowing.

We talked about America, Greta Garbo and constant sunshine, as one by one; the women excused themselves to go home. It soon was Trudy and three men. I invited them to be my guests at the restaurant I'd heard about. They agreed and were ready to join me, when one of their colleagues, a short youth with a moustache that seemed more hopeful than robust, walked in and spoke to Dietrich and Hans.

"Someone has killed the Obersturmbannfuhrer," he said, his voice almost cracking.

"Where?" they asked, almost in unison.

"In an apartment on Reiter Strasse," he said. "They say Frau Bartok discovered his body, but no one is supposed to know that."

"That pig," Dietrich said. "He was always giving us talks on purity and maintaining the Aryan bloodline." Dietrich's cynical laugh seemed to stay with the table after the three had hurried off.

"That's very funny. The Obersturmbannfuhrer gave us those long lectures and he was involved with a Hungarian whore." She looked exasperated.

"Now I know what, but who is Frau Bartok?" I said.

"There aren't supposed to be brothels in Germany, but she has a large one over near the train station. It's full of Polish and Hungarian women. We always wondered why someone hadn't closed it down," Trudy said.

Trudy looked like she wasn't in a hurry. "We were supposed to be working and so were Hans and Dietrich," she said, accepting my offer of a Camel. "They probably will receive a lecture for not being at headquarters," she said, taking in the Virginia tobacco and blowing a perfect smoke ring that lingered for a moment before dissolving. "Everyone in the SS knows this is the place to be when you are not in the barracks, so you can be found quickly if a Jew needs beating or someone must be intimidated." Her face held a look of studied revulsion.

"It sounds like noble work. Let's go someplace for dinner and put some distance between this bar and ourselves," I said. I thought again about that Oscar statuette, but this time I imagined I won it while speaking in a French accent, clad in an ape costume. "I would like to thenk the director Pee air..."

"Are you asking me on what Americans call a date?"

"Yes, I said, picking up my coat. "It's starting when you stand up."

CHAPTER SEVENTEEN

The next day, promptly at two, I stood outside the Obersturmban-nfuhrer's office. "We will go upstairs and you can look at them," said a thin, balding man, as he emerged from the office and hurried up the stairs. "It seems the Obersturmbannfuhrer was going to arrange this after his lunch hour. It was lucky his assistant had heard of your conversation. Herr Himmler would not have appreciated any oversight."

We entered a small room with lights pointing in at a wooden chair. The smell of human sweat was oppressive. Standing in the corner next to some shackles were two gaunt children who probably would be very handsome if they'd had enough to eat.

"What is the name of your uncle in America?" I said.

"Johan." They said the name as if they might be punished for it.

"What was your father's name?"

"Robert, but he's dead," the girl said.

"Is your mother in the place you are living?" I said.

"Our mother is dead, also," the boy said, with a look on his face that seemed to say; "I have no more tears, I've run out of them."

"Where does your uncle live?"

"Kalifornia," the little girl said. I wanted to hug them both and tell them everything would be all right, but my character (for that's the way I saw this version of Tommy Babcock) wouldn't have hugged a Jew.

"Are you satisfied?" the officer said.

"Yes," I said. Even if, by chance, the Germans had somehow rigged this as some kind of cruel joke, the children had been starved and probably beaten, so I wanted to get them out of Germany no matter who they were. These children had just put on their yellow armbands with the Star of David and I couldn't imagine any Gentile parent allowing their children to be dressed as Jews.

"You will not wear those armbands," the SS man shouted as he ripped them off their arms. He turned to me and said, "I don't want anyone to know we released these Jews or that they were ever in our custody. Do you understand? You will be taken to Bremerhaven, where you will board a ship bound for Cuba shortly after midnight. You will be guarded by my men at all times. You will speak to no one, especially other members of the Gestapo. Do you understand?"

"I understand," I said. "Thank you for your help." Because we were to be guarded continuously by plainclothes Gestapo, I wouldn't be able to tell the children I was a friend of Jack's until we were at sea, and then only when we weren't being watched. It was going to be a couple of weeks of hell.

Two hours later we were on the road to Bremerhaven, that German port adjacent to the North Sea peninsula that became Denmark. We traveled through Giessen and Marburg, in a rain growing in intensity. It was as if the Creator kept sending storm after storm to wash Germany's blood from its hand's, but there was always new blood, so the task was fruitless. The atmosphere in the car was as bleak as the German landscape. I was in the back seat between the children. The two SS men, both blond and seemingly selected for their resemblance to some Aryan ideal, relaxed in the front and told stories.

"There was this Jewish cow who tried to get food for her sniveling son yesterday near the Hauptwache," the taller of the two said. "She had taken off her star to pretend she was like us. She actually looked a little German, so they were going to sell her some meat when a woman recognized her and screamed 'Jew, she is a Jew. My sister used to work for her.' I was in the shop and asked the woman if she was sure. If she had been a German woman I would have said she was attractive, so I took her behind the store and screwed her before I beat her. Her face was just a bloody pulp when I was done. Then I had her shipped to Dachau. By the end of the day we had found her son. He was about seven or eight, and we had him shipped to Buchenwald."

The other man laughed and said, "You screwed a Jew?"

"I have kept your secrets, Willi. You keep this one," he said in a plaintive tone, now sorry he had told the story.

"You were taking a chance," Willi said.

"We did it in Dachau. I know you did the same thing to a woman we caught over in Sachsenhausen."

"But not behind a building. If you had been seen by someone and reported," he said in an admonishing tone.

I didn't speak, figuring that silence was the best way to handle this matter. Himmler had ordered the children released, and I was someone these rapists had seen in the movies, so they treated me with some deference.

"Herr Babcock, your sister is like a Princess. Many of us were very proud when we learned your Grandmother was from Germany," Willi said.

"Yes, from Wiesbaden. I went and looked at the house she grew up in a few days ago," I said.

"German blood always shows," Willi said. "Is your sister as beautiful as she looks in the films?"

"She looks much better in person. People say her skin is perfect, but the camera can't capture it in black and white," I said.

"It is impossible for her to look better in person. She is a goddess," the other man said. "She is very popular in Germany," he said. After a pause, he added;" so are you, of course."

The idea of these animals drooling over my sister made my stomach turn, but I said, "Thank you. The German public has paid a lot to see us, so I am also happy about that."

They laughed, before they again began talking among themselves. When we reached Hanover, they filled the tank with gas at an SS facility. While they were both out of the car, I squeezed Karl and Liesel's hands and told them to be patient, they would soon see their Uncle Jack. They didn't know whether to trust me or not and were afraid to say anything, which actually worked in our favor.

"Did your mother die at the same time as your father?" I said.

"No." Karl said, in a voice that was emotionless. "She died in Dachau. She was in another part of the camp, but a woman told us she had no doctor and died from the bullet that hit her on Kristalnacht."

Liesel began to cry and Karl said, "Don't cry, they will beat us."

"Schade," I said, expressing my sadness. "I heard your mother was a wonderful woman. Your uncle Jack said she had the prettiest hair in Germany."

When I said that Liesel actually squeezed my hand back, but Karl was looking for a trick, the real reason they were being taken in this car. He believed they were being taken to another camp, or worse. How, I wondered, would these children ever be without fear? They both seemed deeply scarred, although Liesel had apparently not given up hope. Karl simply wanted to survive to protect his sister.

"Don't say anything while there are Germans around us," I said, although they had certainly learned that already. "The ship is a German ship and they will watch you there also."

They acted as if that was to be expected.

"I will sometimes say some things so they can trust me. Try to believe that I do not really mean those words," I said. "Have you ever seen a film? If you have, pretend this is a movie. That's what I do." I then realized Jews probably hadn't been allowed in movie theaters for years and felt stupid. Neither one of them seemed to find it comforting.

We were covering half of Germany on our trip from Frankfurt to Bremerhaven, so after they got back into the car they handed me some warm bratwurst for me to eat on the road, with a brewery glass of beer to wash it down. There was nothing for the children, but I dared not ask for anything. I knew the children were starving.

Willi said," Would you, perhaps, send pictures of your sister to us so we could put them up in our rooms?"

"Of course," I said, "Anything for the Fatherland."

They laughed and went back to telling stories that made my skin crawl. Liesel had fallen asleep because I could hear a child's little snore next to me. Karl was apparently not going to sleep because he thought he had to be vigilant. I wondered if he knew more than I did about life and the nature of man. I was glad, at least, that I had purchased winter clothes for them this morning so they were dressed warmly. They hadn't been allowed to shower, so the look was incongruous; children with nice clothes and dirty hair who looked half dead.

We were stopped by a roadblock south of Bremen and my heart went into my mouth.

The SS men with us showed no fear, but they had their orders to keep this trip a secret, so they slowed the car down. A heavy man with a black leather coat, holding an umbrella, walked over to the car. He looked into the car, recognizing my face.

"Is that the American movie star with the beautiful sister?" he said, smiling. "He should feed his children better."

"Arschloch," I said. "You should remember that I speak German."

Our SS men gave the man a look that clearly challenged his authority. He wasn't cowed, but probably thought picking a fight was not in his best interest at that point. After all, they both ultimately reported to Himmler. As we pulled away, I could see him going to a building, most certainly to make a call to Berlin in case something happened.

"He had no right to speak about you like that," Willi said. "As you can see, he looks like a Jew." He was speaking of the man's swarthy complexion, which did not fit the SS ideal. I wondered if that made the Gestapo man even more dangerous.

"Forget it," I said. "I took care of the fool. He looks like he comes from inferior stock anyway."

When we arrived in Bremerhaven, a cold wind was blowing off the North Sea. I was chilly, but the children didn't seem to notice. They probably hadn't worn warm clothes in months. We were taken to a building on the waterfront and put in rooms on the second floor, the children in one room and me in another. Our guards said we were waiting for the ship to finish loading its cargo of machine tools. I figured the boat would return to Germany with sugar cane to supplement the country's own beet sugar and with fresh cigars for Goring. At about three a.m. Willi and his sidekick took us down to a pier where the tramp steamer was moored. In English the boat's name would have translated as Wilhemina's wind. Just before we headed up the gangplank, six men in long black leather coats surrounded us. It was clear the Gestapo had been looking for us and guessed I was leaving the country with more than I had when I arrived.

"Let me see your papers," said a tall man with a scar across his right cheek.

I handed him my passport even though I knew he didn't need it to identify me. Willi appeared ready to bow to superior force. His partner, on the other hand, looked ready to resist.

"Where are the passports for your children?" he said.

"I don't have my children's passports," I said. "I forgot to bring them on the boat coming over." If he was stupid enough to buy that snake oil Hitler should throw him into Dachau. This cockamamie crap of mine was going to get all of us killed.

"The boy looks at least twelve. When were you married? We always heard that you and your sister weren't married when you made your pictures," he said.

"I never acknowledged them as my children. Their mother and I never married. I met her in Germany and she stayed here," I said.

The men laughed. One grabbed Liesel's arm and pulled up her sleeve. I could see numbers burnt into her arm and felt ill. They were branded like cattle.

"They are promised safe passage by Reichsfuhrer Himmler," Willi said, finding some courage.

"You expect me to believe that the Reichsfuhrer would let this actor take Jews from Germany to spread their corruption?" the man with the scar said.

"Our Obersturmbannfuhrer received directions from the Reichsfuhrer himself," the other SS man said.

"Obergruppenfuhrer Heydrich has no knowledge of this," the scar said. "He told me to stop you." Heydrich had a reputation for trying to obtain files on every Jew and Communist, as well as on those in Hitler's inner circle.

"I advise you to call Himmler," I said, trying to keep the anger out of my voice and failing. "Heydrich reports to Himmler, so call the Reichsfuhrer."

"Take them back to wherever you are holding them," the scar said to the SS men. "I will call Berlin and my men will accompany you."

With that comment, my spine felt like a January icicle in Syracuse, frozen stiff with good weather at least six months away. We were marched back to the building and placed in our rooms. I had heard stories since my arrival about Heydrich's lust for power and desire to control information in the Reich. Von Taunus once said he had an insatiable desire to make the Jews of Germany as miserable as possible.

The hours went by and I grew tenser worrying that Himmler had changed his mind. According to Von Taunus, who had confided in me before I showed my slimy side, Heydrich had once worked for Canaris and there were rumors he was setting up a rival intelligence agency, if he hadn't already done so. If the boat left without us it would give Berlin a chance to look more closely at the arrangements. I did pushups with my suit jacket on because of the cold, worrying I would rip out the exquisitely sewn armholes on this bespoke masterpiece. I found myself pacing as the hours dragged on. I wondered what the children were thinking. It probably wasn't very different from what they thought about every day in Dachau, except they hadn't been beaten or called offensive names for a day. It was amazing how silent they were, as far removed from childhood as octogenarians.

I started tap dancing and one member of the Gestapo, a short brown haired character who looked like a farmer, opened the door.

"Practicing for my next movie," I said. "Does anybody out there speak English?"

He looked puzzled for a moment and then tried to speak.

"I know, you think meine Schwester is beautiful."

"Ja," he said.

"I want to teach you this line from one of my movies," I said in German. "Here it goes, Say Sieg Heil Sucker"

"Say Sieg Heil Suu Ker."

"Try it again, Say Sieg Heil Sucker"

"Say Sieg Heil Suu Ker"

I gave up and quickly moved into the steps from the biggest number in *Christmas in the Rockies,* after bringing the two children into my room without incident. I danced my heart out, hoping that it would help distract the children from their fear. Of course, I was apprehensive, when I wasn't trying to hold in my anger. It was the best performance I ever gave, for the most appreciative audience. At first, Karl didn't know what to do, but the minute Liesel saw me do a buck and wing she was hooked. She smiled and looked fascinated, her brown eyes growing wide. After a series of difficult moves, I stopped dancing and broke into my biggest song, *Love's on the Top of My List*, a ballad with which Bunny Berrigan had great success. Bunny had inserted a trumpet solo before his own strangely arresting vocals. However, everyone associated the song with me and at nightclubs they would frequently greet my arrival with a rendition of the song that had already become a classic. I winked at Liesel when I changed one of the lines to include "Ich liebe dich" in place of the English lyrics and her smile almost broke my heart. If I couldn't touch them physically, at least I could reach them this way. I finished the song and noticed the SS had opened the door and were standing in the hall. When they clapped I knew Himmler had informed Heydrich we would be going to Cuba. They stood outside while I sang some other songs from my pictures in order to cement my relationship with my audience. All of a sudden the spell was broken when the farmer sang out, "Say Sieg Heil Suu Ker" and I couldn't wait to get the children on board. After they apologized for detaining me, the children and I headed for the ship. It wasn't until later I realized I'd become the sweetheart of the Gestapo.

The voyage across the Atlantic improved the farther south we sailed. We stopped in the Azores to pick up supplies, but we didn't leave the ship. I gave the first mate money and a telegram for Jack, informing him about the children's impending arrival in Cuba.

Jack had connections to some Jewish gangsters who ran casinos in Florida. These hoodlums would go to Havana to party and they knew the Jewish community there, so I assumed Jack would get on the phone to a friend of his named Meyer Lansky and get some advice on what to do with his niece and nephew.

We weren't in the Azores long before we cast off for Cuba. Because we were still on a German ship we were as much in Germany as if we were walking down the Unter den Linden. I usually had my meal with the crew and would pick up some food for Karl and Liesel to eat in their cabin. It was in that cabin I would say the things I really felt, because I was confident the children had no interest in talking to the ship's crew. The crew would never have allowed Jewish children in the mess or even allow them on deck. The day we left the Azores, I brought them dinner and clued them in about the status of their journey.

"I sent a telegram to your Uncle Jack and he will be there when we get to Cuba," I said to them. Liesel smiled. "Did you keep kosher in Frankfurt? Will the family you stay with have to be orthodox?" I was sure Jack had the arrangements figured, but thought it would be good for me to know such things.

"No," Karl said, "we are not orthodox."

"Just like Germany is cold and has lousy weather, Cuba is warm and you can walk on the beach all year round," I said. "The food is really good and you will hear a lot of music and see people dancing. I'll dance with Liesel when we get there, if she'll let me," I said to Karl. Liesel looked very shy, but I had the impression she was glad I had mentioned it. Karl wasn't buying this trip to paradise, because since he could remember, Jews were treated like scum. It must have been like growing up in jail.

CHAPTER EIGHTEEN

We ran into a heavy storm when we were about a days sail from the Bahamas. I ran the risk of going next door, locking the door from the inside and hugging Liesel as the ship rolled and slammed into oncoming waves.

"I'm right next door and everything is going to be all right," I said. I didn't dare try to pull Karl into the hug. It was partly me, but I figured he wouldn't have known what to do, either, whether out of distrust or just because he already felt like a man. After an hour, I went next door, after telling them I'd knock on the wall softly every half hour so they'd know I was there.

I lay there and realized what Jack, a childless man in his fifties, wanted in his life. None of his wives had given him a child, so I guessed Jack was shooting blanks. These two were almost his flesh and they had heard about him from their first years when their father told them of someday going to the Goldene Medina, and living with him. I realized I had developed strong feelings for these two children and hoped this didn't indicate I would soon do something rash like marrying just to have offspring of my own.

How much I wished Karl and Liesel could experience my childhood on the farm in Connecticut. "The Farm" ceased to be a segment of traditional agriculture the day my grandfather bought it. By the end of the 19th Century, anyone with a lick of sense had left New England for the west if they wanted to farm for a living. You had to reach the Tully-Homer Valley in Upstate New York before the soil was good enough for a decent crop. Unless your idea of heaven was milking cows every day, you moved well past New York. Those hardy souls who remained in New England struggled or found another way to make a living. The folks who'd sold their farm in Honeyback, Connecticut, to my grandfather knew to "git when the gitten was good."

Grandpa turned a working farm into a rural oasis without the toil and unpleasantness that usually accompanied country life. To my grandfather, the farm was a reward for a lifetime of work and he relaxed into it. There were elms that added dignity to the area between the house and the barn. The creek that flowed past the stone patio on the southeast seemed to say, "I'm in no hurry to reach the Connecticut and you shouldn't be either." There were milk cows serviced by the hired man, while my mother grew corn, squash and root vegetables on a plot surrounded by chicken wire seven feet tall to keep deer away. If that failed to deter those pests, my grandfather would go out shortly after dusk and then send at least one of them to the butcher for processing the next morning. After seeing what those pests could do to a crop, I always looked for venison on restaurant menus. Unlike most farmhouses, ours had a library that yelled 'move over" to the Morgans and Vanderbilts of this world. No one really knew how many volumes there were but it had taken three summers for a group of Yale graduate students to put together the card catalog.   Unfortunately, right after they'd finished the project my grandfather learned the widow of well-known Wesleyan professor needed some money and was willing to sell her husband's collection, one that required an entire boxcar for transport. Grandpa had a large addition attached to the house, next to where the original library stood. It had high ceilings, oak library ladders and a cupola with skylights to spread sunlight on the new collection.   Another shift of Yalies was soon summoned.

The back of Sandy, the paint Grandpa purchased for me on a trip out west, was my second home.   There was nothing finer then the times Ginny, my best friend even then, mounted Gabriel, her Morgan, to race me across the hills and pastures that weren't fenced in by those crazy few still trying to pull a crop out of New England's sterile ground. I would spy Ginny, with her hair trailing in the wind like a rich brown windsock, and feel complete in a way I never would again.   It was a world in which only America existed, where a trip to New York City was the equivalent today of taking the Queen Mary to Europe and the only Germans I knew were people like my Grandmother who'd migrated here in the 19th Century.   In fact I once believed racial intermarriage was the mixing of the prestigious Mayflower blood of my grandfather with the blood of the people Americans would learn to call "The Hun."

Ginny never knew fear. If I impulsively broke into a gallop, she computed the risks and then decided whether to ignore them. She knew what she would have to do to beat me, including cutting me off in full canter, while I simply stoked Sandy's boilers. When she won, as she usually did, I would always put it down to her advanced age and experience.

The real reason for her victory, I later understood, involved her ability to rein in her mind and concentrate on tactics, in addition to experiencing the rush of adrenaline. Perhaps that was why I was adrift since her departure. I had been able to play the wild youth for too long, while she was the architect of our career. (My success involved the skillful conservation and investment of income. You can take a Yankee out of New England, but you can't teach him to waste a buck.)

Ginny was as beautiful at 13 as she was at 21, when she made jaws drop on Broadway, where rich, important men waited at the stage door with offers of matrimony. Ginny, with her dark brown locks and aquiline nose had the face and bearing of an aristocrat. She was on her way to becoming the woman many men think is the most beautiful creation of the century.

Nothing has seemed as perfect as those summers. The soul of my sister held my heart. I found myself admiring her corporeal beauty when my mind would drift to some different time or place, only to return abruptly to reality. Then, during that moment of clarity, I'd feel I was present at the moment when Aphrodite first stood on the half shell. My mother and grandmother were attractive women, but Ginny was from a mould the Lord used every 10,000 years.

Ginny had easily moved beyond the idea of the farm because she carried a degree of peace and comfort in her own being that she can transfer from place to place and experience to experience. I believe, however, the joy of a gallop through a world of utter peace will never come my way again.

If Karl and Liesel could have experienced those years of peace they'd have something to build a life on. Would these children ever be able to trust? Liesel could probably get past some of what she'd seen. Jack could provide love and give her experiences to help counter what she's gone through. Karl, though, might be like an exposed nerve for the rest of his life. What would he think about when he turned off the lights at night? What would he imagine when footsteps got too close behind him on a poorly lit street?

CHAPTER NINETEEN

It was sunny and warm as we sailed into Havana Harbor, with the historic Morro Castle on the port side and La Punta with its ancient cannon to starboard. We were not far from where the battleship Maine sank, thus giving newspaper magnate William Randolph Hearst a tool to pressure the American government into a short war with Spain, which ended with the Philippines and Puerto Rico as the spoils of war. As we grew closer to our pier, I could see Jack, standing next to a very short man with a hat. There were also two larger men standing slightly behind them who appeared watchful.

When we had docked, I thanked the captain and the first mate for our transport and quickly took the children down the ramp.

"There's your Uncle Jack," I said to Liesel as we got to the bottom of the gangplank. He walked quickly to his niece and nephew and picked them up, placing each of them in an arm. Liesel had never seen Jack and Karl had been very young the last time Jack was in Germany, so they looked surprised by the greeting.

"Don't say anything to me, Jack," I said in English," until we're alone." He caught on and told me to shake hands with the man to his left.

"I'm Meyer Lansky," said a man who couldn't have stood much over five feet. He was wearing a suit and tie, despite the bright Caribbean sun, and looked like a Jewish accountant. I, of course, understood this man ran casinos on the east coast of Florida and was the financial mastermind behind organized crime in America. "Welcome to Cuba," he said. "Havana's a great town. You'll like it here."

"Have you found a place where the children can disappear into the fabric of this island? I said.

"Sure," he said. "There are some Lithuanian Jews who came here about ten years ago. They're from Grodno and are distantly related to my dad's family. Don't worry, they're in a different area of finance from mine," he said.

"That's really nice of you to set this up," I said.

"Don't worry about that. Jack and I go back a long way, to the lower east side of Manhattan. We do favors for each other," he said. "I understand that you're a hero, as well as a hoofer," he said.

"Maybe," I said. "We need to get someplace private pretty quick."

At his signal, two heavyset men came up behind him. "Make sure you've got his luggage off the boat. I imagine the kids won't have anything worth keeping."

"Not even a doll for Liesel," I said.

"The Nazis are killing my people," Lansky said. "It's going to get worse before it gets better. I thought the Cossacks were good at pogroms, but Hitler and his fascists are much better organized."

Where the pier met the island of Cuba, a man cut from the same cloth as the two men with Lansky waited in an old Cadillac. Jack, the children, and I entered the car with one bodyguard, while a Lincoln pulled up to transport Lansky and the other bodyguards to a meeting with General Fugelnico Batista, the island's strongman. Havana seemed like a bright summer festival as we drove through streets full of pretty women and open fronted bars that catered to American tourists. It had been a vacation spot for Europeans, but rumors of war made it a refuge for those who had already fled.

We drove out of town for a half hour on sun baked highways that turned to dirt outside the city limits. Jack thanked me three times and told his niece and nephew that I was his best friend. He explained I didn't want the Nazis to know I was helping them because of our friendship. He did all this in German, which, luckily, neither man in the front seat understood. Liesel, who had accepted me in passage, asked me to sing her a song. I told the guys in the front seat that I was going to sing to her, so they wouldn't think I had lost my marbles in the Fatherland.

"This is a song two friends of mine, Jewish guys, wrote but I never got a chance to sing in a movie. It's all about a Cuban dance that drives a man crazy because he can't get it out of his head. It's called 'Just Anotha Rumba.'"

Liesel smiled and I showed her how to use my stomach as a drum to go along with the rhythm as I sang about the dance having gotten my "numba."

She enjoyed turning my stomach into a conga drum, which made it harder to sing, but there was something powerful in watching her, as she enjoyed her freedom.

"You can call me Uncle Tommy now," I said.

"Onkel Tommy," she said, using a German accent on my title.

"Do you know that at your age, you can learn English and soon you'll be able to speak it without an accent?" I said. "When your uncle isn't being careful you can still hear the Hessische behind the English."

"I don't have an accent," he said in English that actually had more of the lower east side of Manhattan than German in it.

"That's not what Louisa said. She told me when you lose control she thinks she's in the goddamned Black Forest."

"You didn't teach these kids English did you?" Jack said.

"Not a word," I said. "We spoke their mother tongue all the way over so they could concentrate on taking care of themselves. They don't speak very often. I think you're going to have to spend a lot of years getting them to trust anyone. Liesel may actually get a childhood, but the older one is probably in a world of simple survival where not being starved and beaten constitutes a good day."

"I'm not sure what to do for him," Jack said. "I've got a lot to make up for with these kids. Any suggestions?"

"He's pretty strong for being treated like a human punching bag," I said. "How about playing baseball down here while we're finding a congressman to sponsor a bill making them legal immigrants?"

"By the way, I got a call from your buddy, Willkie. He tried a lot of things but couldn't make it work. I think he's really good guy.

"But I've given up doing this in an above board way. I've already got a congressman in my pocket and Meyer owns a couple of them in Florida and New York," Jack said. "If they handle it carefully we can get them to America in a few months. We won't have to deal with the anti-Semites in the State Department. I think a bill in Congress could immediately make them citizens."

"I can't believe that Roosevelt let them send back that ship full of German refugees," I said. "All the Jews will end up dead. I can feel it. Those animals will end up eliminating every one. There is a feeling in Germany that a need for a blood purge of so called 'inferior stock' is preordained and is justified."

"If you spend time growing up there, you know they're thinking 'I'm being nice to this dirty Jew because I need something,'" Jack said.

We reached a nice home in the countryside that sat amidst mature palm trees and had clay walls covered with jacaranda.

"The woman who came out looked like a Jewish version of the pinked cheeked, pie baking mother some Americans had and others always wanted. The woman's dark haired husband stood behind her without any discernable expression on his face.

"I am Esther," the woman said to Liesel as she picked her up and gave her a hug. Her husband shook hands with Karl and welcomed him in German.

They shook hands with Jack and me and we followed them into the villa.

"Your German is good," I said to the husband, whose name in his adopted country was Roberto.

"Both of us also speak some Polish and Russian.   In Lithuania you never know who will occupy you next week." He said it with a laugh, so I assumed from his irony they had been in Cuba for awhile. They'd probably picked up an easy language like Spanish while clearing customs.

The children were taken upstairs to clean up and put on the clothes Jack had purchased for them in Havana.

"Meyer set them up in this house for me. They've got a smaller place, but as a favor to him they're staying here with the children," Jack said. "I set up an account in Havana and am paying them well. They can be trusted to keep a low profile, and a couple of Meyer's men will be here the next few days. I'll be here for a month to make sure they adjust."

Since Jack was probably worth ten of Meyer's men in a crisis, I decided everything was going to be okay.

"I guess I'm all caught up in the children, trying to figure out what's best for them, but I guess they're not my problem any more," I said.

"The children and everything you saw in Germany got to you, didn't it?" Jack said. "If you want, you can come to Havana and see them while we're waiting to bring them into the States."

"There's a lot more going on you don't know," I said.

"I figured that," Jack said. "Someone just doesn't waltz out of Germany with a couple of Jews, even if they're six and twelve. They think you work for them, don't they?"

I didn't say anything and he knew he'd hit pay dirt.

"Do you still have the key to my place?" Jack said.

"Yeah."

"You know that I collect guns, and I know you know how to use them. I've got a key hidden inside a copy of "The Pickwick Papers" in the den. The key opens a closet downstairs in the back of the pool room. All the guns and ammo you'll need are in there."

"You read the Pickwick Papers?"

"No. I hollowed the pages out before I had a chance," he said.

"Have you read any of those books?" I said.

"No," he said. "I've left them to you in the will, so don't worry about it."

"The only thing that's going to kill you is too many wives," I said.

"You want them now?" he said. "Why don't you drive a truck over there and take them back to Encino."

"I can wait," I said.

"Okay, since you won't take my books, you'll have to take this other present I got for you," he said.

"What's that, one of your used wives?"

"Funny guy. Funny guy," he said. "You're starting a picture in three weeks. It's a private eye movie for Magellan. You have to practice not smiling for the next three weeks. Stop being polite and don't let spying get in the way of completing the picture," he said, half sarcastically and half earnestly.

"You put up the money for the picture, didn't you?"

"I gave you a hint that night when you told me you were going to England. I didn't have all the loose ends tied up then, so I was about to call you when I got the cablegram."

"What if it loses money?"

"Make sure it doesn't," he said.

"The private eye sings?"

He looked exasperated until he saw my smile and realized I was jerking him.

"Don't smile. I have to support two more people now."

"I want to get drunk and lie in the sun," I said. "They always say that hell is hot, with flames, but it's actually cold and it rains all the time." I was quiet for a minute, which always surprises everyone. "Is that rum on the table there? It looks pretty dark."

"Darker than Judy's heart," he said.

"Wife number three was the worst of all. She looked like Olivia De Havilland and had the soul of a southern slave owner," I said. "The rum looks fantastic."

"I'll get the limes from the counter. Find the glasses in the cupboards," he said.

"Give Karl a small glass of rum," I said.

"He's twelve years old."

"He's older than either one of us will ever be," I said, taking the rock glasses from their shelf. I looked out the window as some clouds obscured the sun and wondered what it would be like to be Karl, and was thankful I didn't know.

CHAPTER TWENTY

When I saw America from the deck of the ship, I realized how lucky my whole life had been. I left the ship in Miami and waited for a porter, then checked to make sure my steamer trunk full of British clothes was unloaded. If Churchill is right, I won't be tailored by Savile Row any time soon. While I arranged to have the trunk placed on a north bound train, a handsome man sporting a large moustache and wearing a linen suit, waved at me and approached. An Egyptian cotton shirt with a tie that shouted British public school accompanied him.

"We have a common friend at Chartwell," he said.

"You know, you couldn't look more British," I said.

"There aren't any Nazis around, if that's what you're worried about, but I'm now going to ask you to sign here," he said, handing me an autograph book. "I'll meet you at the Boca Raton Hotel and Club later this evening. You have a room reservation in your name. I'll come up to your room after nine," he said, moving away, after loudly thanking me for my graciousness. He disappeared into the crowd in a way that surprised me. I then set about making sure my steamer trunk found the train for Boca Raton, which if memory serves me right means "mouth of the rat."

CHAPTER TWENTY ONE

The train first stopped at Fort Lauderdale, before pulling in to the station in Boca Raton. Boca was a resort destination rated just slightly below its neighbor, the internationally known Palm Beach. I was met at the station by a hotel representative and transported in a wooden sided auto to a large edifice, that spoke of northern money entrenched among the plantation south. I was reminded of the Greenbrier, a hotel I'd enjoyed in West Virginia, and the Hotel Del Coronado in San Diego, because the hotel's bearing and understated urge to please imbued its design and presentation. Once in my room, I took a shower and then put on a seersucker suit, a linen shirt and a silk tie I'd purchased in Havana. On the first floor there was a soda fountain proving I was once again in the land of the brave and the free, so I indulged in a banana split with a "whipsa cream and a walla nuts." After sitting for awhile in a deck chair to watch the surf, I wandered over to the bar, where I fell into an old fashioned with just the right consistency of muddled fruit and Angostura bitters. It was great to be an American. The bartender recognized me and proceeded to tell me a story about Clark Gable I knew couldn't be true.

The maitre d' then showed me to a table, where I devoured the first good steak I'd had in months. Returning to my country had turned me into a glutton. After a glass of a very old Port, I retired to my room to await my British colleague. On the way up, I asked the hotel to make sure I wasn't bothered by the press and was disappointed when the desk clerk told me there'd been no enquiries about my visit.

CHAPTER TWENTY TWO

He arrived promptly at one past nine dressed in a tattersal shirt woven for the tropics, perched above a pair of slacks we called "white ducks." I pulled out a bottle of Merryvale's best and put some ice in a glass for each of us.

"The Great Man figured something special was going on when you didn't return to Chartwell and England, so Winston talked to your brother-in-law, learned about Cuba, and asked me to meet your ship," he said, pulling out a cigarette that was oval, sought my permission, and then lit its tip.

He told me his name was Saunders, omitting a first name. I told him about the struggle to get the two Jewish children out of Nazi Germany, outlining their relationship to Jack. For the first time, I talked about killing the Gestapo man in Frankfurt.

"Unfortunately, a lot of Anglo Saxons are going to find their hands around the throat of a Hun or be forced to kill many of them to save democratic societies," he said

"I was surprised at how easy it was. It just seemed like the most rational thing to do," I said. "Before I saw what evil they had done,

I might have hesitated. Now they need to be killed before they do more harm."

"It is going to take a long time until your countrymen will agree with you. The Germans will do anything to keep America neutral. For that matter, our populace will do anything to keep us out of war," he said. "But the few of us who rally around the former First Lord of the Admiralty believe push will again come to shove and we will be forced to fight Germany again. This time the Hun will be a lot nastier than those who raped the Belgian nuns."

"I thought the stories about the nuns were British propaganda," I said, causing silence. I waited a moment and asked, "What are you doing in America."

"I've a title at the embassy in Washington, but I'm supposed to forge ties with people in army and naval intelligence, but at a very sub rosa level. Chamberlain, of course, wouldn't want the little corporal getting mad at us."

"Are you MI5 or MI6?" I said, referring to the two, often squabbling intelligence agencies Britain had created before the First World War. "Five" was supposed to confine its efforts within the Commonwealth, while "Six" operated on foreign soil.

"Seven, actually," he said, before laughing at my bewildered look.

"In other words, you're not going to tell me," I said.

"It's not that, it's just that at the moment neither service is covering itself with glory, what with Chamberlain as PM. We're walking around on little cat feet, as one of our poets might say."

"To be honest, that's one of our guys," I said. "You would think everyone would understand what the stakes are in all of this."

"It wasn't a cakewalk for you Americans, of course, but it's hard to understand what losing whole generations of village men did to the British people," he said. "The Frogs will never come back from it. Their country is like a park. Outside of Paris, there isn't anybody."

"It sounds like you're listening to Churchill," I said.

"I know too much not to be with him, but any information I get to him is transferred in the most circumspect manner. He's literally loathed by many of the most important people in his own party, and his views on India make him a creature of the nineteenth century. In fact, his war was in the nineteenth century." I thought of Churchill, as a very young man, escaping from the Boers, grabbing great headlines and realized how old Churchill was. In many ways he was a throwback to the age of cavalry charges and white feathers.

"How do you see me fitting into your operation?" I said.

"The first thing you have to comprehend is that you might be looked on as a traitor if you're working for a foreign power," he said. "Had you thought about that?"

"It won't be long until we're all in this together," I said.

"I hope that's true, but until then you're taking a risk," he said.

"Okay. I'm willing to do that. What else should I know?

"We're not sure what they have in mind for you. Have you made it clear that you want no attention drawn to your support for Germany?" He washed the end of the sentence down with the rest of his scotch, which I quickly refilled. I found myself liking Saunders. I had the feeling he wasn't born into the aristocracy, probably a boy from solid middle class stock who rose on pluck and luck, never acquiring the superiority complex so common to those at Jimmy's level. It always seemed the class system had more to do with what we called "British reserve," than some genetic traits of Anglo Saxons.

"The Abwehr, their intelligence service, is run by a very canny Admiral named Canaris. He has used the German American Bund to place his people in your country. It won't be long until you'll be hearing from them," he said.

"Do your people talk to the FBI?"

"I guess the answer is yes and no. Roosevelt and Churchill have begun talking, but Winston isn't in power and therefore isn't in the position to ask for anything" he said. "There isn't enough support in this country yet for collaboration, but Hoover began going after the Bund last year. He knows we won't be the enemy if a war comes," he said.

"But it still doesn't mean you feel comfortable telling him about me.   Anyway, since Churchill isn't anybody in your country at the moment, I just might as well be working for Shirley Temple," I said.

"Actually, Heidi has more influence than Chartwell's owner, so pretend you're aboard the *Good Ship Lollipop* and make yourself comfortable," he said, downing his drink and standing up. "I think you should pick up some tradecraft before we pipe you and Shirley aboard, so meet me tomorrow at eight in Pompano Beach at this location," he said, handing me a map. "Here are the keys to a Ford we've parked outside the hotel. The house we've rented for our training has old slave's quarters behind it and sits far back from the road. The road itself is dirt, with few autos on it at any time. We should be able to work in private."

"Anything else I need to know?"

"Yes. Don't wear your tails or tennis whites. We'll want to make sure you're ready for the real thing. I do hope dancing has kept you in shape," he said. "By the way, in that that scene on the Pirate Ship where you climbed the rigging did you do that or a double?"

"I never used a stunt man, except for the scene on the biplane in "Brazilian Barnstorming.""

"I can't say I saw that one," he said, opening up the door.

"That's okay. Very few other people did either. That was one of the ones I did without Ginny," I said ruefully.

"I suppose it's tough to have half of a team walk away," he said.

"Actually, Magellan Pictures wants me to make a private eye picture. I don't have to sing, dance or look moonstruck," I said. "I guess I just have to pull my Borsalino down low and buckle my trench coat.'

"Make sure you do. We have a difficult time being taken seriously unbuckled." And with that, and a wink, he was out the door.

CHAPTER TWENTY THREE

Europeans, who've either read "Gone with the Wind," or seen movies about the Civil War, seem to think that the south is Virginia, with cotton plantations and singing slaves. When they think of Florida, they picture either rich people from New York asking each other if they want to play tennis, or alligators swishing through swamps looking for a 'cracker' to dine on. Florida is, of course, those things, but it is also the South, with its legacy of slavery and continuing mistreatment of Negroes. It may be 1939, but in parts of Florida it is barely 1866, so I wasn't surprised to see the former slave quarters, with the faded whitewash and areas overgrown with vines. Native plants that could survive without cultivation had taken over.

The mosquitoes must have left an early wake up call, because by the time I reached the location, every exposed part of my body felt like it had been bitten. I longed for Southern California with its mosquito abatement districts and arid climate. This place had all the appeal of the Amazon. One day right here and everyone from Manhattan would be dreaming of snow.

"Where's the Panama Canal?" I said.

"Ghastly place isn't this?" he said, mopping his forehead. "If the colonies were like this place, you wouldn't have had to pour tea in the Harbor or fight Cornwallis. We would have paid you to take this colony off our hands."

"You have to come out to where I live and appreciate a great climate," I said.

"I'm going to show you some jiu-jitsu today. I understand you've used a gun since your youth, so I'll just urge you to go to a range out west to make sure you haven't gotten rusty."

"I started hunting when I was eleven and learned to handle a pistol when I was on Broadway. I'd head to Connecticut and practice with a handgun to relax," I said.

"In England you'd have trouble getting your hands on a pistol, but you Yanks seem to emerge from the womb with one in your hands," he said.

"I lied about my age to get into The Great War. I was only sixteen, but after I qualified on the range, no one ever thought twice about my youthful appearance."

"Who taught you?"

"My grandfather grew up on a farm in Northern Maine," I said. "He had to go out and bring back dinner from the time he was 12. Then he was in our Civil War where he killed more men than he wanted to remember. He taught me. Luckily, the Great War ended before I had to use those skills. I'm not sorry now that I didn't get to go over there. I've remembered lately that my grandfather said sometimes when it got late at night he could still see the Confederates getting shot. Some nights he said he would see the same men falling over and over again, until the sun came up."

"The trenches were even less civilized," Saunders said, his face darkening.

"I'm glad I didn't get to find out."

"Many of our countrymen may get that opportunity again," he said. "Tomorrow we'll work on some communication skills, but today I'll show you some tricks. Someone I served with in Shanghai lives in Los Angeles and will continue with your training. He'll come to your place in the evening and keep quiet about it. But he doesn't know why you need these skills. He just understands it's to be kept quiet. He's good with a knife, too. Your grandfather didn't show you how to kill a man with a knife, did he?"

"No. He believed in keeping his distance."

"I'm afraid that in this business, we don't always get to choose how death occurs," Saunders said, putting his foot behind my ankle and pushing me over like a piece of straw. I got up and threw myself at him, but he stepped aside and let me fall into a puddle of rainwater.

It happened more than I wanted to admit. Something snapped and all those forces that were always bottled up broke through and took over, which only made it easier for him to move out of my way.

He played with me, like a cat with a mouse, until the surges were less insistent and I felt quieter inside.

"Do you feel like you have too much energy sometime?" he said.

"Yeah, that's why dancing has been a godsend. I don't think I could sit down at a desk or work in an office," I said.

"I noticed last night that your mind seems to wander off," he said.

"All the time," I said.

"My brother, James, was like that. My father was devastated when he dropped out of Oxford," he said, his facial features tightening.

"What's he doing now?" I said.

"He got the Victoria Cross posthumously for running against a Jerry machine gun nest in No Man's Land. He killed all the Hun in the nest and brought back his lieutenant's body," he said.

"I thought he died?"

"They say blood was coming out of his mouth as he fell into the trench. He died shortly thereafter."

"A brave man," I said.

"Yes, brave, but he would get like you were just then. No one would know when it would happen, but an explosion would go off inside him and there would be trouble. He said he never could tell when the dam would burst. James said he could keep the lid on it just so long. It's interesting that his leg would move up and down as yours does, all the time," Saunders said.

"I wish everyday I wasn't like this."

"He said the same thing and said I would never understand what it felt like," Saunders said. "My parents took him to many specialists. One on Harley Street called it attention deficit disorder."

"Some days," I said, "I can't get moving fast enough to stop the engine inside. Those are the days I'll try anything to slow it down."

"Make sure you take some Nazis with you when it happens, won't you?"

"I promise," I said, and let Saunders show me how he'd used my movement against me.

Late in the afternoon, I finally said uncle and we headed for a bath and then to the hotel bar. Saunders told stories about his brother and I knew he cared more about him than he'd ever care about anybody else. I understood, because I felt the same about Ginny. For some reason, listening to stories about somebody with my condition took away part of a special fear I'd held for a long time. His brother had won the Victoria Cross and hadn't wound up in some loony bin talking to the walls. My biggest fear is of a time when I can't control it anymore and people get hurt. It's funny to be worried about your own energy, I know, but maybe I could do something like his brother when it happened.

"My brother ran incessantly. My parents thought something was really wrong with that," Saunders said.

"I'm sorry you don't have your brother in your life anymore. When Ginny stayed in England, it was as if she kept a part of me there and it didn't seem very fair and I was angry and hurt."

"A war takes people indiscriminately. I could have died many times on the battlefield, but the devil that hid inside my brother and that churns inside you drives you to take risks like charging a machine gun nest in no man's land. You can't have tea with a Victoria Cross. It can't hold your children in its lap, and it won't be there to share childhood memories when you need them most in a world gone mad.

"I want you to call Von Darmstadt, your contact in America, as soon as possible, maybe tomorrow." He thought a bit and said, "I've heard the Germans are interested in a Santa Monica aircraft plant and I want you securely within their organization, so you can find out just what is going on."

"I was going to wait until he contacted me."

"This is too important to wait on. You were given his number and it's up to you to show how much you want to work with them."

"Okay, I'll do it tonight," I said, realizing I needed to start the new movie. Balancing both parts of my life was going to be difficult.

"The plane operation is just to get you in the door. They've something big planned," Saunders said. "I want you to be trusted by them as quickly as possible, so you can alert us and we can stop whatever it is."

"Don't you have any more details?"

"That's your job," Saunders said.

"This is Tommy Babcock," I said. "Do you still want to work with me?"

"Of course we do," said Von Darmstadt.

"I'll be at my ranch within the next few days

"I pass along my regards from our mutual friend, Von Taunus. I am planning to be on your west coast in a week and wonder if we could get together and talk?" he said. His English bore only a slight German accent.

"That would be fine. It's best on the weekend and best if you can come to my ranch in the San Fernando Valley," I said. "That way we'd have our privacy and could talk in an uninterrupted fashion."

"I can be there next Saturday," he said.

"I would pick you up at Union Station, but that might not be best for either one of us. Take a taxi into the Valley and have him drive down Ventura Boulevard until he comes to Rancho Diablo in Encino. My place is at the end of the road," I said.

"I had your address, so I obtained a map of the area and think I will be able to manage.   I will be there by twelve, or 'noon,' as you say."

"I look forward to it.   I have everything but Apfelwein."

"Thank God you don't. I might be obliged to drink it out of politeness," he said, laughing.

"I'm sorry you disdain Hessen's noble beverage," I said.

"It is good that the Fuehrer is a teetotaler, because that is some- thing someone of his class might like. We would be obliged to drink it every night," he said.

I was surprised by his comment, but, of course, this was America, where we don't have many people who'd go running back and report him. I knew that members of his class believed they could use Hitler in 1933, but had been surprised.   Now Adolf controlled their fate.

CHAPTER TWENTY FOUR

I boarded a train in Jacksonville and slept for about 14 hours, my muscles still sore from where I'd landed on the Pompano dirt. When I awoke, I found that Jerry Taft's Swing time Ramblers, a band I once worked with at the *Criterion* in New York were holding forth in the bar car. This collection of Lotharios and practical jokers were coming off an Eastern tour and heading west to make a picture. They wanted some insights into the mores of the female population in the land where the Santa Monica Mountains kiss the blue Pacific, so I acknowledged a civic duty and provided some commentary.

"What's the story with Mary Astor?" said Trummy Smith, the skirt chasing trombonist from Little Rock.

"Overrated," I replied.

"How about Claudette Colbert?" said vibraphonist "Too Tall" Garrison?

"Underrated," I said.

In this manner, I helped them focus on what lay in store for them. They pulled out their instruments, so I sang along with them. After a few minutes, some very attractive women joined us with the intention of assisting our migration out of the Deep South. We realized the importance of maintaining our Embouchures, or ongoing lip conditioning, so we continued exercising with them until we spied the Hollywoodland sign or their husbands.

The subject of the day seemed to be Glenn Miller and his hip sound. Glenn had experienced trouble filling small dance halls three or four months ago, but now the sun was shining like seven hundred bucks and the news was traveling from tour bus to tour bus. They say he found a way to use his clarinets to produce a sound people couldn't live without.

We told vaudeville stories and put away some sour mash whiskey that a trumpet player, Jimmy Landon, had picked up along the way.

Finally, after many of us had damaged large portions of our cerebrums, we arrived in Union Station, where Francisco was waiting with the wagon and his cursory hello. He manhandled my steamer trunk into the ranch wagon's cargo area and we drove back to my little spread in the country. I started telling Francisco about my new movie, but he didn't show much interest so I concentrated on our descent into the San Fernando Valley. It wasn't until we were halfway up Ventura that I got him talking by inquiring about the Honey Tangerines we were experimenting with. They were so sweet; he thought we should put in another acre because water was dirt cheap. I had a fan in the nursery business in Arcadia who gave me a good price on trees. (After the delivery of the last ones, I even sang at his kid's wedding. When folks heard about his connections in Hollywood, they elected him President of the Arcadia Rotary Club. His Rotary Ann (that's what he called his wife) has raised her head especially high at St Bernard's church since the nuptials). Francisco wanted to put more Honey Tangerines in before it got hot. There was still at least a month of potential rain, so I said yes and asked him to also try to find some Clementine trees. I was surprised to hear we were making decent money. Since I'd begun accepting the ranch as an ongoing opportunity to throw money down a rat hole, I felt all of a sudden as if I'd jumped on a gravy train. (The best thing, by the way, about getting drunk with musicians was picking up the newest slang, and Jimmy Landon always had it first) So when my enthusiasm was greeted by silence, I started singing in the hope I could *piss off* Francisco. Then I realized I needed to conserve my energy, because the Nazis were the guys who really *pissed me off.*

CHAPTER TWENTY FIVE

As soon as we reached the house, I opened a package from Magellan and began to study my lines for next week. Later that evening, tired of memorizing dialogue, I gave in to the impulse and dialed a number in Chinatown.

"Wei," the woman said. It was Feng Feng's mother.

"This is Mr. Blodgett from the Superintendent's office. May I speak to Miss Fang Fang please?"

"It is Feng Feng," she said, politely. "I will see if she's here." Her mother took a couple of minutes to get her daughter to the phone.

"Hello Gorgeous. I have returned from the Continent," I said. "I hope you're doing well. By the way, my name is Mr. Blodgett and I'm from the Superintendent's office."

"Thank you very much, Mr. Blodgett. I love teaching them, also."

"Could we have lunch tomorrow? I start a film on Monday and I'm sure you've got church and family obligations all day Sunday. Did you think about me while I was gone?"

"No, Mr. Blodgett, I honestly didn't," she said, beginning to enjoy the conversation.

"How about this? I'll meet you at the Brown Derby at one tomorrow. Take the bus up Wilshire. You'll recognize it because the building is shaped like a derby," I said.

"How clever."

"Please."

"How many other teachers will be there?"

"I'll get us a booth in the back. No one will see you. I promise."

"Yes. We're related. That's my dad.   I'll tell him," she said. "Thanks for calling." She hung up.

I was left wondering whether she'd show up, but I knew it was my obligation to study Chinese culture, just in case Churchill sent me to Singapore to save the British fleet.

CHAPTER TWENTY SIX

"The person who is joining me in the back booth is Chinese and I want her treated with respect," I said to the maitre d' at the Derby. "If anyone, in any way, makes her feel unwelcome, I will make his or her life a pile of shit."

When I first came to town, I developed a reputation for swinging on chandeliers and dancing out of the way of assholes before grandpa's patented roundhouse left them seeing stars. I'd changed a lot, but sometimes the evil you do has a way of sticking with you, providing you with an advantage. In truth, I would have made anybody's life miserable who treated her disrespectfully, but I have been working out on the bag in the barn to make me less explosive. Think of Bogart attending finishing school.

The maitre d', who was a good Joe, told me he'd take care of that and went off to speak to the employees Feng Feng might encounter.

She arrived fashionably late and was escorted to the booth by the maitre d,' who treated her as if she was Bette Davis and his most important customer.

"What happened?" she said, sitting down. "Did I wake up white this morning? I've got to go look in the mirror."

"Maybe people just recognize true loveliness," I said.

"Yes, I'm sure that's it," she said, breaking into a smile that would melt Harry Cohn's heart.

"I thought Chinese women were supposed to be quiet and inscrutable. Did you get your sense of humor from the movies?" I said.

"We started seeing talkies in English in 1932. Joan Blondell taught me how to speak American. Claudette Colbert in 'It Happened One Night' is my role model," she said. Joan Blondell was a funny choice but a fascinating one. Her fast talking blonde was certainly a strong example of the tough cookie with a heart of gold, the new American woman.

"Chinese humor is different?"

"We have this genre where two men talk to each other in a story. It's very different than Bob Hope," she said.

"I'm glad you could come. It's a long drive from Encino," I said. "I took a chance that you'd show up. You're worth the effort, but if you hadn't come, I'd probably have had too many Rob Roy's and ended up sleeping at the Ambassador Hotel."

"You know, for a man who is always a fast talking playboy in the movies, you don't have a bad reputation. You don't have a stain on you like Errol Flynn and some of the others I heard about on the set.

I believe what you said is true. But why me? Where's the future? I'm not going to sleep with you. Getting involved with a 'Chink' would make you persona non grata at Hollywood parties. I'm flattered, but I don't know why you're going to all this trouble. Soon my parents will find me a suitable man and I'll get married."

"Maybe I'm crazy. Maybe you'll charm as many men as Madame Chiang or the other Soong sisters and it will make everything rosy?"

"None of the Soong sisters married outside their race. They loved everything American, but ended up with guys who knew chow from lo mein."

"It takes me longer and longer to forget about you every time I see you," I said.

"Then we'd better stop seeing each other, after dessert. I'm really hungry and I skipped breakfast to make room," she said.

"Let's order some shrimp cocktails, New York steaks, and champagne."

"OK, but, as you know, I'm not much of a drinker. It's not a trait associated with a proper Chinese woman," she said.

"What is?"

"We're deferential to our husbands in public, handle the money, and make a lot of decisions we've been able to convince our husbands were originally their decisions. It's an art form. American women are getting more and more rights, but Chinese women might as well be living under the Han Dynasty. Only the communists treat women as equals, or at least partly equal."

"Mei ling Soong seems to be equal," I said.

"The minute the Generalissimo loses control of the Kuomintang, she's just another pushy Chinese woman."

"Do you want me to tell you about my new picture?

"Sure, who do you dance with this time, Greta Garbo?"

"It's a kind of a detective movie," I said. "Bogie was scheduled for the part, but Warner's wouldn't release him, so they called me. I said yes and so we start shooting Monday."

"Is changing genres good for your career?"

"When I went overseas I didn't have much of a career left," I said. "This is a new start. I don't sing. I don't dance. I just beat up bad guys."

"Can I feel your bicep? If you're going to be a tough guy, you have to have muscles."

"Sure."

"Boy you're in good shape. I bet you could make moo shu gai pan out of a lot of guys," she said, surprised.

"A dancer also uses his upper body. I do 75 pull ups a day and lift every other day," I said. "People frequently think I'm going to be a pansy, before they end up flat on the deck," I said, warming up to my favorite topic; me.

"They think I don't know much either, but I can't sleep well, so I consume books. I was reading in German while I was over there. Because I learned the language so early in life, most of it is easy. But I still carried a German/English dictionary with me."

"Under different circumstances, I'm sure my father would really enjoy talking to you, she said. "He speaks German and Japanese, as well as Mandarin, Shainghainese and English. Back home he was a revered scholar at Peking University," she said, daintily shoveling in more steak, before continuing. "We're here because my dad understands the Japanese, so when they took Manchuria and he could see Chiang wanted to fight the communists, not the Japanese, he accepted a standing offer from UCLA. He is a realist, but he was surprised that when the Japanese raped Nanjing, killing thousands and thousands of people, the world didn't step in and do something. He now knows his country is lost, unless the Japs get crazy enough to go to war with America. He understands their ambitions, but thinks the Japs will realize they don't have a chance against this country," she said, trying some champagne. "We've all applied for US citizenship and UCLA is making sure our applications are moving swiftly."

"You're a proud person," I said. "It must infuriate you the way you're treated in America. The places you can't go, the people who won't wait on you in stores..."

"I've gone from being the daughter of an important scholar, with an important family background that goes back to the Han Dynasty, to a woman people look at and remember their shirts need to go to the laundry. The Chinese value education more than anything and being Professor Chung's daughter made me special. Here I'm looked on as if I came from a sub-human species," she said, taking a larger sip on her champagne. "But my country will never go to war against the United States. If I don't steal, or otherwise break the law, I won't be thrown in jail. We eat well, and in the Chinese community we're respected. We've all learned Cantonese, so we'll have more people to talk to."

"All Chinese can't speak to each other?" I said.

"No. Most of the Chinese in this country speak Cantonese, because they're the descendents of men brought in to build the railroads. Mandarin and Shainghainese are just two examples of other languages spoken in China. People from the North of China cannot converse with the people in the south. It makes it hard to unify a country, although the Dynasties somehow accomplished this, until the Qing Dynasty fell and the man you call Sun Yat Sen tried to establish a democracy. Americans don't know that even though he was a hero, the warlords still ran parts of the country, before the Japanese began turning us into a vassal state like Korea," she said.

"I didn't realize things were that complicated or so brutal there," I said.

"If the communists ever took over, my family would be under sus-picion, because of our social class. It's funny, because at least the Communists are fighting the Japanese, while Chiang is only try-ing to kill communists. I kind of admire the communists, but they wouldn't think highly of me," she said.

"How come you don't have any accent?"

"My father insisted we learn English and German from the time we were three or four years old, so I went to schools run by American missionaries, where we were taught in English," she said. "In fact my teachers kept working on taking Joan Blondell out of my pro-nunciation," she said, digging into her steak. "I think they thought Claudette Colbert was okay." She pressed her napkin to her beautiful lips in a way that made me believe I was in the presence of a princess. Those Methodist missionaries probably trained her to follow the Soong sisters to Georgia Wesleyan and sit primly during afternoon receptions with sherry and tea.

"What did you think of the men and women who came to bring you Jesus?" I said.

"They were very good people who treated us well, but they seem to have been trained never to be comfortable with joy. They were surprised that so prominent a scholar as my father would drink and enjoy long banquets with Chinese they did not see as righteous. My father once said to my mother that 'Methodist missionaries seem to believe you have to be constipated and unhappy to live a good life.' Of course the philosophers he wrote about had different ideas of what

'righteous' meant. Some of his career was spent translating and inter-
preting many important works of Confucius, and the man you call
Mencius, into English. He felt he had to learn English and German
to understand western philosophy, so therefore his children learned
English very well and German not quite as well."

"Kant, Hegel, Nietzsche, Feuerbach?" I said.

"You've read them?" she said.

"Mostly in English, some in German," I said.

"I thought you didn't go to college and started dancing on Broadway when you were seventeen."

"I told you I don't sleep well and always have something to read," I
said. "Anyway, my genes are good enough that I didn't need to learn
the 'Whiffenpoof Song' to understand what lies between the covers
of a book."

She seemed to look at me through new eyes. I was still Caucasian
and off limits, but now it bothered her.

"Ask your father if he thinks the link between Hegel and Marx
goes through Feuerbach?"

"I wish you two could meet?"

"Anytime you think it's a good idea," I said.

We finished up with Baked Alaska and I finished up the champagne. I noticed that even the small amount of the bubbly she had consumed had affected her.

"Can I drive you part of the way and then have you catch the bus near Chinatown?" I said.

"I've got a silk scarf I could wear, and you could leave me where Wilshire meets Figueroa," she said.

I thanked the maitre d' and tipped everyone generously. The valet brought my Cadillac to the front and we began our drive down Wilshire.

"What's your number? You can't call my house again. I'm going to get married to a nice Chinese boy my parents will find suitable. If people found out I was seeing you, it could ruin my chance of getting someone really good."

It didn't take long on a Saturday to get to Fig. When I pulled over on the corner, she put my face in her hands and kissed me.

"I wanted the memory," she said, her body shaking.

She got out of the car and walked to the bus stop. Feng Feng gave me a smile that was a cross between that of a girl who'd just gotten off a Ferris wheel and a woman who'd met Prince Charming while bussing tables at a country club.

CHAPTER TWENTY SEVEN

At five a.m., Ginny called.

"I never sleep, except tonight and you had to wake me up." I said, grouchy as a bear whose hibernation had been cancelled by Mother Earth.

"I'm coming to California," she said.

"Why?"

"Your sister is returning and all you can say is 'why?'"

"Okay. It will be great to have you back, but what about Jimmy?'

"He brought up the idea, because he's sure hostilities will start very soon," she said. "I think he was a little surprised at how quickly I jumped at this."

"You're going to have the baby in Santa Monica?"

"Yes, I'm eight months and I'm flying out on a Pan Am Seaplane tomorrow, before the war breaks out, which Jimmy says is soon," she said.

"I'll buy a place for you in Santa Monica, and live there with you until the baby is a couple of months old," I said.

"Longer than that, I hope," she said. "I've decided I like Chinese women, so don't get all worried."

"Why did you say that?"

"I said it because I'm not stupid. Have you seen her?" she asked.

"Yeah." I didn't like where this was going. "I'm not marrying anyone, if that's what you're thinking."

"It's amazing how little you understand yourself," she said, laughing. "If anyone knows you it's me. I've never been prejudiced, you know that. Grandpa would have killed me."

"When do you get here?"

"When the seaplane hits North America, I'll hop on a train," she said.

"I'll find something like a pre-nanny, unless you want Mom to come out,"

"I hate to be bossed around. Find me someone I can boss around, without feeling guilty," she said.

"I'll call a realtor when I get off the phone," I said.

"By the way, I opened a letter from Churchill to Jimmy about you."

"When you get here you can't talk about it," I said.

"We've always kept secrets," she said.

"But this one could get me killed and hurt the people closest to me," I said.

"Does that mean me or Feng Feng?"

"Both, as well as Winston Thomas" I said, trying to scare her.

I hung up the phone.

CHAPTER TWENTY EIGHT

I spent Sunday memorizing the lines for Monday's shoot. The script required me to show the explosive inner Tommy Babcock. Showing it without eliminating it through action frightened me. In reality, that power would emerge from nowhere, moving like a flash flood that filled a desert riverbed for a short time before it disappeared.

For those who haven't experienced something like this, it's hard to explain the need to seek peace by working manual labor, or praying for an illness to flood the inner engine. It also might stop if you passed out after getting blotto. But the engine inside was stronger than you were and if you couldn't outwit it, you'd come apart.

I didn't work out much the night before, so I couldn't sleep. A couple of Ales trucked down from Canada kept me company at first. They had the full, rich taste American men used to expect. The worst aspect of prohibition, I believed, wasn't the years of having to sneak a drink; it was the expertise of brew masters and the spirit of unique breweries lost forever.

I still couldn't sleep so I opened a book about how Negroes are mistreated in the South. I knew victims closer to home than Mississippi.

In the early thirties I would go down Central Avenue to listen to Jazz. More than once I saw the cops roughing up colored people and shaking down the joints for cash. If the owners couldn't or wouldn't pay, the cops shut them down. They'd beat up almost everyone in the place but me. The cops would order me out of the club before the carnage began and warn me to stay in my part of town, where it was safe. Only a fool would believe I was in any danger. On the other hand, a colored man who went too far down Central into Compton was in deep trouble. "Don't let the sun go down on you in Compton," Negroes were told. In America, being colored was a lot more dangerous than having skin like mine. My grandfather would have been outraged and begun looking about for someone to cane.

These thoughts sent me to a bottle of JW Dant, whose contents I mixed with water from the well I tapped just for this and making coffee. I nursed that drink until four a.m., when sleep dropped by, wrapped its arms around me, and held me down until six, when I got up and enjoyed three cups of dark black coffee made with a metal pot Jack brought back from Italy with wife number two, the Renoir collector; or was that wife number three, the tennis pro collector?

The chill air made sure I was awake as I drove over Sepulveda to the studio.

I'd never worked at Magellan Pictures, so it was lucky the guard was a fan. He pointed out a parking spot marked T. Babcock. I hoped today wouldn't inspire executives to paint it over.

On the soundstage, Reed Strickland, the director, was there to meet me. He was pleasant, but I knew I hadn't been even his fifth choice, and that he would never completely understand how I'd picked up the lead. I was polite to everybody and found a couple of cameramen who'd worked on my pictures and said hello. However, my body was a pressure cooker, with the steam almost visible.

It reminded me of the day my mother pulled me away from a tree I was (for some strange reason) punching, and told me to dance that energy away. Then she bandaged my bleeding hands after dousing them with alcohol. (Here are words to live by; if you decide to take on a tree, pick a poplar instead of an oak.)

Today's dialogue involved a scene between the hero/tough guy and two punks who were shaking down his client, a rich, mysterious woman. Strickland probably chose this scene to immediately show the studio, and me, just how out of my league I was.

The setting was a roadhouse bar. It was raining outside and the set was darkly lit.

When I walked up to the bar, I already wanted to take the heads off both actors. I looked at them and said, "Stay away from Mildred. She's had enough trouble already."

"I don't know what you're talking about," one guy said.

"You must be Jimmy Scalese. They described you as short, with a face that scares small children," I said.

Scalese sputtered, while I said to the other guy, "You must be Sammy Leone. They said you were the muscle, with the brain of a prairie dog in heat."

Leone moved towards me and I grabbed the middle of his trench coat, picked him off the ground and held him in the air, saying, "You stay away or I'll make sure both of you end up floating down the Los Angeles River. But don't worry about drowning, you'll already be dead."

As I said it, I let myself imagine an outrage fit for the record books. Sam Wyatt, the guy playing Leone, looked like he was actually scared shitless. His head had fallen through the trench coat collar and he was lost somewhere inside.

"Don't think you can push us around," he choked out. I sneered, put him down right before he fell out of the coat and watched Leone and Scalese try to salvage some of their pride as they walked out the door into the rain.

The bartender said, "You're McDonald. I've heard about you. You almost sounded like you'd enjoy taking care of them."

"No," I said. "I'm just a peaceful guy trying to help out a dame." The look on my face had turned from menacing to distant. People on the set told me that look was scarier.

"It's too bad I've got to go back to LA. It might be nice to take a boat out on the lake when the rain stops," I said, throwing some bills on the bar and headed out the door.

The bartender looked down at the money and said to himself, "If I took a boat ride with you, I'd worry I'd end up floating face down, out near the Island."

"Cut and print," Strickland said. "Everybody can go home. That's all I had planned for today." Strickland had expected 40 bad takes. I'd screwed up the schedule.

Jim Tierney, a cameraman who was one of my old pals, said, "The only other hoofer who could have pulled off that scene was Jimmy Cagney, and you scare me more than he ever did."

"I just haven't had my coffee today," I said, smiling.

"Strickland thought he'd been dealt a bad hand. I bet he thinks differently now," Jim said, before walking away.

Strickland came over and said, "I think this picture might make some money. Just don't lose that edge."

"You don't need to worry about that," I said. "You didn't mind my throwing in the bit with the trench coat, did you?"

"No, it was a great touch. But I think we'd better show you how to pull a punch before we go any further. I'll have the stunt men work with you tomorrow and we'll shoot again on Wednesday," he said. "I don't want any of my actors getting hurt."

"Thanks for worrying about me," I said.

"You weren't one of the actors I'm worried about," he said.

I smiled and headed for my car. I looked forward to a quiet afternoon on my paint, riding across the Valley. I hoped Francisco had been exercising her, because I wanted to see how fast the quarter horse could go. After I lunged the thoroughbred for a couple of days, I might be ready to really risk my neck.

CHAPTER TWENTY NINE

Two days later, the Examiner and the Times featured comments about the "new" Tommy Babcock. One quoted a source who had been on the set. "He scared the pants off me. He picked up one actor using the guy's trench coat. Believe me; he's in a class with Bogie and Cagney." The other paper said, "It's clear Columbia made a big mistake taking Tommy Babcock off contract. If his acting is as good as they say it is, Columbia will have to pay as much for just one film as they were paying him in an entire year."

No matter how good that sounded, no one knew what the average American would think about a has-been hoofer turned private eye. Clearly, some people would go to see it, to check whether any of this promotional stuff had truth in it. If they liked the picture, not having a contract would be a blessing. I could make the movies I wanted, and my agent could get a decent price. But I stopped this wishful thinking, remembering that in Hollywood many of yesterday's stars were trying to find ready cash to pay the pool man. One thing was sure, I would get at least one more picture based on this PR. With the ranch making money, I could put some more bucks into a rainy day fund.

Two days later I had a love scene with Louisa Bordeaux, Magellan's new sex siren. Three years ago, before she'd hitched a ride to Hollywood from Juarez, her name had been Maria Lopez. Even back then she had bubbled like oil on a hot grill. Yesterday, I saw her walk towards her trailer and the sensuality traveled fifty feet. I took stock of my situation. First I kiss a Chinese girl, and then I kiss a girl from Mexico. I was starting to feel like the only member of the League of Nations who liked his job.

Louisa had long dark hair that shone like a seam from a strip coal mine. She had large eyes and a full mouth that invited you to make contact with it any way you wanted. She was five six, with breasts hiding under her low cut blouse that seemed to imply they were flowers waiting to push through towards the sun.

They'd set the soundstage as an intimate restaurant. I saw Jim Tierney standing there. "I've never been in a picture lit this darkly," I said.

He looked at me and smiled. "You're waiting for the spotlights and the stairs that light up as you step on them, aren't you?"

"Well in those movies I was sure the audience would be able to see movement on the screen," I said.

"You can see what's going on in Warner Brother's pictures can't you?"

"Yeah," I said.

"Think Warner Brother's," he said, walking away.

Louisa was already seated at the table, looking as edible as a meal at El Morocco.

I sat down next to her and looked into brown eyes that grabbed your attention like a homing beacon on a dark night.

"We're supposed to be in love. Can you imagine that?" she said.

"Most of the men in America will believe I'm in love with you."

She moved closer and began to stroke my thigh, moving up until she found home plate.

"I don't have to stand up in this scene, do I?"

"No, don't worry," she said. "And that's good, because part of you would get caught on the table."

"I don't know what came over me," I said, as she raised the tension another notch by removing any impediment to closer contact.

"You're certainly ready for a big scene," she said. "There are a couple of other actors who must like boys because nothing happened when I did this to them."

"You should be the final test for choosing Scoutmasters."

"We're supposed to be in love. It should look real," she said. "Anyway, when I saw you I thought I could really enjoy this."

"What happens if I lose myself in the role?" I said.

"Don't worry. When I saw you walk towards me, I'd already decided to help you out in the trailer after the scene."

"Then do me a favor and stop for a while, so I have a chance of surviving until they yell 'cut and print,'" I said.

She looked into my eyes. "If you don't hold on, I'll tell everyone you're a fairy."

I leaned back and tried to think about honey tangerines. I tasted my drink, expecting tea. It was about four fingers of Cutty Sark. I looked across the room and saw Tierney give me thumbs up. He must have figured this for a tough scene.

I didn't know if the camera could capture the sexual tension, but I was glad Feng Feng was looking for a nice Chinese boy, so I didn't have to feel any guilt. Louisa had a way of making a man lose control. If she was Mata Hari, the Mexican government would know every country's military secrets. Part of my body throbbed during the scene, but it wasn't a difficult part to play.

After a couple of takes, we made Strickland happy. When he was happy, she turned to me and gave me a kiss that seemed to use her entire body. She smiled, told me where her trailer was, and walked off slowly, letting everyone enjoy the movement of her hips. I waited until my lower body said I could emerge from under the table. I finished the scotch and drove home. My life was too complicated to add in Louise Boudreaux.

CHAPTER THIRTY

"And now, from deep within the lovely San Fernando Valley, it's Nazi time. This is your host for tonight, Ludwig von Kinderkiller." I suddenly realized I'd said that out loud and was glad I was alone on a ranch.

I had decided to make sure Francisco wasn't around, by telling him a famous, married female star, who was paranoid about being discovered, would be visiting Saturday and Sunday. In actuality, of course, it would be just me and the Third Reich.

Von Darmstadt wasn't wearing striped pants and spats; he showed up dressed like an upper middle class American businessman with an exceptionally good tailor. His hair was blond and he looked like someone who taught skiing in the Alps. Standing about six feet tall, he had an athletic build with broad shoulders.

He was accompanied by a woman in her twenties whose beauty would take the breath out of Jesse Owens' lungs. Her blond hair touched her shoulders, flipping outward at the ends. She had eyes that captured the blue of the sea and her bee stung lips must have come with her birthday suit. Her breasts were fighting to get out of her blue dress, while her skirt seemed to hold other as yet undreamed of pleasures. Her waist was too tiny for her upper body, as if she'd sent it to the dry cleaners and they'd put extra water in the cleaning solution.

I could see her as Heidi in a dirndl made of silk and velvet, with a matching handbag. If you wanted milk from her goats you'd have to mortgage the Fifth Avenue town house. I'd learned in Hollywood that women who looked like the girl next door had unimaginable secrets, but there was no denying that her animal magnetism put Louisa Bourgeois in the supporting actress category.

Von Darmstadt introduced her as Meike Schultz, an American native from Pennsylvania whose parents were German immigrants. Apparently her parents had taught her German from the time she could talk and she'd spent two years with her grandparents in Munich. I wondered what her job was at the Embassy, and why her English made me want to see her passport.

I took my eyes off Meike and invited them onto the screened in porch, where I'd laid out sausages and cheeses, some cold bottles of St. Pauli Girl, and a good Riesling.

"Did you leave your bags at the train station?" I said.

"We had a colleague take them to the Biltmore Hotel," he said.

"It's very nice here," she said, "Especially when you've left New York and its chills."

"Believe it or not, this is about as late in the year you'd enjoy sitting on this porch in the daytime," I said. "From June on the weather is too hot. I have a place in Santa Monica in the summer."

After a couple of beers for the men and a glass of wine for Meike, they got down to business.

"You said you are still willing to work with us?" he said.

"Absolutely," I said. "I think Roosevelt wants to bring us into a war on the British side as soon as he can."

"We believe the British will never go to war against us, but one can never be too careful," Von Darmstadt said.

"What can I do?"

"We've been reading how you're going to be a big star again," he said.

"Everyone in America seems to want to get close to movie stars, including politicians," he continued. "It would be nice if you could go to Washington and make some friends. You could develop contacts who would tell us how to operate in this country and what to do about Roosevelt. Taft or Dewey will not be problems for Germany. The danger lies in another term for Roosevelt."

"Do you have other people working on this?" I said.

"We are waiting on what could be an important development," Meike said, touching my shirt and looking into my eyes as she talked. If I hadn't seen so many actresses do this I'd believe she was experiencing love at first sight.

"Is it something positive for Germany?" I said.

"We believe so," Von Darmstadt said.

"That's good to hear," I said.

"I'm ready to take a trip after the movie wraps," I said.

"Wraps?" Von Darmstadt said.

"It's when the picture is all tied together and ready for the final edit before it hits theatres. They've been pumping details on the movie to newspapers to create anticipation. It sounds like you've been reading publicity?"

"You don't seem much like the Tommy Babcock I saw at the movies," Meike said.

"People always seem to confuse the actor with the part he plays," I said. "For example, you wouldn't believe what miserable human beings comedians really are."

"I think it would be nice to find out what an actor is really like," she said with a smile of Shubertian sweetness. She could pull in a man the way a Redondo fisherman reels in a striper.

"Meike will be your contact in Washington," Von Darmstadt said. "You can't come near the embassy, so the embassy will come to you.

Before that, however, we'd like to find out more about a bomber that Douglas Aircraft is building in Santa Monica."

"Why do you want to know about it? America isn't thinking about entering any wars I know of," I said.

"No, but they could sell this plane to the British to use against Germany," he said. "We want you to obtain the specifications of the plane and its engines."

"I thought you said you wouldn't have to fight the British?"

"This is just in case I'm wrong," he said, bringing out some documents and going over them with me, while Meike twisted curls in my hair with her fingers.

CHAPTER THIRTY ONE

The next day I called Saunders to talk about the bomber.

"Have you got a crystal ball?" I asked.

"I'm glad you've come to appreciate my greatness," he said.

"I'm talking about the transportation in Santa Monica. They want me to get the skinny about it," I said.

"Are you supplied with funds?"

"Oh, crap. Churchill can't pay me, so now I have to pay to be a spy?"

"There's a former RAF officer who got into trouble passing Winston information and had to resign his position," Saunders said. "He doesn't have a farthing."

"And..?"

"He's not a British government employee, but he knows everything about planes, and if Churchill calls Donald Douglas, whom I know he knows, then we can find out about the plane."

"Okay. I'll call Jimmy and ask him to give money to whatever his name is?"

"His name is Lachlan McLean and he believes we're right about the future, so he'll be here in a flash," Saunders said.

"You'd already set this up, hadn't you?"

"Oh ye of little faith," said Saunders.

"I'll pay his expenses in America, but he has to arrive like a ghost and disappear, because I don't know if I'm being watched," I said. "Why is Donald Douglas going to give him information?"

"If he wants to sell planes to England, there has to be an England, and people like Douglas think Churchill's the man to save our sceptered isle."

"I love America and I have no intent of giving the Nazis our secrets," I said, fury rising in me in the way it has a tendency to do.

"We won't give them the truth, don't worry about that," he said.

"I better not be a patsy here," I said.

"You've already shown you can kill and I have a wife and kids I'd like to see again," he said.

I hung up and called Jimmy.

CHAPTER THIRTY TWO

It was the second Friday after that scene with Louise Boudreaux when my barn phone rang shortly after I'd finished exercising.

"The newspaper said you have a girlfriend. In fact, every newspaper says you are in love with that French woman," Feng Feng said. "Are you trying to get to all the continents?"

"Mexico is in North America, or don't they teach geography at San Jose?" I said.

"She has a French name."

"I thought you were going to marry a nice Chinese boy," I said.

"Is she there?"

"Yeah, she's mucking out the stables," I said.

"What's mucking?" she said.

"She's not here. You know, after a quick shower, I could head for Chinatown."

"You know that's impossible," she said.

"The publicity people at the studio place these stories to build up the box office," I said.   "Its 8:30 and the people of Encino have already rolled up the sidewalks."

"I just wanted to find out about you and this French, or whatever, girl."

"That's the sign of a good friendship, when someone looks out after you," I said.

"Why did I have to have lunch with you?" she said.

"Because sometimes life isn't as simple as it should be," I said. "Look, I promise never to call you again. If you don't call me we'll both get over this. You've made it plain nothing could happen between us."

"You would never marry a 'Chink' anyway," she said.

"If I married anyone, a Chinese woman would be just fine," I said.

"You're just saying that because you know it can't happen. I've run out of money for the payphone and have to hang up," she said, sounding as if she was going to cry.

"Thanks for calling," I said, as I heard the payphone click off. Why was I doing this? Marriage just wasn't for me. I decided I needed to work the bag for awhile in the hope some crazy feelings would pass.

CHAPTER THIRTY THREE

Tuesday evening I stopped into the screening room to watch the "dailies." I sat in the back, while one of the assistant directors poured me a scotch and soda.

The "edginess" beneath the surface of Tommy Babcock, boy dancer, looked like a mooring line ready to break. I was a coiled snake carrying venomous potential. (I could certainly see why everyone liked Ginny better) The guy on the screen looked dangerous. In romantic scenes, that tension somehow enhanced the chemistry with Louisa. It seemed plausible that people could imagine me throwing her down on a table and having my way with her.

I knew then this picture would be a hit and I'd have no trouble working again. That layer of pseudo gentility had been peeled away and what remained was the boy bloodying his hands against the tree.

The buzz had been right. You can never tell in this town whether you're being fed bullshit or not. I felt better watching myself in this picture than I'd ever felt watching all the others combined.

The screening finished and they turned around to look at me.

"You didn't know whether to believe what you were hearing; did you?" Strickland said.

"No."

"This picture is going to make the studio a lot of money, make me a big-time director, and bring you back from oblivion, bigger than you were before. You know that?"

"Yeah." I swallowed my scotch and stood up. "I thought when you were washed up; that was it. No second acts."

"How did you change your style so dramatically?" said Jenkins, an assistant director.

"I guess what you saw is me," I said.

I was walking out the door when Jenkins said," That's downright scary."

Pointing to my chest, I said, "You ought to be in here. You'd piss in your pants."

CHAPTER THIRTY FOUR

Saunders and McLean flew into L.A. and drove out to a rundown motel in Malibu. I wasn't taking any chances.

To make my life even more complicated, Ginny was arriving tonight. I was a silver sphere in a pinball machine.

I put the top down on the La Salle and headed up Highway One. I pulled off once at Sunset and again at Topanga and there was no one following me.

I reached the motel to see a youngish guy sitting on a desk chair he'd apparently pulled out of his room. The Brits are suckers for sunshine, after they figure out what it is.

"My name's Tommy," I said, stepping out of the caddy.

"Clark Gable," he said. You could tell he'd been a flyer by his attitude, the kind of attitude which allowed him to go up in the air knowing he might not return.

"Where's Ronald Coleman?"

"I'm right here," said Saunders, from the other side of my car.

"How'd you do that," I asked.

"That's a fifth level trick and you're still in the basement," he said.

"There's a roadhouse down the highway. If we can't get some privacy, I don't want to hear an English accent. Just stay quiet and drink the crummy American beer I buy you," I said. "Drink it as fast as you can and we'll leave."

They both laughed, but knew it was a good idea.

"It's hard to believe you were a dancing movie star," said Saunders.

"This is the new me, except that it's really the old real me,"

The roadhouse on the way to Pt. Mugu was practically deserted. We sat as far from the cash register as possible and had chicken fried steak and some Budweisers.

"When are you going to Douglas?" I asked.

"He's got an appointment at 11," Saunders said.

"What do you think he'll find?"

"I think I'm going to find a plane that can't fly. From what I've heard from Saunders, the plane is so big, the Yanks may not have an engine big enough to get it off the ground," Lachlan said. He was a good looking guy that had a way of inspiring confidence, so I listened carefully.

"No one's ever tried to build anything this big before. If we had it, we could linger over Berlin and drop a lot of bombs on the Nazis," he said, "and then go on to obliterate Hamburg. That is, we could, if no one had invented the fighter plane."

"I guess someone would have to invent a long-range fighter to go along with those beasts," Saunders said.

"I just got my spy license, so I'm listening to you guys," I said. "I only fly to look at the cabin attendants. Everybody would like to have a nurse around."

"Pretty soon all the nurses will be on battlefields. They won't have any leftovers for airplanes," Saunders said.

"That's wonderful news. I can't tell you how great it is to have a cheerful man in the room," I said. "I've got to drive you back and pick my sister up at Union Station. Then I have to study my lines. After work tomorrow, I'll be back with my trench coat on."

"Next time, wear something under it, won't you?" Saunders said. "We aren't all debauched Americans."

"If you can see through this suit, you'll be a great asset to whatever side you end up on," I said, as I motioned them out the door into an onshore breeze.

CHAPTER THIRTY SIX

Ginny looked radiant.

"Ni hen pang," I said.

"You too, buster," she said. "Is that something Bong Bong taught you?"

"You know her name is Feng Feng, and I just told you you're fat."

"The bundle from Britain is resting comfortably, despite having a gone-to- seed uncle," she said. "Let's get in the car before people remember that they're fans"

We drove down Wilshire, through Beverly Hill, and back into Los Angeles, before finally reaching Santa Monica. We took a right on 6th St. and pulled up in front of a sprawling house that looked like it belonged in Massachusetts, somewhere near Marblehead. My grandfather would have approved of it. I stepped out of the car and introduced an attractive woman in a maid's uniform.

"This is Teresa. She cooks really well and she loves babies,"I said.

We walked into the foyer and Ginny said, "I'm home. I'm really home."

"I'm really glad you're here," I said, hugging her.

"I guess you're really busy," she said.

"I have two jobs and one of them really stinks," I said.

"I'm here to have a baby and support my little brother," she said. "You always pretend nothing's important, but everything's actually really important to you. Are you scared? Don't give me your phony tough guy act," she said.

"It has its moments," I said. "At the moment I'm supposedly working for one foreign government, while really working for another foreign government, while hoping against hope I'm not doing my own country any damage."

She pulled me close and I felt stronger than I'd felt in days.

"By the way, I had to call Jimmy and it didn't sound like it originally was his idea that you'd come back here," I said.

She focused those big blues on me and said, "We'll talk after you kill some more Nazis. At the moment I hate Churchill and can barely tolerate Jimmy for the mess they've put you in."

"I found you the best obstetrician in Los Angeles. I've also hired a car which will pick you up at ten and take you to your appointment, and after that take you to Schwab's so you can get discovered again."

"Go learn your lines for tomorrow while I settle in," she said, barely holding tears at bay. I truly had no idea what those tears were all about.

CHAPTER THIRTY SIX

"What did you think about the plane?" I asked.

"I have some of the specs and I'm convinced this will take years to build and then they'll discover it won't fly," Lachlan said.

"I guess that's good news for me, because I won't be selling my country out no matter what I do, but I still will have to lie to them," I said.

"Not completely. Not if we make up an engine that could turn this into the biggest weapon in history. If the Nazis then try to duplicate it, they'll waste a few years until they find out," said Saunders.

"These Germans didn't just fall off the turnip truck," I said.

"You've forgotten we have these two places called Cambridge and Oxford," Saunders said.

"I don't have a lot of time to wait for the dons to come up with something," I said.

"I brought the plans for an enormous engine that has a fatal flaw which won't be discovered until someone tries to build it," Lachlan said.

"How come you have it?" I asked.

"Until I resigned, I was trying to get the British government to rise from its stupor. I saw all the designs. This engine looked like the greatest thing since buttered scones, until an aeronautical engineer by accident discovered this problem with it, a really big one that no one had thought about before," Lachlan said.

"Don't the Nazis know about it? I asked.

"Loose Lips Sink Ships' didn't just go in one ear and out the other. Except for the friends of Russia in our midst, very little information gets out, believe it or not," Lachlan said.

"That would work as long Hitler and Stalin don't get chummy. Do the plans look they're British?" I asked.

"The plans these were copied from did, but not these. All the spelling is American."

"So I'll take the plane specs and combine them with this engine design, and give it to the Hun," I said. "What's the chance I'd get caught?"

Lachlan and Saunders looked at each other and away from me.

"Great," I said. "If I end up dead in a ditch, it won't bother you." I left the room and reconsidered what I was doing for an avocation. I was really angry and worked at getting under control. England wasn't my country and I figured if the Germans invaded it would all be over in a "fortnight."

I drove home and kissed the Queen of the Cinema, before closing the door in the room with the phone.

Von Darmstadt picked up the line in Washington.

"I got it," I said. "When I can break free, I'll bring it to you," I said, hanging up.

CHAPTER THIRTY SEVEN

The studio threw a party at the Beverly Hills Hotel for the cast and crew... The ballroom tables overflowed with bottles of Dom Perignon, shrimp as big as your fist and roast beef shipped over from Lawry's, a new restaurant getting a reputation for quality.

When Ginny walked in on my arm, the room exploded. I left her alone to be fawned over.

I had invited Feng Feng to come the last time she called and told her to tell people her name was Rose Yuen and that she wrote for Asian newspapers. This might keep the press from alerting her parents, and any prospective bridegroom, to her attendance. We never touched, anyway, so I hoped it wouldn't look noteworthy. She'd appeared in *Hello, Hong Kong, Hello*, but, although it made money, very few people really went crazy for it, so I doubted she'd be recognized. Her father had required her to use an alias on the credits, because Chinese movie actresses came from the lower classes.

"I've heard you're going to Washington. You can use my suite at the Hay-Adams," the president of Magellan, Sam Weinstein, said. "I think it's the best address in Washington, so if you're going to make friends, stay there and entertain them. It's on me. In fact, maybe you might take something from the industry to FDR." He paused. "We're really glad you agreed to do the sequel, although it's unusual to have a non contract player. Your agent, unfortunately, did a good job of negotiating your salary. I expect, however, that we'll get it back in a couple of weekends."

"If you'll get it back in a couple of weekends, he didn't ask for enough," I said.

Sam ignored that, saying, "We've had some of our people look at the rushes and a quick edit of the whole movie. It wasn't the edit we wanted yet, but they were crazy about this picture."

"I guess everyone believes your publicity people, because all of a sudden, I'm being invited everywhere," I said. "I couldn't have gotten arrested in this town three months ago and now I'm almost Clark Gable." My conservative side, the one that saved my paychecks, wasn't ready to buy into the accepted wisdom quite yet. "I like the picture and think it's great, but this is a tough town. Tomorrow I could look like an opossum who got hit by a delivery truck."

"I have to make money off the movies or my investors will have me hung on a meat hook," Weinstein said. "At first, I cast you in the picture for Jack, who had a belief in your abilities [read that put up the money]. Then I saw the first day's rushes and I knew we had something. Day after day I became convinced," he said. I noticed his Hungarian accent emerged when he seemed to be speaking about something in which he believed. The rest of the time he was concentrating on sounding like he was born somewhere between Washington, Iowa and Kansas City. It would be interesting to see if this would be a tip-off when you played poker with him. Then, I realized you couldn't pick up an accent on 'raise' or 'call' alone.

"If you entertain in Washington make sure they send me the bill," he said, moving off to buttonhole Louisa. He probably needed to relieve some stress before he went home.

Just then I saw Feng Feng walk in, the eyes of many men appraising her. Whether they were racist or not, they could still appreciate quality. She was wearing a blue suit with a simple white shirt that looked like a ball gown to me. Since no one on this crew had worked on *Hello, Hong Kong, Hello*, I'm sure she went unrecognized. Most Caucasians never bothered to note the differences in Asians. "They look all the same to me," was the common phrase.

"Where'd you tell your parents you were going?"

"I told them the school district had chosen me to receive extra instruction," she said. "They were very proud, but told me not to let all this new recognition go to my head."

"That doesn't sound very nice," I said.

"That's very Chinese. They make us feel we can strive harder. Chiang's mother probably told him he never quite made the grade, so he can't stop until he's invaded Japan," she said, laughing.

"You seem fine to me."

Just then Ginny walked over and kissed Feng Feng on the cheek.

"I know all about you. We should talk tonight," she said.

"Your brother told you about me? Feng Feng asked, astonished.

Ginny pulled Feng Feng close so she could whisper in her ear. Feng Feng had another astonished expression and refused to look in my direction.

I didn't like this one bit. Luckily, the publicity man brought over the press releases and glossies I'd requested.

"Let me see the pictures," Feng Feng said, very quietly. "What a surprise, they're all of you."

"If you start a Chinese 'Tommy Babcock Fan Club' you'll get a lot more copies."

"Did they make you wear the trench coat to cover a pot belly?" she said.

"No, they did it to keep the women on the set from going over the edge with desire."

"The next time I see you, even in the summer, you should wear it," she said.

Ginny was breaking up. I guess she thought Feng Feng was almost as good as she was at making fun of me.

"Does my presence make you feel like the humble shepherd watching the Princess riding by?" she said.

"Ke Neng," I said using the only words I knew in Chinese.

"I'll 'maybe' you, buster" she said.

Ginny looked at Feng Feng and thought she'd found a soul mate. Feng Feng wasn't brought up to reach out and touch Ginny, but Ginny took care of the problem by hugging her.

"You didn't notice I was Chinese?" she asked Ginny.

"Holy Mackerel," she said. "I wondered why you were so pretty."

"Let's get some shrimp," I said, "and champagne as well."

"What should I do with this shallow prose and the ugly pictures?" she said.

"I'll carry it. All I want is some champagne. You can carry your drink and a plate. I've arranged a bungalow where you can interview me," I said. "They'll roll in a meal."

"I hope you don't have any funny plans," she said.

"You're safe. Only the Japs would have the insensitivity to rape an emissary from the Emperor's court."

As we were heading out with a bottle of champagne, Louis La Grange, the publicity man, came over and said, "Miss Yuen, I don't know when we'll get the picture to China because of the war. Will you hold the interview until then?"

"Of course, I'm in the Tommy Babcock fan club," she said. "I want everyone to see his pictures. Thank you so much for arranging everything."

As we exited the room, Louis looked like he had just met Greta Garbo and was savoring the moment. He immediately rose in my estimation.

At that point, Ginny decided to give us a little privacy and went back to be idolized.

We went to a bungalow, which was exquisitely decorated, and sat around a table, drinking champagne, while we waited for a lobster dinner to arrive.

"Who is Rose Yuen anyway?"

"No one in America has seen her. They just know that she's beautiful and can move the Asian film market with her reviews."

Feng Feng looked around the bungalow and said, "You must be paying a fortune for this?"

"I'm not paying for anything. The studio looks at me as a meal ticket," I said. "Because I don't have a contract, I'm being wooed. I'm going to Washington next week and the head of the studio is lending me his suite at the Hay-Adams Hotel, as well as bankrolling any entertaining."

"You're going to Washington?"

"I thought it was time to become part of the democratic process," I said.

"How come?"

"I've been reading Walter Lippmann and the Federalist Papers. Now that I'm making a lot of money, I walk into bookstores and walk out followed by a clerk loaded down with volumes. He puts them into the trunk of the new roadster I bought. I learn a lot every night," I said.

"Can you remember what the page looked like, where the information is, and where it is on the page?" she said.

"Of course, that's the way to remember information, isn't it?" I said.

She smiled and took a sip of champagne.

"I think your sister is wonderful. She's really as beautiful as they say," Feng Feng said. "When is the baby expected?"

"She's due in a couple of weeks. Maybe you could stop by and visit her. We've got a Nanny, already, so that's not what I'm implying. Ginny doesn't trust the women in Hollywood and she needs a woman to talk to."

Feng Feng looked like her world had been turned upside down.

"What did she say to you?"

"There's no way I will ever tell you," she said.

"How's the marriage process going?" I said.

"They think they may have a boy for me, the only Chinese boy in his class at Johns Hopkins Medical School. I've said I would like to wait a year to organize my thoughts before marriage. He may be introduced to me this summer. His father teaches at Cal and is also an expert on Chinese philosophy."

"He sounds perfect. Are you excited about this?" I said.

"I suppose."

"That doesn't sound excited," I said. "If I felt that way before getting married, I would immediately pack my bags for Cairo and leave her a note."

"You'd leave her a note?"

"No. I was kidding about that. I'd go tell her in person. I'm not that rotten," I said.

"I don't think you're rotten at all. The only time you kissed me was when I kissed you after the Brown Derby," she said.

"Making love to you involves too much responsibility, in your words. If I want sex, that's an easy thing to get in Hollywood. Part of me feels like I'm protecting you from me," I said.

"If you were Chinese, I'd be in love with you," she said.

"I'm not going to comment on what that really means," I said.

Tears were falling from her eyes. I went around the table, pulled her unresisting body out of her chair and hugged her in a determinedly non-sexual way, as if I was trying to comfort Ginny. I had difficulty suppressing some involuntary physical reactions, but I held her very carefully, without making too much contact. Powerful emotions were moving through me, but I'd been reading about Chinese culture and understood that to do something now would be exploitation. It was harder and harder to hold her without her experiencing my altered physical condition so I probably gave away more than I intended as I pressed against her body. She didn't seem to care. I stroked her hair and waited until she stopped crying, before pulling out her chair and sitting her down.

"You love me too or you would have done something just then," she said.

"The only persons I ever said 'I love you' to were my mom and Ginny," I said.

"It's funny. I really trust you," she said. "And, I know you love me."

"How?"

"Somebody just told me," she said.

"She's been in England, how does she know?"

"She says she's known since last November. She could tell by the way you talked about me. How come you never told me about it?" she asked.

"Ginny's mind has been affected by the pregnancy. Yesterday she thought she was in Lapland."

"I never knew you were such a liar. I just thought you were a big windbag who surrounds himself with pictures of himself," she said.

"By the way, I don't have any of my Broadway posters in my trailer."

"Yes, but that's only because you're trying to change your image," she said. "I said 'I would love you,' I didn't say your ego had diminished. Your ego is so big I can hardly fit into a room with it."

"How can you stand it?"

"Because there's so little space left, it's like being wrapped in blankets," she said, "and for some reason that's comforting."

"I think the movie's going to be okay," I said.

"Some people who got an advance peek say it's a lot more than okay."

"I can't imagine where you heard that. You've got to remember that this is the year of 'Gone with the Wind' and a lot of other great pictures, so I don't know what it will do at the box office," I said.

"Were you always so worried about a picture or a show?" she said.

"No, except for the last two I made without Ginny. Before that, I knew everybody would love Ginny, and my dancing was good. The Gershwins or Berlin always gave us great songs, so it was like shooting fish in a barrel," I said.

"This role seems to fit who you really are," she said. "You were always upbeat onscreen, but there was always tension off stage."

"Back then, I didn't know people could feel that," I said.

"I could," she said. "At first I thought you were just being phony in the movies. I finally realized you wanted to be Tommy Babcock, the dancer and singer, but that wasn't you. You were a great, very athletic dancer, and I liked your voice, but that had nothing to do with who you were inside. You always seemed like Vesuvius about to erupt."

"How do you know all this stuff?"

"I studied psychology, before taking an additional year of college so I could teach elementary school," she said.

"Why didn't you become a psychiatrist?"

"Do I look like a white male?" she said. "Am I wearing a dress and do I have different eyes than you?"

"I guess it would be hard," I said.

"The word is impossible," she said. "Anyway, I like kids and maybe I can help them be ready when people in America don't look at Asians as if they're from another planet."

"You would be a good role model," I said.

"Maybe someday Americans will be concerned when another incident such as the Rape of Nanjing happens. If they see enough of us in responsible positions, not doing their laundry, someone will stand up and say atrocities like that shouldn't happen," she said. "It's surprising, but second generation Japanese think and act just like any other Americans. I met a lot of them that I like. In Japan they think Koreans and Chinese are inferior, so prejudice is a universal problem. In America, the law says everyone is equal, but there is an exclusion law for people with slanted eyes."

"We've got a constitution, though, that's different from a lot of other countries," I said.

"Yes, but it's only for white people," she said.

"Things will change here," I said.

"I hope it happens before I die, so people outside of Chinatown will treat me with respect," she said.

"Let's hope so," I said, wondering what it would take for white America to understand how cruel they can be. I also realized that my life had been charmed. Anybody who told me I wasn't welcome would end up being sorry, one way or another.

We had lobster and more champagne (she had another half glass, so I made up the difference) and talked until 9:30. Then Ginny came in and we drove Feng Feng to Chinatown. I parked down the street, while Ginny walked Feng Feng to her house. (Ginny's progress looked more like a waddle than a walk.)

CHAPTER THIRTY EIGHT

Washington is more like a small southern town than the political equivalent of Paris or Berlin. I could imagine the angst accompanying an assignment to this backwater and could picture how continental liberals might react to the treatment of Negroes. Luckily, the ten-year-old Hay-Adams was a fine hotel with elegant appointments. It endeavored to evoke the Italian renaissance and was built on land once owned by the irascible Henry Adams and Secretary of State John Hay. Lindbergh and Amelia Earhart had slept here, although probably not together. Ethyl Barrymore had visited, but the hotel's history didn't tell me if John had ever passed out in the lobby.

This world seemed far away from the recently signed German-Italian pact of steel and the German-Russian non aggression pact. Americans were concerned, but they had decided it wasn't their problem. The folly of the Great War was part of the national consciousness, while the concept of "The War to End All Wars" resembled a bitter joke.

A long telegram from Weinstein I'd received last night said his friend, Interior Secretary Harold Ickes, had arranged a short photo opportunity tomorrow morning at nine with the President. The studio had edited the film in less time than it usually took the Yankees to dispense with the Red Sox, so they'd held sneak previews in New York and Los Angeles. Louisa Boudreaux (stopping off on her journey to her "village" in France) had driven the audience wild in Gotham. The sneak I attended in Washington last night received a great response. I got a standing ovation after removing my fake moustache and horn rimmed glasses. The wild applause reminded me of vaudeville and Broadway, so I briefly thought of breaking into a soft shoe, before remembering *that* Tommy Babcock had been buried in Frankfurt. After the screening I met with a large stockholder in Magellan who anticipated a rise in the share price. I stayed in character, which to a Titan of finance was like looking in a mirror. As Balzac said, behind every great fortune, there's a crime.

I laid out a good, grey, pinstriped, double breasted suit for tomorrow, with a white Brooks Brothers straight collar shirt and a blue and red, diagonally striped tie. My cuff links were American eagles holding arrows. My Beverly Hills tailor had made sure, as he always did, that I could flash my cuffs. Thus prepared for the next day, I sent for room service and asked for the duck a l'orange and a soda siphon. The room was stocked with everything from Johnny Walker Black to Jack Daniels, but I thought this evening called for restraint in anticipation of tomorrow's meeting. I sat in an overstuffed chair, drinking slowly as the sun went down over Washington, concentrating on my mission and the day to come.

CHAPTER THIRTY NINE

A desk in the oval room on the second floor of the White House was covered with American trinkets and statuettes, from a three inch Maine lobsterman to a four-inch girl holding a sash with both hands that read "California." Sam had sent along a small silver cameraman to join the other objects on the desk and remind the President of West Coast Jews who had supported him with money and votes. While studio heads thought like Republicans, they were still Jews and no one in the GOP had bothered to reach out to them.

The photo session had been called off and I could see why. The President looked tired, with grey circles under his eyes, and I realized what a burden this conversation would be for him. He sat straight in his wheelchair, but looked like he belonged in a hospital or at Warm Springs, Ga., his retreat and rehabilitation center.

He tried to make himself the spunky, hearty man we all saw in the newspapers and heard on the radio, but it wasn't working. I decided we didn't have time for small talk, so I let him begin.

"I hear you're turning from a hoofer into a private eye," he said. "You know, it's good to see you, but I wish you'd brought your sister with you, too."

"It's because everyone says this that I've become a private eye," I said, laughing.

"She wasn't supposed to go over there and marry an Englishman, just entertain a lot of them," Roosevelt said. He paused and said," What can I do for you today, Tommy?"

"Sir," I said, "I'd like to ask a serious question, although it's one you probably didn't expect."

He looked wary, but said, "I'm surprised every day Mr. Babcock."

"Hypothetically, if an American was asked by a British politician and writer to pretend to work for the Nazis to pick up information, would that make his work treasonous?" I asked.

"I did read where your brother-in-law is a friend of Churchill," he said. "You speak German, don't you?"

"Both are true, but I didn't realize the public knew I spoke German," I said.

"Do I remind you of a farmer from Nebraska?" he said, pointing around the room, as a very thin Harry Hopkins popped in, left some papers and popped out again. "I am the public. I have to be in order to understand the people of this great democracy. But I've got a country to run, so I need to know as much as I can and that fact about you was hidden somewhere in this brain of mine."

"What do you think, Mr. President?"

"Hitler is a menace. I would like to believe that war will be averted. I would like to believe that we will never have to face Hitler in a battle for our way of life," he said. "But then I would like to live in a world without Borah, Nye, Taft, or Dies, and the Lord has not answered my prayers about them." Borah, Taft and Dies were isolationists who would like nothing better than to replace Roosevelt with someone who would not let Americans go overseas, much less fight in Europe.

"So, they think you'll help the Fatherland?" he said.

"They think I hate my brother-in-law for taking Ginny away and that anyone exposed to a German grandmother could only have one possible choice to make."

"It's strange to think they actually believe all the ridiculous things they say," he said. "Now I think we could beat them. They're too stupid to win."

"I think I may have my answer," I said.

"In the Great War the British Naval Attaché in Washington was Captain Sir Guy Gaunt. I was assistant secretary of the Navy and saw how well Gaunt worked with American intelligence. I have no question that we could have our intelligence systems work that same way again.

"There are, however, two things you should remember. Don't think that the American people believe as I do, and be careful with Churchill. People tell me he's a drinker who doesn't always act rationally," Roosevelt said. "Many people believe he's an opportunistic politician with an ego the size of Westminster Abbey. I must tell you that in 1918 I went to London and the Cabinet gave a dinner for me at Grays Inn Court. Churchill was a 'stinker' who was very arrogant and dismissive. I didn't like him much," the president said.

"You can make a guess at how I may feel towards the Austrian house painter. I am, however, going to promise the American people their boys will never again be buried in French soil."

His eye had a twinkle and I realized this man could probably have taken a lot of Hollywood producers to the cleaners and act shocked at the outcome. He was my President, but I wouldn't want him in charge of my immortal soul.

"Thank you very much for taking the time," I said, standing up and pulling out the silver cameraman.

"Now, I've got a question for you. So all the communists in Hollywood now like Hitler because of this non-aggression pact with Moscow?"

"I wouldn't speak badly of Adolf with Lillian Hellman in the room," I said. "The communists who're Jews are even getting into step."

Roosevelt got a disgusted look on his face and said," What are they thinking?"

"Mr. President, making movies has nothing to do with intelligence," I said. "Hollywood is all about narcissism."

He smiled and picked up a paper Hopkins had left. I got to the door as he said, "Thanks for coming." I saw myself out, hoping he'd take time for a nap.

Harold Ickes was wiping his glasses as he stood inside the entrance to the White House, apparently waiting for me. I stuck out my hand and Ickes shook it. I had the strange feeling of facing another man who had difficulty keeping his inner anger much below the surface. I heard he was pugnacious and unrelenting, but I had not seen him in action, so I kept my own counsel.

"The President just called down and said you were someone we should stay in contact with. I didn't realize he was such a fan," Ickes said.

"I guess we talked about more than just show business," I said. "But I made sure he got Sam's gift for his desk. You certainly steered us right on that one."

"The president seems to think about you outside the realm of show business, which makes me think I should give you my home and office number, along with the numbers of people who will always know where I am," he said. He pulled out a Waterman's pen and carefully wrote down some numbers on his card, handing it to me after checking them over again. "It could come in handy," I said, smiling.

"I take it you're on our side," he said.

"Apparently in a lot more ways than I'd expected," I said.

"Apparently." He shook my hand again saying, "I have to talk to some people about Yosemite," he said, "right after I stop in the oval room. It was nice to meet you."

He began to walk away and stopped, turning his head to say, "My neighbors went to the sneak preview. They liked the movie and their teen aged daughter wants to marry you."

"Tell her I'll wait," I said to Ickes' departing footsteps.

I decided to walk around the riot of color that was Lafayette Park before going to my rooms at the Hay-Adams, in case anyone else had gone to the sneak preview. There is nothing like staying close to your public. I knew the President would understand.

CHAPTER FORTY

I was just about to put in a call to Saunders, when the phone rang.

"How are you enjoying Washington?" a female voice said.

I pretended I didn't recognize the voice. "I apologize, but you've got the advantage on me."

"How soon men forget. You were just entertaining me on your front porch a few weeks ago and now I'm a stranger," she said.

"Meike, how great of you to call," I said. "You are right on top of everything."

"Not always on top," she said, laughing.

"What are your plans?" I said.

"I thought you might like to come over for a late lunch at my flat," she said.

"That would be great, but I need to have Von Darmstadt there. I've been holding something too long. If it's close I could be there in a flash," I said.

I decided to take a shower before heading over. The humidity had gotten to me after the walk in the park and I realized how California had completely spoiled me. I'd opened all the windows in the room, but had yet to sense a breeze. After showering, I splashed on some Bay Rum cologne a friend had sent me from Bermuda, put some Pinaud tonic on my hair, and slipped into fresh underwear. The fresh scent from the Old Spice soap on a rope had left me reinvigorated, so I put on a Turnbull and Asser Egyptian cotton shirt and tied a four-in hand knot on the silk tie I'd purchased at Liberty of London.

I put the plans in my briefcase and walked to her apartment where I was greeted by a kiss on the cheek.

She wore a silk lounging outfit that somehow was fitted at the top, but loose enough at the bottom so her legs frequently appeared through a side slit below her tightly cinched waist. She had that Heidi look on her face, which sent off alarm bells in my Hollywood tainted mind.

"Did you enjoy your meeting with the President?" she said.

"How did you know I met with his nibs?" I said. "I didn't even know it was going to happen until yesterday."

She smiled, but said nothing.

"As you would figure, the Jew's greatest friend had time to meet with a representative from his lobbying arm, the motion picture industry. They make movies about the people who vote for him. They root for those people and carry the communist line to America,"

I said. (It was funny, if they thought Roosevelt was on the side of the Jews, wouldn't he have made more visas available to the people Hitler blamed for the ills of the world?)

"We know where he stands and who he represents," she said. "He lies to us and tells us we won't have to fight again over there, but we all know he wants American blood spilled to crush the Germans."

"You say 'the Germans,' but don't you consider yourself German?" I said.

"My parents are German, but I'm a loyal American," she said. "I just work for the Embassy because I speak the language."

"But you don't share the feelings of your employer?" I said. "It seems to me that anyone with half a brain would see they were right." I had an exasperated look on my face.

She hesitated a moment before saying, "of course they may have some points but I think some ideas may be extreme," she said.

"I've made up my mind," I said. "I have to put up with Jews because they control my career, but you can be honest. I'm very disappointed. I thought you were someone I could talk to about these issues."

"Anything you tell me is safe," she said. "Ever since I saw you at your ranch I've been thinking about you. When I came out of the theatre after the sneak preview I was very frustrated by seeing you on the screen and from the audience instead of sitting next to you."

"I need to talk to Von Darmstadt."

"He's in the living room," she said.

I walked in and closed the door.

"It's good to see you," I said, putting my briefcase on the coffee table.

"It's great to see you also," Von Darmstadt said, showing even teeth. He must have had his teeth fixed, because everyone in Germany has teeth that resemble broken picket fences or mountain ranges.

"I got what you wanted, but I had some tough times doing it. It always seemed like I'd get caught. I'm glad the war hasn't started yet. Then, it would have been impossible to get any information."

"Is it as big a plane as we've heard?"

"It looks big to me," I said. "But then you sent in a guy who has never flown a plane to get you the plans. I wouldn't take anything on my say so."

"You have the specifications?" he asked, seemingly holding his breath.

"Of course, the XB-19A has a wingspan of 212 feet." I said

"Why did you go to all this trouble for us?"

"Because you asked me and because I don't want this country in another European war. As it is, I feel like a traitor," I said, my face turning into an angry scowl.

Von Darmstadt moved in quickly to defuse the situation. "You don't have to do that to yourself. We'll soon have something that will make a war between our countries highly unlikely."

"What is it?" The look that seemed to scare a lot of people was still plastered across my face.

"I can't tell you right now, but if these specifications and designs are accurate, then you'll know very quickly."

"I hope I passed the test, so I can find out what the big deal is all about." My sarcasm spilled out the way water crests over a New Orleans levee in a hurricane.

He gave me a worried look, before opening the door to let Meike bring in some drinks and cold cuts.

"He's done a great favor for the Reich," Von Darmstadt said. "I want you to understand that."

"I'll make sure he understands how much he's appreciated," she said.

"I'm going right now, because there is a Forscher on a ship that's leaving this evening," he said. "I want Goering's people to look this over."

Meike showed him to the door. She then moved in very close to me and pulled my lips down to hers. She was like a tiger that had caught her prey. I put my arms around her, letting my hands drop down to her hips, which were hard and firm.

"I want you right now," she said, undoing her lounging outfit. Before this, I had figured that I'd seen the best there was, but I was mistaken....

Later in the afternoon, we awoke and she got some Veuve Cliquot Champagne out of the icebox. We sat up in bed and drank champagne until the doorbell rang.

"It's the food I ordered from 'Chez Lafitte,' she said, putting on a robe, grabbing her purse and heading for the door. We had Rock Cornish game hen, broccoli au gratin, and a spinach salad, followed by Napoleons for desserts.. We got back into bed for awhile, until I decided it was time to get back to the Hay-Adams so I could organize tomorrow. She gave me a kiss at the door that was pure lust and I promised to call her the next day. Walking back to the hotel I found my mind straying from tomorrow's plan to thoughts of the afternoon's passion.

CHAPTER FORTY ON

The only way Meike could have known about my visit to the White House would have been if I were being followed, so this presented complications in meeting Saunders. It seemed only appropriate to have the professional tell the amateur how to proceed, so I called him on his special line at the Embassy. With his height and manner, he could have been related to my friend, C. Aubrey Smith, who lived in Santa Monica, a British enclave.

"Saunders," he said, in a voice that sounded like he had his briar pipe in his mouth.

"It's your acolyte," I said.

"You understand you're not alone," he said.

"Yes, so what's next?" I said.

"I'll have to slip out of the embassy, change my appearance and slip into your suite," he said.

"You must have had practice," I said.

"Actually, this particular maneuver, had always involved access to the fairer sex," he said. "Even in those cases it was usually not a good idea. However, your lack of materials with which to disguise yourself makes it necessary."

"How did you know I was followed?"

"We were watching to see if anyone was watching you. They were good, but we were behind them. By the way, I'll have to teach you how to use cabs to get around this problem. I can only go through this once," he said. "If you're wondering whether they're listening, we vetted the women at the hotel switchboard. Surprisingly, they are both British émigrés with no ties to Ireland. A bit of luck, what?"

"Yeah, that is lucky," I said. "I'll leave the light on so you won't hurt yourself."

"We must teach you British humor," he said, hanging up.

About 11:30 I heard a soft knock on the door. I put the chain on and looked into the face of a tall, black haired man with no facial hair.

"It is I," Saunders voice said. I let him in quickly and marveled at the change in his appearance.

"I've been in Hollywood long enough to spot a wig, although in this case, I would have had to have seen you before and have the expertise to spot it," I said. "However, how you did that with your lip is beyond me," I said.

"I've been told I have a splendid moustache. So I had the choice of a beard or shaving it. I, personally, always assume a beard is a disguise, unless they're a Prussian professor," he said.

"I bet it hurt."

"You have no idea," he said.

"It takes ten years off you," I said.

"Thirty-eight isn't quite senior enough in England. I'll have to grow it back before I cross the North Atlantic again," he said, frowning.

"Was it necessary?"

"Yes, there's man in a Plymouth parked across the street. He moves occasionally but I fear he'll be there all night," he said. "They're apparently trying to ascertain to what extent they can trust you."

"I was virulently anti-Semitic with the woman who seduced me this afternoon. She says she was born in America, but I'm not buying it," I said.

"She was, actually, but her father took her back to the Fatherland when she was seven, after her mother died and he lost his job," he said. "Her name is Meike Koenig and she's a rarity in intelligence, a woman actually attractive enough to match the myths about spy craft. Before she came here, she'd led a lot of men to trains headed for concentration camps after they made the mistake of trusting her.

Every intelligence chief wants a secret weapon and Canaris found one."

"Do you have a doctor at the Embassy?"

"Yes."

"Could he check me from time to time? It sounds as if I'll be going into tunnels that have seen a lot of traffic," I said.

"I think, though, that it beats fighting from a trench," he said, laughing."How would she function in Hollywood?"

"Believe it or not, she would be a big star," I said.

"For some reason, I find that very upsetting. No one knows about what you're doing, do they?"

"Nobody except Jimmy and Churchill," I said, leaving Jack out. I needed to call Jack one night and inform him about Meike and her charms. He would never knowingly say anything about what I'm doing, but might give away my real attitudes.

"That's good. Let's keep it that way," he said. "I hadn't altogether believed the tales I'd heard about her before, but you've just attested to their veracity."

"If you didn't know her connections, she could lead any man down the garden path," I said, "except in Hollywood. In Hollywood no one really completely trusts anyone."

"The people there are our guides to the future. California is exhibiting just the birth pains of a world in which Richard III would always come out on top," he said. His reference to an odious character (albeit a real historical figure) from Shakespeare made me wonder if there was any point in preserving a future for a world like that. I made myself a note never to inflict such a world on my offspring.

"Von Darmstadt seemed really happy with the airplane specs," I said.

"This is going to get you in the inner circle," he said. "Did you learn any more about the big thing on which they're working."

"I think if Goering's guys like it, I'm in," I said. "I don't want to think about my future if they catch the flaw and realize I've stiffed them."

"For a devil-may-care hoofer, you worry a lot," he said.

"I'm probably a traitor whose days are numbered and you're making fun of my apprehension? We spent two hours going over how to use multiple taxis to lose a tail. My memory would retain it; I just hoped the adrenaline would kick in to help my concentration. Concentration hadn't always been my strong suit.

"You are going to have to be patient, while continuing to stay close to her and von Darmstadt until you figure where they're going to concentrate their efforts in America, "Saunders said.

"I've never been good at waiting," I said, as he got up to leave.

"It sounds like you did all right with Miss Koenig," he said before he opened the door.

"I guess I have to continue in order for you to justify losing the moustache," I said.

"Make it worth it," he said.

"By the way, I still don't feel very comfortable with giving them that engine design. I have a strong feeling that they're too smart to be taken in."

"I don't have any questions about it," he said, disappearing down the hallway like an Anglo-Saxon ghost.

Without the accent, it would have sounded like the bullshit it was.

CHAPTER FORTY TWO

Jack picked up the phone on the second ring so I knew he was sitting at his desk in the library.

"Have you married anybody I know lately? I said."

"You are a putzallah," he said.

"What do you hear from Cuba?"

"Lucy Siegel was in Havana and stopped in to see them," Jack said. "Liesel seems happy and Karl is learning how to play baseball, but he doesn't look either happy or sad. She says he doesn't look like he knows how to feel anything."

"What's happening on their immigration status? I really need to see them," I said, surprising myself.

"I think this congressman is going to come through for me. I just gave him another campaign contribution and he knows there won't be any more if the children are still in Cuba," Jack said.

"I miss them," I said.

"You ought to get married," he said, "so you can have a child like Liesel."

"I can see her face in my mind. I worry about Karl," I said, feeling the distance from them.

"By the way, if something happens to me I want you to give a girl named Feng Feng Chung a ranch as a wedding present."

"How am I going to give her a ranch?"

"I left it to you and I want you to transfer it to Feng Feng, after you've socked some money away for Karl and Liesel from the sale of my horses and a couple of houses in Hancock Park I've been renting to folks who want to look like they've got more cash than they really have. My parents have all the money they need and enough for Ginny too, so I don't have to provide for them."

"Karl and Liesel are already going to be the richest refugees in the world," he said.

"Yeah," I said, "but your ex-wives could do anything, or you could die while you're on the honeymoon with a new one."

He ignored my comments, saying "what's the story with this Feng Feng and where does she live."

"Her father's on the faculty at UCLA and they live in Chinatown. I know you've got the ability to find anybody."

"This sounds crazy to me. Who is she marrying?"

"She's marrying a doctor," I said.

"Okay, but how am I gonna know you're dead," he said, milking this for everything it was worth?

"Would you miss me?"

"No, anybody who goes around giving Chinese girls large wedding presents is too meshuganah to be friends with. You couldn't find a nice Jewish girl who deserves a wedding present?"

"Yeah, Liesel. By the way I met with Roosevelt, so I'm going to New York tomorrow to see Wendell Willkie," I said.

"Good. After you hang up I have to get ready for the Pope. He's coming by at seven to circumcise me," he said.

CHAPTER FORTY THREE

Meike answered the phone with a sultry voice that ignited me like a match in a drought weakened forest.

"I think you should consider Hollywood," I said. "You could make a fortune with that voice and everything else that goes with it"

"Where are you today? I called the Hay Adams and they said you weren't around," she said in an accusatory tone. "I thought we could have a long dinner to match our long lunch the other day."

"I had to go to New York on business," I said. "I'll be back to Washington in a couple of days."

"Herr Von Darmstadt would also like to see you at my apartment," she said, the irritation barely suppressed.

"I hope it isn't for the same reasons you have. I needed to meet with some of the studio's big investors to tell them about the new movie," I said. "I'm doing it as a favor to Weinstein. You know how the Jews can be about money."

She paused before saying, "I could come to New York and keep you company when you weren't working."

"It sounds great, but things are too busy here," I said. "I'll see you in a few days."

"You left town. You won't let me join you," she said. "Didn't the last few days mean anything to you?"

"I thought you and I understood each other. You didn't just fall off the turnip truck and neither did I. Wait a couple of days and we'll be together again," I said, hanging up the receiver on the payphone. It was lucky I wasn't in my twenties anymore, because I would have believed all this crap shoveled in my direction. Thank goodness for age and its companion, cynicism. If I'd been in Germany and one of her first victims, my ashes would be spread over the Fatherland.

I'd been serious about Hollywood. She would have singed the fabric on every casting couch in town. It would serve a couple of guys that I knew right if they got screwed over by a Nazi. The kind of guys who would kill careers just because they had the power would be completely blindsided and she would destroy them before they could lay a glove on her. I decided that dwelling on this wouldn't be constructive, so I went down to the Metropole and had a drink while I listened to Sidney Bechet. My meeting with Wendell wasn't until eight.

CHAPTER FORTY FOUR

Wendell Willkie had impressed me the first time I met him. He'd been looking for an actor to be the spokesman for the electric utility industry when the New Deal started to put projects such as the TVA together. I'd been an early supporter of Roosevelt so it didn't fit right, and as much as I liked him personally, I actually admired the TVA concept of giving low cost electrical power to people with little money. Most other utility executives had as much imagination as the head of an Elks Lodge in Buffalo, so I never understood how he could stand the business. He'd been an attorney when he was picked as President of the utility holding company and I knew he was not the kind of man who would have wanted to work his way up in that business,

When he opened the door to his pied a terre I was once again impressed by his charisma. He stood six foot one and weighed about 200 pounds. With his dark black hair and blue eyes he had the gift a person with presence has of making you feel you are his whole world when he looks at you. With people like that you always feel disappointed when the attention moves on. He gave people an absolute confidence in his abilities.

Tommy, it's great to see you," he said, his warm Hoosier smile pulling you in like harbor lights on a dark coast

"I'm lucky to have someone of stature in my place," he said. "All I do is peddle electricity, but you're lighting up the screen."

"Arthur Krock of the New York Times and Raymond Moley think you ought to run for president," I said.

"It's nice to be well thought of," he said. "Just because I've become a Republican doesn't mean I'm going after that man in the White House."

"Well he's gone after you before," I said.

"It was never really personal. I was just expressing a different point of view on government," he said, "even though his boys Corcoran and Cohen weren't very respectful to people who got in their way." Tom Corcoran and Ben Cohen had stepped on a lot of toes to get the TVA through. It still stuck in Wendell's craw. Roosevelt had done a lot of good. Sometimes, however, in incidents like his crude attempt to pack the Supreme Court with people favorable to the New Deal he overreached on a grand scale.

I told him that I'd been reading about some of his recent appearances. "You didn't sound a lot like Taft or Dewey in the articles I read. People think you sound a little like the New Deal with a governor on the accelerator."

"You wouldn't believe what people think I am," he said. "The problem is I'm not liberal or conservative. Some things work in one arena that don't work in another."

"What about Europe?"

"Now there's a problem, Tommy. No one wants to have us fighting there but it may be inevitable. I don't like what I read about Hitler and I think we're slowly angering the Japanese in ways we don't understand. How can we have diplomacy with a nation whose emigrants are treated like dirt in this country? Eventually things may come a cropper," he said. "Both Germany and Japan are going to want more and more. Czechoslovakia and the Rape of Nanjing both are portents of things to come."

"I agree. I just don't know if we'll wake up in time," I said.

"The other issue we've got to face in this country is that we treat the Negroes shamefully. Some places they can't vote. Many places they can't get a decent job or live where they want to," he said. We have to face that issue head on. People have a problem with me because I represent big business. I may think a little differently than a lot of executives on some things but I'm convinced business is the engine of this country and the people who run these businesses have something to say."

I knew I was in the presence of a great man, but felt a lot of businessmen couldn't see beyond the balance sheet. There probably weren't a lot of other Willkies out there.

"I guess you're the Great White Hope of liberal republicanism," I said. "Roosevelt should have been smart enough to figure a way of bringing you into his tent."

"He never made the least effort, but I had Commonwealth and Southern to protect and he couldn't make peace with that."

"I hope you run. You have risen to the top without picking up all that extra baggage and because you weren't born with a silver spoon in your mouth you understand the people of America."

I looked around the room and asked the obvious question. "What about Irita. Does she live here with you?"

"This is her place," he said. "Every reporter understands that I live here with her. It's an open secret. She edits the book section of the Herald Tribune and entertains all the time. Anyone who didn't know it would have to be missing all the sensory functions except taste."

"No one in journalism has any taste. You know that," I said, laughing.

"Irita does, and Walter Lippmann thinks he does," Wendell said.

"Wait till I tell Winchell he wasn't on the short list. You can't run for president and have a mistress," I said.

"Well then I can't run for President."

"I guess I wanted a man of principle to run for President," I said. "The curse, the Chinese say, is to get what you ask for."

"In Elwood, Indiana, you either have integrity or you don't. Just because you come to New York City and learn how to fight the New Deal doesn't mean you leave your values somewhere in the Pocono's or the Delaware Water Gap."

"I know. I'm supposed to be a Hollywood star, but I've got a Civil War hero wandering around in my cerebrum," I said, holding up my empty glass.

"There's only one answer for that. One more Johnnie Walker Black straight up before we have my driver take us to the biggest steak in Manhattan," Wendell said, as he filled my glass and his to the top.

CHAPTER FORTY FIVE

I went up to Connecticut to see my parents. After a couple of pleasant days I returned to the city and took the train from the vibrancy of New York City to the quiet southern town that passes as our national capital. Why a nation would place their government in an area which boasted a section called Foggy Bottom was beyond me. I could imagine a new French ambassador saying, "Drive me tout de suite to Foggy Bottom so I can present my papers to the Secretary of State." It sounded ludicrous. New York had been the capital, as had Philadelphia. Both cities had something more to offer than just being the seat of government. Boston, the "Hub of the Universe," also said much about our history and stability as a people. Well, L'Enfant, Washington's brilliant designer, had done his best. He couldn't help it that the District of Columbia brought to mind a white goateed former slave-owner snoring on his veranda. If FDR had anything to say about it, it would soon have a population of ten million governmental employees, so perhaps I should withhold judgment until all the lawyers in America made it their home, thereby luring restaurateurs from Europe to cook their meals for congressmen, ensuring culture would follow filthy lucre.

I planned to meet at Meike's with von Darmstadt and then catch a train for the land of orange blossoms, Catalina Island and the glitter factories. After a hot train ride, I caught a cab to the Hays Adams and took a shower before setting off. Arriving at her doorstep, I knocked and waited while the discussions underway were concluded, with at least one person raising his voice to push his point. When that ended, von Darmstadt opened the door with an apologetic smile as if he had just finished disciplining young children. I entered the living room to find two men and Meike sitting on the couches across from her fireplace. One had the look of a Prussian soldier, with a rigid posture and a sneer on his face that made you glad to be an American, but not necessarily a British spy. The other man looked like an accountant who fronted for a horse parlor or a 24 hour crap game. You didn't know why you didn't trust him but he gave off a whiff of immorality topped with an unctuous approach to human relationships that a ten-year-old trust fund baby could spot with her eyes closed.

Meike and the guy who looked like Francis Pangborn playing an ax murderer had beers in front of them while the Prussian had water. Von Darmstadt apparently wasn't drinking anything. Meike opened a Ballantine Ale for me and poured it into a mug featuring a German eagle. I picked it up; thankful it didn't have a swastika on it. The Ballantine tasted like ale suffused with carrots, a taste I surprisingly liked.

"How was your trip to New York?" von Darmstadt said. He may have been a Nazi but he was a friendly one. I had to work at not actually liking him.

"It was a good trip."

"This is Hans," he said pointing to the Prussian, who actually was from Landsberg, "and Gerhard," he said, motioning towards the weasel. I wasn't going to have to fight my emotions over these two. Meike gave me her milkmaid smile, which somehow always struck me as erotic. The men were barely civil.

"It is nice you can meet with us," the weasel said sarcastically.

At that point I couldn't hold the energy in anymore. I hated being a spy and I hated the Nazis. The train was out of control and I was no longer in charge.

"I guess so, since I'm a movie star and you're a civil servant who's on the clock," I said, treating him with the disdain I felt. The Germans expected a big shot to sound like one and he really did make me feel big. The weasel looked surprised and sank down into his chair. He appeared to be a man who got on in life by holding Satan's coat while his boss gathered souls.

"Gerhard," von Darmstadt said, "there will be no more of that. The Reich isn't paying Herr Babcock; he's here because he believes our cause is right. There's a good chance he's done something really important for the Reich."

Hans said nothing but looked like he wanted to teach me who really was part of the Master Race. In a gangster picture he would have been the muscle who was the last to die. Meike seemed to be anxious about the whole experience. She shot me a look that said "shut up."

"It's good your movie is doing so well, Herr Babcock," Von Darmstadt said. "When it's time for you to help us in an important task, everyone will certainly let you in the door."

"It sounds like you'd chosen me to be a courier," I said. "That's a new part for me. Eddie Robinson recently told me he's going to be in a movie called 'A Message to Reuters'. I should call him and ask him if I could play one of Reuter's pigeons, now that you're willing to train me."

Von Darmstadt laughed and said," it's more like you'll be playing von Ribbentrop." He was talking about the man who always showed up with Hitler's demands before he sent in the troops, so I guess that should make me feel honored.

"Good, that's a part I like. Gerhard can carry my coat in the picture," I said.

Meike began to laugh and Gerhard gave her a look that implied he could kill her after he killed me, but I'm sure it really meant that Hans could kill her after he killed me.

Von Darmstadt didn't know whether to laugh or calm the waters. He was having a difficult time but Gerhard wasn't allowed to give him a look, so I figured it wouldn't be long before he'd turn into a puddle of dirty oil. I knew I should let up and forced myself to suppress my feelings before I queered the whole deal but it was late in the game.

"I'll be explaining the plan to you in detail when I come out to see you in September," Von Darmstadt said, apparently unsure if they knew enough to trust me completely. "Today we're going to explain some of the communication techniques by which we'll be able to contact each other in case the FBI has decided to track our movements. The next few hours will be very important, so we'll move ahead. You'll be able to leave for California tomorrow."

We went over and over the procedures for four hours because they thought it was a fluke that I absorbed everything the first time. It eventually dawned on them they were teaching an Olympic swimmer to doggie paddle, so when I became completely exasperated, Hans and Gerhard left and it was just Von Darmstadt and Meike.

"It took Hans and Gerhard a week to learn all that information," Meike said, "and I think that made them mad, along with everything you said."

"They were mad at me before they met me, so it's no big deal," I said. "What's their story, anyway?"

"They are some of the best that National Socialism has to offer," Von Darmstadt said, irony in his voice. "From what I've heard, Hans grew up in southern Germany in Landsberg, not far from the prison where Hitler wrote Mein Kampf. His was a Roman Catholic, deeply conservative, family. After his father died at 14, food became scarce. Rumor has it he and his mother were forced to work many hours to support themselves. Hans idolized his mother, so when he discovered she was entertaining a city official for money and the prospect of employment, he beat her and left home, but not before the city official died of a slashed throat. It was a good time to commit murder. As the depression grew deeper, Hitler sensed it was his time to strike, so his supporters were looking for thugs to help his rise to power. The Nazis found Hans before the police did, put him in a black SS uniform and created a lifetime adherent to the Nazi cause."

"It sounds to me that he isn't your kind of German," I said.

Von Darmstadt said, "Even for the SS, Hans is unusually brutal. When he helped break up a communist rally, someone would usually die, to be discovered by police the next day. If other politicians needed to be forced off stage, Himmler would make sure Hans was among those sent on that mission. When it came time to destroy the SA and the perverts who ran that organization, Hans was in charge of forty men who systematically killed all the sleeping SA men they could find. Because everyone knew how loyal Hans was (and how vicious) Himmler forced Canaris to agree to Hans' posting to Washington to keep an eye on my operation."

"What about the weasel?" I said.

Meike and von Darmstadt laughed. Meike said, "When I was in Germany recently a friend of mine obtained his file for me. I think

I was able to read through the lines and I found out this much. Gerhard grew up in Hanau, which lies upriver from Frankfurt on the Main River. His father was placed in prison in the 20s for alleged embezzlement from the local brewery. Gerhard obtained a job with some accountants. His job, at first, was as an office boy, but then one of the principals noticed he had a mind for figures. They let him do computations and bookkeeping chores. They were supportive of his efforts to become accredited and made him an accountant. In 1932, he became one of Himmler's accountants, tracking the funds the SS received or had appropriated. He had asked and was allowed to observe torture sessions. Gerhard learned he enjoyed watching pain inflicted on others and wished to become involved in torture himself. Here's where it gets into conjecture. There was a note in his file that implied one weekend he stood outside a café in Berlin in the evening and waited until a woman came out alone. He apparently approached the woman and before she realized it, he held a flick-blade knife against her throat. He took her to his car, drove her out of town, where he tied her down and filled her mouth with cotton, so he could use the knife to remove flesh from her body. After the night grew long, he stuck the knife in her heart and threw her body out of the car. The police wanted to question him, but they couldn't get near him. The next day he apparently applied for torture detail and Himmler, who was sorry to lose a good accountant, reluctantly allowed him to follow his dream.

"Coming to America in 1936, Hans and Gerhard found they had much in common and became roommates, settling in to watch my operation and carry out as many intimidations and executions as were needed. Gerhard regretted torture was now such a small part of his job description, but suffered for the good of the party."

I listened in amazement that such clearly troubled criminals had risen in the ranks of Germany's bureaucracy. It was as if the Lindbergh kidnapper and Al Capone were in positions of power.

Von Darmstadt left a few minutes later and I was soon in the arms of Meike. We made love with the kind of wild abandon that had marked the last night we were together. The pull of her sensuality was undeniable and I was engulfed in it. After a lot of additional physical activity, she turned to me and said," I never thought I'd tell a man I loved him again."

"You really don't know me very well. Who was the first man who heard those words?"

"He was an important official in my city, Cologne. I was nineteen and he was in his early forties. He had a wife, but he said he really loved me," she said, with a bitterness which made her look less like Heidi and more like a Val Kyrie.

"One day he told me it was over, that he had just played around with me. I protested and told him I would never love anyone else. He hit me and threw me out of his office. A couple of SA men marched me out of the building as if I were a tramp begging for scraps. A few days later I saw him in the street and tried to talk to him. He sent a man over to take me in an alley to beat me before raping me. I didn't understand. He had told me that he loved me. It took two weeks before my face looked somewhat normal."

"What happened to him?"

"He was arrested and shot," she said, a small smile crossing her face.

"What did he do?"

"I don't know what you mean. He was shot and he died," she said.

"I mean what was he accused of doing?"

"He was accused of stealing from the Reich," she said.

"By the way, you told me you were a nice Pennsylvania girl," I said.

'If you believed that, you'll probably die this year of chronic naiveté," she said. "I could tell you didn't believe that. You're a much better lover than actor, at least in person," she said, reaching over and kissing me.

I accepted the kiss and the passion that went with it. "Did you have anything to do with the man's downfall?"

"Yes," she said.

"How did you do it?" I said.

"Let's just say my face was the last one he saw before being marched out into the courtyard. He begged my forgiveness and said he had always loved me. I spat in his face," she said. "He was quite a cow-ard. He cried and begged for his life in front of the SS."

"It's hard to know what's true when you're 19," I said. "However, very few women ever have the satisfaction of turning the tables."

"My determination to see him pay drove me to become something. If he hadn't done this, I'd be married to a nice civil servant," she said. "I think very often of how nice it would be to be that 19-year-old girl again. There are many things which have changed about me that I don't like."

"Why are you telling me this? I can't believe everyone gets this oral history."

"Even Von Darmstadt doesn't know this," she said.

Why me?"

"I would think you'd remember what I first said to you," she said looking hurt.

"Why do you think you love me?"

"When a woman is too young to be able to discriminate, as I was, they don't necessarily make decent choices. But when a woman has seen the world for what it really is, they recognize certain things about someone. Why does a woman ever love a man? Because she believes she can't live without him, because if she can't have him she'll spend the rest of her life with part of her heart missing.

A woman whose life has crossed the path of many men knows when she's met the person perfect for her," she said.

I was stunned. When you're in the motion picture business you hear some crap that sounds pretty but you know it's crap. An actress acts like she's in love with you while the cameras are rolling or while you're shooting a picture, but you know that even if she believes she feels something, it's an illusion. The delusion is exposed when she doesn't answer your calls. For some reason, this didn't seem to fit here.

Of course, my experiences with women have been ones of befuddlement and terror, amidst plenty. Being Tommy Babcock has had its advantages, attracting both the starlet whose career is so important that she'll do literally anything and the star struck fan who wants someone to tap dance through their upstairs' rooms. Loneliness, that bane of man's existence, has never reared its ugly head. However, my judgment never was good, so I'm always jumping out the window just before I'm permanently tied to a gold digger or tramp. The initial days are always fun; it's the denouements that take years off your ticker.

Cherry was the roughest to escape from. Her milky white skin and perfect figure brings back memories that have to be beaten and incarcerated before they precipitate disastrous actions. Julie had a hunt seat mere mortals could only dream of, while the way her hair emerged from under her riding helmet could, by comparison, have left the Goddess Diana with a feeling of inadequacy and ruined a lot of hunts. Both had hearts of ice and an instinct for exploitable vulnerability.

The prize, though, went to Judy (nee Utka)Goldberg from the Pest part of Budapest), whose indescribable figure and large brown eyes pulled a man in like a riptide, leaving him as limp and ineffective as Buster Keaton hanging off a downtown clock. It wasn't until my business manager caught her in his office checking my assets and liabilities that I could arm myself against her. She should have controlled herself a little longer. I was thinking about driving her to Reno and making her an honest woman. The guy she got to marry her had obtained one leading role, terrible reviews, and finally, two, one way, tickets to Barstow. The last I heard, he'd disappeared and she was hanging off the arm of a low level grifter who ran a book in Hollywood.

An alarm bell should have been going off in my mind, but all I could hear was silence. This woman couldn't be this good at dissembling, but Saunders had given me the word, so I suppose I was still the rube, the kid paying money to see the "egress" at the fair.

"I think you've just really met me and perhaps you feel that way because you saw the movie. The guy on the screen isn't me."

"But he is," she said, "with the same hard edged idealism. I don't know what you're doing with us, but it doesn't feel right. Maybe that's part of your appeal."

"You're fooling yourself. Don't go about making something from the little you've seen," I said.

"I've never had a man tell me why he isn't good enough for me," she said.

"I don't want to be tied down," I said. "This has been great, but I'm going back to California tomorrow."

She said nothing, but grabbed me and pulled me to her. I could feel her entire body beseeching me to stay. I held her tight for three more hours, unable to put this experience into perspective. Saunders' warning fought with my experience. Her surprising admission about who she really was caught me off guard.

"I've got to go back to my hotel, because I'll be leaving on the train this morning."

"I don't want you to leave," she said. "When you were in New York I missed you terribly."

"We live three thousand miles away from each other. You've got a role here in America that you can't perform where I live," I said.

"I can come out for awhile. I'm sure Rudi would approve it," she said.

"You call Von Darmstadt, Rudi?"

"I'm the only one who does and then, only when no one else is around," she said, laughing. "Are you bothered by that?"

"You can call me Tommy Babcock."

"Even children on the street call out 'Tommy Babcock, Tommy Babcock,' so there is nothing special about that," she said.

"Then you can call me Herr Babcock," I said, buttoning my shirt.

"I'm coming to California, maybe next month," she said.

"I'll save some sunshine for you," I said, uncertain of how to discourage this visit. If truth be told, this woman had scorched me like a prairie fire and I couldn't protect myself when I was in the same room with her.

I kissed her long and hard and then let myself out the front door. I went down the steps, lost in thought. The temperature was bearable and there were stars. Just then, I heard a sound behind me. At the same time a large man with a stocking over his head stepped out and began to punch me, throwing jabs and crosses to my face, before stepping back so he could kick my balls. I was in pain from a kidney punch, but I'd cleared my head of the mental cobwebs, blocked the kick and went on the offensive. He was surprised by the agility and the timing I'd picked up on the speed bag, so I began to land some really fine punches. I felt like I could take this guy so I pressed my advantage, throwing combinations that seemed to pick up power as the motor turned me into a fighting machine. He was gonna go down, I could feel it.

Just as I moved in to make pulp out of whatever was under that stocking, something hit me from behind. Sure there was pain but I was angrier about being cheated of victory. I seem to remember trying to hang in and go after the stocking face until the pain got worse and my world turned to darkness.

CHAPTER FORTY SIX

When I awoke, a beautiful woman was standing over my bed, her hand stroking my hair. Then the angel smiled and a few moments later I realized it was Meike.

"You look like a goddess. What am I doing here?"

"Thank you for the nice words. As to your question; I heard noise from outside and found you lying in front of the house," she said.

I didn't say anything as I tried to put everything together. Then I fell into a pitch dark well with no bottom.

I then opened my eyes and Meike was holding my hand. "I must have passed out for a minute," I said in apology. I didn't feel exactly like the famous, witty, charming Tommy Babcock.

"Tommy, that was yesterday. I'm going to go get the doctor," she said, leaving the room.

A middle-aged nurse with short black hair came over next to the bed and said, "I sure wish I had somebody love me that much. She's been sleeping in a chair since you were brought in here. She's always holding onto your hand as if she can send you something you need.

I've only seen this kind of dedication a few times in my life." She shook her head in wonder at my luck.

"Do people know who I am?" I don't know why I asked that, because I don't think I had any photos to sign anyway.

"Yes, all sorts of reporters keep trying to sneak in here, but this Senator made sure there are always two policemen outside your room 24 hours a day. He even came in here and had his picture taken standing next to your bed. Meike liked the idea of the policemen but I could tell she didn't like the idea of this Senator getting in the paper by appearing to be your protector.

"The reporters wanted Meike to give them an interview and have her picture taken next to the bed but she wouldn't do it. Imagine that, a girl who doesn't want to be famous," she said.

"She's a good woman," I said, my brain barely able to keep up with everything I'd just learned.

"The movie studio has a good looking publicity man who sits outside and talks to the press. Meike lets him come in and talk to her once a day, but he hasn't had much to tell the reporters, which, apparently, just makes them just want it a lot more," she said.

"How long have I been here?"

"Seven days today. I saw your motion picture last night and it was good. I don't much like singing pictures, but I like you in this one. You looked tough and I like that. Meike, she's strong, like a rock,"

I lay there looking for words, as the door opened and Meike walked in with a young doctor clearly in thrall of her. He looked like he felt he was walking with Betty Davis. But as he approached the bed, his doctor role took over and the love struck boy disappeared.

"I'm Dr. Naismith. We're very glad to see you opening your eyes." He had a soothing voice which made him sound older and very experienced. "We'll have to see what the blow did to your brain. You have what is called an aligned skull fracture, the best kind to get if you have to have one. When you woke up yesterday, I was really pleased. Looking at you today makes me even happier. By the way, Meike has been watching you like a hawk and Nurse Givens and her counterpart on the other shift have had little to do. They say that she doesn't really sleep very much."

"What do you think is going on?" I said, pointing to my skull.

"We think you got a serious concussion from being struck with a tire iron. There seems to be an indentation in your skull, but when your hair grows back no one will be able to see it."

"Tire iron?" I said.

"That's what it appeared to be. I had a pathologist come in and look at it and he agreed with me," Naismith said. "Meike, could you excuse us a minute, please."

Meike stepped away and Naismith continued. "The pathologist's name is Jim McGinty and he told me to tell you that the only times he's seen this before is during an autopsy, so you should be really happy. Also, he wanted to know is Louisa Boudreau's tits were real?"

"Like Honeydew melons," I said.

"He'll be happy to hear that. Get her to send him a picture if you can. He'll stop by to give you his address."

"How did he know I'd come out of the coma?"

"He didn't. He left these instructions if you came out."

I swallowed hard, trying not to think about it.

"By the way, the police want to talk to you, but I won't allow them to do this for at least two more days. They're interested in catching who did this, but I'm interested in getting you well. However, I want you to keep listening to Meike for awhile and even if you don't talk I don't want you going back to sleep for awhile. She is supposed to keep you awake."

"Has Ginny called?"

"You're an uncle to an 8 pound, four ounce boy named Thomas," Naismith said. "She's still in the hospital, but you can hear the worry in her voice. She'll be home when you get to go home."

"Thanks," I said. Talking was a pain in the ass, so I tried to keep the words down to the bare minimum. Naismith hurried out of the room and Nurse Givens followed him.

"Kiddo, what do you think."

"I think you made Hans and Gerhard very angry," Meike said. "Rudi talked to them for a long time, but they kept saying they'd been playing cards at the time. He sent them to New York and brought in two other men. You should be more careful about who you laugh at."

"You're probably right, but I couldn't stop it. I forgot these guys got used to killing anybody who made them angry, but I'm not sure it would have made a difference, either"

"I don't like Gerhard either, but I'm not lying in a hospital bed."

"Hans is his boyfriend?"

"National Socialism would not allow homosexuals to serve in such delicate assignments. When Hitler killed Rohm and his SA lieutenants, tolerance of queers ended," she said.

"I bet the publicity boys are happy about this story," I said.

"La Grange, the publicity man, said that the movie is 'a run-away success and this is really good for the picture, unless you die.' I got really angry when he said that."

"Sam Weinstein must be shitting bricks about this. He had another movie that was supposed to start next week," I said.

"La Grange talked to him on the phone and he said it was as if Weinstein had the concussion. He said they've arranged for a rail car that can be outfitted as a hospital to take you back to Los Angeles as soon as you can travel."

"That sounds cushy," I said.

"They said I can go with you and make sure you're comfortable," she said.

"Who are they?" I said.

"Weinstein and Rudi," she said.

"Sounds like a team I worked with in Vaudeville," I said.

"It sounds like an unlikely combination," she said.

"They talked to each other?"

"Of course not. Rudi said I could travel with you after this man Weinstein said I could be on the train to keep you company. Weinstein communicates with me through Louis."

"The nurse said the PR guy is good looking," I said. "Is that why you're coming?" I said, kidding her.

"Of course, because we're going to make love on your hospital bed when you fall into your next coma."

"Nice German girls don't do that," I said.

"Nice German girls didn't used to be spies either," she said. "Times change."

"Did I snore while I was in a coma?"

"No, why?" she said.

"I'd hate to disturb you and the publicity man," I said. She laughed and squeezed my hand.

It was the voice that had launched thousands of dreams for adolescent boys and for some who had a lot more mileage on their odometers.

"I'm really worried about you. The tabloids here have you close to death," Ginny said, with tears in her voice.

"You've seen me miss enough fences to know I'm indestructible," I said. "Call Jack and you know who, and tell them I'm fine, okay?"

"Of course I will. You know that if I hadn't just delivered Thomas I would be on plane to Washington".

"I thought it was Winston Thomas?"

'I changed my mind," she said. By the way she said it; I knew there was a bigger story there

"Can he sing yet?"

"He cries on key."

"They won't let me talk very long. Do me a favor and sing 'Indiana Autumn' for me," I said, "but blow your nose first. If you are plugged up like you are now, it will sound like you have a water glass in front of your face."

"If you ever had a chance of hearing me sing, you just crapped out."

"C'mon. I was close to death."

She started into the first verse, quietly, just as she always did. It was hard to hear her until she reached the bridge and raised the volume. The last thing I remembered was the beginning of the third verse, "When it's autumn...in Indiana...The skies..."

CHAPTER FORTY SEVEN

After five more days of observation, Dr. Naismith was finally satisfied that I wasn't going to expire the minute I walked out the hospital door, so he let them take me to my private railroad car. Soon Meike and a nurse hired for the trip were escorting me across the country.

I hadn't spoken to Saunders for ten days. He was good at his job, so I hoped he knew I now had a Nazi girlfriend. For a reason I couldn't quite fathom, I worried about what Feng Feng was reading about me in the papers. I had this gorgeous storm trooper who treated me like gold and I was thinking about a girl I'd only kissed, who was going to marry somebody else. I tried to put it down to the basic stupidity of man.

At every stop we came to there were women and kids standing on the platform holding signs like "Get Better Tommy" and "We're Praying for You Tommy." I guessed the publicity boys were going to wring every tear out of every eye in America before I reached California. Once again, I marveled at the lack of shame in Hollywood. I should have died just to spite them and turn off the money machine. Of course, the signs actually were pretty nice.

Not to be outdone, Weinstein had sent the chef from the executive's dining room to cook for us on the train. If I ever doubted how bankable I was, it ended when I saw Jacques. He had purchased the ingredients in New York and ridden down to Washington with them on the day of departure. We had Coquilles St. Jacques and dishes that were unpronounceable for an uneducated boy like me. I couldn't have the wine, but Meike pronounced them excellent.

In Denver, Sam Weinstein and Louisa Bordeaux got on the train and rode the rest of the way. Meike discreetly declined to be included in the photographs, only adding to her mystery quotient. At one point, Louisa offered to take care of my needs on the trip to Los Angeles and Meike told her she'd kill her if she tried. We were all one happy family on that leg of the journey.

CHAPTER FORTY EIGHT

As we pulled into Union Station, Meike slipped into a car, after the publicist made sure no one from the press had hidden themselves aboard.

An ambulance had been parked right outside the station's side entrance so the reporters were watching it while we hopped into a Pontiac which had been pulled up on the other side. I could walk just fine and to fool the press I sported a white moustache, a cane and a large straw hat. I got in the back seat, behind Meike who was sitting in the shotgun seat next to the publicist.

Meike had a sweet smile on her face; as if she really was Heidi and her grandpa was waiting outside. I guess the best way to explain that face and hair was to say she looked like a cross between Jean Harlow and Alice Faye. Her hair was naturally blond and her skin was lifted from a Pond's ad. Believe it or not all those elements were there when Meike first emerged into the light of day. The fact that she looked better to me now than when we first met was unsettling, because that day she had looked beautiful.

"I'm sure Ginny is home now, so I'll get some support for my recovery," I said.

"What am I if I'm not support?" she said. "I will get a hotel room and come over every day to nurse you back to health."

"You will have to talk to Ginny about that. She may have different ideas," I said.

"I love you and you need me, so I'll be there," she said.

She clearly hadn't met Ginny if she thought she could steamroller her, but that was something they could settle. I just wanted all my brains back.

I hoped Ginny had figured a way to sneak Feng Feng in without the Val Kyrie finding out.

CHAPTER FORTY NINE

"It's about time you called," Jack said. "When I read about the angel of mercy, I figured it might be the woman you told me about, so I stayed away."

"That was a good move," I said. "If we looked like we were in close touch, it might have blown the story I used to get Liesel and Karl out of Germany. It also might get me killed."

"It looks like they already tried," he said.

"I pissed off a couple of Nazis, but they weren't important enough to worry about."

"I said the same thing once when I was in the garment business and ended up with bullet holes too close to my balls to think about," Jack said.

"It might have saved you some alimony if they had hit them," I said.

I guess it was because I was sick, but he didn't say anything about my comment. "So, how're you feeling? I can see the blow didn't improve your comic sense."

"It sure sold movie tickets," I said.

"I'm making a lot of money, but I've got production money already into the second picture, so don't take any more chances.

"Too bad," I said. "Another blow to the head and Gable would drop to second place."

"You can get yourself killed after the movie is all wrapped up," Jack said. "I'm looking forward to owning a ranch." He paused for a second and said," By the way, you are going to be on an Oaties cereal box starting in three week."

"Couldn't you make it a gin bottle?" I said. "How come you put me on a cereal box?"

"When I put in the money, I kept the licensing rights. Everybody thought I was crazy so they gave me anything I wanted. Since you are repeating your character from the first picture, I continue to own the rights and I may make a fortune off your ugly mug," Jack said.

"Do adults eat Oaties?"

"None that have any taste buds," he said. "Each oat flake is surrounded by half the Cuban sugar crop. But kids go to the movies and they bring their parents. You are going to own the Saturday matinee. Make three pictures and you can buy the biggest ranch in Colorado."

"I didn't inspire any kids to be dancers, so I'll just teach them to skirt the law a little bit," I said. "What happens if J. Edgar Hoover tells people I'm a German spy?"

"I'll get your face plastered on Nazi Oats. Every country they take over is a new market," he said. "None of my people are going to eat your goddamned cereal, though. By the way, I planted a grove of trees in Palestine in your name. You can tell your German buddies how pissed off you are about it."

"Are Jews able to get to Palestine?" I said.

"Not very many right now," he said. "I gave some money to the Zionists so they could tell Italian Jews to get out of Italy and French Jews to get out of France, but there aren't many takers. They think they're Italian or French and don't realize to the people of Europe, they are just Jews."

"I hope you're wrong about their prospects," I said.

"So tell me I'm wrong. You've been in the belly of the beast."

"You're not wrong," I said, getting depressed. Naismith said I might be more susceptible to dark moods as I was healing.

"Every day I'm on the phone raising money to put up housing in Palestine or smuggle Jews out of Czechoslovakia," he said.

"Somebody once told me the hardest person to get money from for charity is a Gentile doctor. The easiest to raise money from are Jewish businessmen."

"I get a bunch of them in the room and tell how much I'm putting up and ask them to give just as much."

"Does it work?" I said.

"In the movie business, all the big shots were born in Europe. They remember what it was like to be a Jew there," Jack said. "If they've forgotten, I show them pictures we smuggled out of Germany. When they see corpses with swastikas carved on their stomachs, they remember quick."

"I'll come over to your place in a couple of hours if I'm sure I'm not followed. I've just got a few things to finish up at the studio. They need to figure out how to cover up the part of my skull that's shaved."

"A long blonde wig might be nice," Jack said.

"Maybe you *should* get married again," I said, hanging up.

I then dialed Saunders and found him in his office.

"How's your upper lip?" I said.

"My moustache is a shadow of its former self. I can't twirl the ends yet. I look like Olivier with his version of peach fuzz," Saunders said, ruefully.

"I guess this call tells you I'm alive," I said.

"I assume our friend Meike is your Florence Nightingale," he said.

"Yes. It's funny but she told me about her past and what she did," I said.

"Confession is good for the soul."

"You don't think that's surprising? She also told me that those two Nazis are the ones who put me in the hospital.

"You're not stupid. She would have calculated they would be first on your list. Didn't you think they'd done it?" Saunders said.

"Of course," I said.

"There is nothing more reassuring than stating the obvious. Don't let down your guard. There are a lot of men in concentration camps and coffins who were taken in," he said.

"Okay," I said. "I'm listening to you, 'Master Spy.' She really has fooled a lot of people into thinking she's in love with me."

"So did Mata Hari," he said, an air of impatience in his voice. "Keep your guard up or you'll end up in the ground along with the others, and my country will be the worse off for it.

"If you want me to be able to get away from the studio, I'll have to bring a person I trust into the picture. With Meike watching me, the only breathing space I have is when I'm at work. She shows up outside my house and follows me to work. This guy can arrange location shots and other excuses for me to get away," I said. "I've never been in a situation where a woman was intent on watching all my moves. If she doesn't go back to Washington I'm going to feel like I'm in prison."

"Prison?" he said.

"Well, a prison with frequent conjugal visits," I added.

"Is she really that alluring?"

"Take what you've heard and raise it to the ninth power," I said.

"That's truly frightening," he said.

CHAPTER FIFTY

Her arms encircled me as we sat in her hotel room and watched the sun head for the Hawaiian Islands, leaving the West Coast in darkness. Her upper body had somehow placed itself between me and the back of the couch as her breasts pressed into my back. She then straddled me with her two legs coming around my hips. This unlikely position was typical of how Meike switched gender roles as her lust took over and I absorbed her overwhelming sexuality. I had begun to feel comfortable with someone whose desire had no off switch. Given the way my energy flowed through me in so many undesired ways, I was glad of the opportunity for release in our innumerable couplings. It was like an addiction, which bothered me when it wasn't happening. While it was happening, it was like tall bourbon without branch water.

"It's quite remarkable," she said. "You feel the same way about me that I feel about you."

"And that is what?" I said.

"We are destined to be together," she said. She then wrapped her arms around my neck and kissed me. "You could feel that. I feel that. Why are you fighting it?"

"I'm not the marrying kind. You are German. I'm an American who just happens to work for the Germans out of ideology," I said.

"I'm not going anywhere," she said. "All that would happen is you'd be miserable and follow me like a puppy dog."

"Where are you getting this? I don't think I'd do that at all," I said.

"I'm not leaving Santa Monica," she said. "You wouldn't know what to do without me."

"Have you been like this with every man you've ever known? I think this is scary"

"Only the first," she said. "Every other time I ended it."

I thought about what had happened to the first guy and inwardly shuddered. If I hadn't committed myself to Churchill, I would jump into a car and drive north, where I couldn't be found.. To be honest, the level of passion in this relationship had been scaring me before this outburst. And I was starting to be worried about the addiction to her that seemed to ratchet up daily.

"I know what is best," she said. "If you can't see it, you will. This is not going to end." She held me tight and kissed me in a way that made me feel I was going to be devoured. I needed to think this through, but I decided to turn this moment over to my body, just as men have been doing since Eve pulled the apple off the tree.

CHAPTER FIFTY ONE

"Miss Feng Feng is here," the guard said.

"I'll come out to get her."

She was waiting by the gate in a red dress that would have inspired half the men in the world to climb aboard a plane to Shangri La. We shook hands and quickly walked to my bungalow on the set.

"I'm glad you remembered who I was," she said as we entered my quarters. "When you are being ministered to by angels, it must be hard to concentrate on old friends."

"I thought Ginny was keeping you up to date on what's going on?"

"She is, but this "Angel" of yours is still hanging around."

"How is your fiancée?"

"He isn't, at least not yet," she said. "I told my parents I needed a little more time."

"I thought he practically sat on the dragon throne," I said. "What are you waiting for, a bolt out of the blue to awaken you."

"Actually, I've been thinking about you," she said.

"Given what is going on in my life, it's nice to hear that someone is thinking about me and not checking to see if there are bullets in all the chambers," I said.

"You're the biggest movie star in the world."

"Next to Clark Gable," I said.

"The biggest movie star in the world, next to Clark Gable," she said. "And you're complaining about your life."

"I've got lobster and champagne coming."

"At least I get to eat well," she said.

"Tell me what's going on," I said.

"When I saw the newspaper with your name in big letters, I thought I was going to collapse. I called the hospital, but they said you were unconscious. When you finally were out of the coma, they wouldn't let me call in," she said. "I realized how much I loved you then. Oh God, I told myself I wasn't going to say that." She began crying and I held her for a few minutes, until the sobbing stopped. "I was with Ginny when she was having Thomas. She called and sang to you while I was in the room, so I felt a little better, but not much.

"I'm in a funny situation right now," I said. "Things are more complicated then you realize."

"Did you get married to this woman?"

"No. There are some things I can't explain to you for awhile, probably a long while. If I were you, I'd get on with my life," I said.

"Is that why you were attacked?"

"Yes."

"Could it happen again?" she said.

"Not if I'm careful," I said.

"Is this woman part of it?"

I didn't say anything. I pulled out her chair so she could sit down at the table.

"What were you doing last winter in Europe?" she said.

"Visiting my sister," I said.

"I think it has something to do with your visit there," she said. "I think Ginny knows what's really going on, but she won't even hint."

"Stay away from this topic or it could get very bad for both of us," I said.

"You are just crazy enough to try to do something noble," she said. "It's the same as when you treat me like I'm some kind of great lady whose honor can't be sullied."

"What is the word in Mandarin for sullied?"

"Unmarried," she said.

"I do care about you and that's why nothing is happening between us," I said.

"Is that what you said to this angel of mercy?"

"I don't seem to remember saying that," I said.

"Can you lock the doors and close the blinds?" she said.

"I told you that it isn't good for you to be around me right now," I said, surprised.

"I didn't mean that anything was going to happen here. I just want to know that it's just us. Can you understand that?" she said.

"I guess so."

"I'm going to have a lot of champagne and we'll pretend that we're in Paris or Macao and the rest of the world has disappeared," she said. "But nothing funny is going to happen."

I called the guard and said I wasn't to have any visitors and told the switchboard operator not to put through any calls. I opened the door long enough to get the cart from the chef and make sure there was a couple of bottles of champagne in the refrigerator, as well as the one we were opening. It was certain to be a wasted effort because I figured two glasses would put her under the table.

Feng Feng talked about her little sister, just 17, and how she was talking like someone who knew much more than the rest of the family.

She also told me her grandmother had somehow gotten out of Shanghai and had joined them in Chinatown.

"I suppose your parents couldn't move close to the UCLA campus?"

"Only if we wanted to be firebombed," she said. "In Chinatown we have people who will talk to us and act as if we're human."

"Knowing what America is like, why are we doing this?" I said. "You are scared stiff about not being treated with respect. I couldn't stand to watch it, so I think we're just bringing both of us a lot of trouble?"

"I told you why I was doing it. I don't want to admit we're not going to be together. Let me pretend a little while longer," she said.

I held her hand and poured her a second glass of champagne. She wasn't exactly inhibited normally, but I could see her opening up, with secrets slipping out like smoke drifting out a chimney.

"You have to believe me this woman could be a danger to you," I said.

"You've spent too long in the motion picture business," she said.

"Ask Ginny if you should be identified by this angel." I said. "Are you ready for the lobster?"

"Can we dance first? I don't want to think I might never dance with you," she said.

"Sure, but there's no music," I said.

"I can sing. We can dance to that."

"Okay," I said.

I put my arms around her and she sang "When I fall in Love" in the most beautiful soprano I'd heard in a long time. As the saying goes, she was like a quail feather in my arms.

She finished the song and said, "Pretend we are in Shanghai and there are no Japanese. The band is from America and we're the last couple on the dance floor. The band wants to go home, but they're enjoying the fact that we're dancing to their music, so they can't stop." She then sang the words, "Someday, when I'm awfully low" and I was caught up in her dreams.

"Are you pretending you're dancing with Fred Astaire? Those are his songs," I said.

"I'm pretending I'm dancing with Tommy Babcock and that he loves me," she said. "And don't tell me it's not true. I'm the director of this movie."

"Okay, Cecil B., take me to the next scene," I said.

"We're going to sit down and look into each other's eyes while I can still see out of mine," she said.

I helped take the meat out of her lobster, and dipped it in the drawn butter, feeding her the first bites.

"No one's done that since I was three," she said.

"How is teaching?"

"I like it," she said. "Another career might be better, but I'm making the most of my options and I love children."

"What do you want your own kids to become?"

"I'm Chinese; so of course I want them to be doctors. If I have enough of them, maybe all the specialties will be covered. That way I'll get house calls for everything."

"What about lawyers?" I said.

"Maybe the last one, but he'll have to promise not to sue his brothers and sisters," she said.

I looked at her closely for a moment.

"What are you looking at?"

"You're starting to look more and more like Joan Blondell," I said.

"You're a wise guy," she said. "No wonder somebody hit you over the head."

I took her hand and kissed it. "You make me think that what America actually does to immigrants is free them from horrible lives. Even with the prejudice, having freedom in the air invigorates people and makes them want something more than their parents had. It makes me sure I have to do something to help preserve this."

"I love America, but remember you are a white man, who never went without food," she said.

"Maybe I don't see things the way they are."

"That's okay, because you see America the way you think it should be, and you can fight for that." She paused for a moment. "I'm going to put my mind back on the dance floor where everything is just beautiful."

"I've rented a junk for a cruise of the harbors?" I said. "There are no Japanese ships in the harbor. There are restaurant boats, though, and you can pick your fish."

She took another sip of champagne and said, "This is wonderful. And to think, it's going to be like this every day."

After another glass, she started to get sleepy, so I put her on the couch. I sang "Good night baby, time to hit the road to dreamland" as she drifted off. I sat at the desk, watching her sleep, hoping her dreams were as good as the world we'd pictured before Bacchus bit her.

CHAPTER FIFTY TWO

I'd stayed overnight in Meike's hotel suite. I awoke early and I heard movement in the closet. I got out of bed and put on a robe and found her packing a suitcase.

"Was it something I said?"

"I wish you worried that something you said could drive me away," she said, sliding into a dress that packaged her hourglass figure like a bow on Valentines' Day roses. "Rudi asked me to take a trip down south for a day or two."

"I'll meet you downstairs for breakfast."

I threw on some tennis slacks and a linen shirt and went down with Meike to the coffee shop. She sat down and picked at her food.

"A penny for your thoughts," I said.

"I'm just sorry I have to go. I'll be taking notes at a meeting in San Diego involving the Ambassador to Mexico," she said.

"At least you can be happy Rudi is using your services. This way he won't be so upset you are spending time here."

"I suppose you are right," she said, finishing her coffee and pushing her chair away from the table. We went outside and she put her arms around me. She wasn't acting sexy, which was a new experience. It was as if my little girl was going to kindergarten for the first time. I stroked her hair until she let go and picked up her small suitcase. I took it from her and went out and put it in the trunk of her car. I watched her drive away, suddenly worried she might be going somewhere dangerous. I decided I would never recount that feeling to Saunders, who would probably have me committed.

CHAPTER FIFTY THREE

Meike had been gone for two days. I woke up at home and decided to join Ginny and Thomas, while I read the paper in front of some bacon and eggs. I brushed my teeth and headed down the stairs. The nanny had put the Times on the table, so after I told her what I wanted, I sat down to read.

The headline said "Anti-Nazi German Slain in Capistrano." The lead went; "The body of an anti-Nazi figure, whose courageous stand against the Third Reich had him marked for death, was discovered in an alley one block from the San Juan Capistrano Mission last night.

"Jonas Fischbach, the legendary 53-year-old opponent of fascism, was found with three bullet holes in his chest by a local woman returning home from work.

"Police said nothing had been taken from his wallet and that the bullet holes, which were described as being in a 'very tight pattern,' were covered by German coins featuring busts of Adolf Hitler."

I had read it out loud, so Ginny had a worried look on her face.

"Do the Germans have a lot of assassins in America?" she asked.

"I don't have any idea," I said.

"You are exposing yourself to a lot of danger. Sometimes in the middle of the night, in my dreams I see people chasing you, trying to kill you," she said.

"If I have a bad dream, I spend extra time dancing around the room holding Tom," I said. "He loves my singing, so I can tell he's really smart."

"Maybe my son has a tin ear."

"Wash your mouth out with soap," I said, hoping we'd get past this conversation.

"Columbia wants me for a new picture," she said.

"Your singing is just as good as ever. If you exercise you can get your shape back quickly," I said. "Who's the male lead?"

"Tyrone Power; they say he can dance a little."

"Are you going to do the picture?" I asked.

"They say I can have the nanny and Tom right on the set, so I can continue breast feeding," she said.

"Feed him within an iron room with no windows that you can lock from the inside," I said. "You know Hollywood,"

"It's funny; Feng Feng is the first woman I've been able to trust completely. You and I aren't the trusting sort, are we?"

"As you once said, we've seen enough dirty deals in this industry, that we only used to trust Jack and each other," I said. "The world we operate in is not noted for its ethics." I said, getting up from the table and heading for my namesake.

CHAPTER FIFTY FOUR

"Can you talk?"

"Sure kiddo," I said. "It was great seeing you the other day. How's your family?"

"Is the 'Guardian Angel" a beautiful blond woman?" Feng Feng said.

"That's what everybody says."

"People saw her outside our house. She must have followed my bus after I left the studio."

"How do you know it was her?"

"Wake up, White man, this is Chinatown. They said she was prettier than any woman in Hollywood and she was looking at our house and she was angry," Feng Feng said. "I guess you figure that happens every day."

"You've got a point. You have to stay away from me. She'll kill without thinking twice. If you're not worried about yourself, you've got a responsibility to your family." I knew that always worked with Asians. They were born owing their parents everything and died with their kids owing them everything. It beat America where you jumped on an outbound freight when you hit sixteen and asked somebody whether your mom was still kicking when somebody from your town happened through.

"Look, if anything happens to you my life won't be worth anything," I said. I caught myself too late, realizing what it sounded like and how I felt just then. I took a deep breath.

"I never figured you'd say something like that." She was more surprised than I was.

"It doesn't matter what I just said. I'm in the midst of something important that could get your parents killed. You've got a responsibility to them. I'll call you to tell you more when she leaves town. Keep in touch with Ginny everyday by phone. Don't go to the house."

Her version of OK wasn't the most upbeat one I'd ever heard.

CHAPTER FIFTY FIVE

After leaving the studio I went to Meike's hotel and found her in her lounging pajamas. She looked as if she had been on a month long vacation at the Fountain of Youth. In contrast to her mood when she left, she looked relaxed. Meike stood up and put her arms around me, pulling me against her and I realized, once again, how incredibly attractive she was.

"How was your trip?" I said.

"It was very boring. I took notes and then typed them up and sent them on a short wave radio the Ambassador had brought with him," she said, sounding very casual about it.

"Well you didn't miss anything here. I went to the studio, came home and went to sleep early," I said.

"How is the picture doing?"

"Fine. The dialogue is very good and this one should do even better than the first," I said.

"Did you miss me?"

"Can't you tell?"

"Yes, I can. It comes off your body in flames."

"Good," I said.

"That makes up for a couple of boring days," she said, reaching her hand down in my trousers, apparently searching for my conscience.

Before things started accelerating, I excused myself to use the bathroom. Once inside, I looked around and tried to practice spying. On a whim, I looked in the trash can and found her expensive blue blouse covered with bloodstains.

Putting it in the trash can, I covered it with the garbage it had been buried under before. I washed my hands and returned to the living room.

We made love as if we hadn't seen each other for ten years. When she relaxed into sleep, I went into the other room and examined her purse. I realize I'd never seen the derringer before.

Returning to the bedroom, I lay down next to a murderer.

CHAPTER FIFTY SIX

One night after a serious game of hide the sausage, Meike lay next to me, her arm on my chest.

"I have to go back east. They won't let me stay any longer," she said.

"I'll miss you," I said.

"This coming year is important in many ways. I have much to do," she said, like a serious schoolgirl ready for the next term.

"At first, there was talk about something major happening in the U.S, but I guess it was just a lot of talk" I said.

"I was told Goering's men like what they've seen so far, so if the information is deemed reliable, Rudy will tell you immediately about our big project," she said. "We're going to use you in its execution, so don't act like a little boy who wants to see his grades."

"I hope talk of our coming to the aid of Europe fades into an unpleasant memory. Our job is to protect this hemisphere and be careful the communists don't gain a toehold north of the Rio Grande."

"Some Americans don't understand it as well as you. The Fuhrer brought Germany back from the dead and he did it by wiping out the communists. You know I don't approve of his treatment of the Jews, but he has made our streets safe from gangs of jobless men and put bread on every Germans table."

"He truly is someone special," I said.

"I've been in a room with him and you could feel his presence," she said. "He always treats women with the utmost respect."

I realized she pictured herself as a patriot, driven by her Teutonic roots. "How good are you with a pistol?"

"I am very, very good. When you come to visit, I will take you to a range and show you how to improve your shooting," she said.

"I look forward to it. I'm better with a rifle," I said.

"I like hunting deer more than I like shooting birds with a shot-gun, but I'm good at that too."

"What's the secret?" I said.

"When you are shooting on the range you have to focus very well and imagine the center of the target is your enemy's heart," she said.

"I'm glad we're on the same side," I said.

"We are much more than on the same side. We are drawn by fate to be together," she said, locking her eyes on mine and pulling us together. "Never forget that."

I went down and hailed a cab. The cabbie took Meike's bags and put them in the boot.

"Hold me tight," she said. "I will think of you all the way across the country."

"It's too bad we won't be on the train together," I said.

She kissed me. The smell of her French perfume reminded me it would soon be less expensive in Berlin, as would a fine Bordeaux.

"Everything is just beginning for us," she said. "I can feel it."

After she left, I could imagine her aiming a pistol at my heart. I didn't look forward to becoming her enemy.

CHAPTER FIFTY SEVEN

One day Feng Feng came by the house, wearing a black hat with a veil. Since she still walked like a queen, it wasn't that good a disguise.

"Are you sure you're not married?" she said.

"Yes," I'm sure. You can't get married in a coma."

"Is there a law against that?" she said.

"It's part of the English common law. The Chinese took it from them."

"In China the woman can get married when she's in a coma if her father wants her to," she said.

"Maybe you're already married to the guy from Johns Hopkins because you look pretty comatose yourself," I said.

"In my country, phony private eyes don't talk disrespectfully to princesses," she said.

"Am I the only guy you get to talk to this way?"

"Yes, but my sister is even getting better at this than I am, so I may send her over to practice on you, or I would, if you were a man of honor," she said, sipping on some tea.

"Two wise-cracking heiresses would be two too many. But you have to understand that this situation is not something you can brush off," I said. "When you told me Meike was outside your house I realized I'd brought danger into the lives of everyone in your family.

Feng Feng sat down next to me on the couch and put her head against my shoulder. I put my arm around her so her face was next to my chest and she fell asleep. Just then, Ginny came by and pulled the door closed.

CHAPTER FIFTY EIGHT

It was the second time I'd gone to the Wilshire Temple on a Friday night. I would pull a yarmulke from the bin at the entrance and sit in the back and listen. Before I'd visited for the first time I'd read a book about the rituals, so I wouldn't look too out of place. At the Roosevelt Hotel, I'd used a makeup kit, applied a moustache and put on a fedora and a nondescript dark suit. No one took any special notice as I watched the service.

"Baruch, ata, eluhanu, melacalom." The prayer was not one I understood, although I'd read about it. However, it seemed to put me in touch with the spirit of those who still were alive in Dachau, the thousands I hadn't freed from brutal captivity. When one of their loved ones died, Jews took the bottom pillows off their couches and chairs, ripped their clothing, and grieved. I was very afraid a whole people would be sitting on springs and tearing their clothes for generations if someone didn't stop this.

When they brought out the Torah, I knew it was my book too, for my religion was founded on that document. I, of course, believed that four hundred years after God last spoke to the Hebrew people, as recorded in Malachi; he spoke to John the Baptist. But if the books that chronicled John's and the Carpenter's journey were taken to heart, everyone should be pounding on the gates of Dachau shouting "let my people go." Unfortunately, the few who cared so far didn't constitute a minyan. At this point, the group's size most resembled a gathering on a Cleveland street corner in February.

CHAPTER FIFTY NINE

September first was always bittersweet because its arrival said summer was departing. Children were dreading the first day of school, while men were driving their families down from Santa Barbara or Arrowhead after a week away. That morning I awakened to a phone call from Feng Feng.

"You must have gone to bed at eight with milk and cookies if you're calling this early," I said.

"I thought you'd want to know that Germany has invaded Poland," she said.

"So it's started.'

"Actually it started when the Japanese raped Nanking and no one did anything about it," she said.

"From now on, the news will just get worse."

"Perhaps then everyone will understand that the world has gotten smaller. The world isn't like it was during the period white men call the Boxer Rebellion. Before now it didn't matter to America whether the Japanese beat the Chinese or whether Ci xi stayed on the throne or not," she said, sending her agitation through the phone. "Now the Germans and the Japanese will be able to split the world any way they want." She rattled off something in Chinese. I'd never heard her slip into her own language without thinking before.

"This day was one I expected, but hoped would never come," I said.

"I hope you're saying you've been cuddling up with Miss Master Race because you want to destroy her people," she said.

"I'm not going to talk about it," I said.

"If that isn't the reason, then I will kill you before the Japanese rapists invade California and do it themselves.

"If I have a choice, I will take my chances with them."

"What is America going to do?" she said.

"Try to make money selling ammunition to England and France, I guess."

"That's all?"

"The American people remember the last time they went over to Europe and how their sons and brothers died for nothing," I said.

"What will it take for this country to wake up?"

"Hitler invading Nova Scotia," I said.

"I'm being serious," she said. "You just joke around while the world is burning."

"Do you really think that's what I'm doing?"

She was sputtering into the phone like a pressure cooker right before the squash hit the kitchen ceiling. I listened as it changed to the sound of a percolator with adenoids.

"What are you going to do about this?"

"You sound like a broken record. Do you want me to fly to the Polish border and tell them I'll do a song for them if they'll stop? I've done my part, at least by keeping a German woman from the front," I said. "What about you? Are you teaching?"

"No, not until next week," she said. "What do you have in mind?"

"Ginny went up north to look at a location they plan to use in her next picture. Is there any way you can get away for today and tomorrow?

"I can't think of a reason my mother would accept," Feng Feng said.

"Use the news of the day and tell her you feel you have to take some action?" I said.

"You are really a man without shame," she said. "Okay, I'll go home and see what I can work out and call you back."

"When does a Chinese woman get to be an adult and control her own life?"

"When her father is sure men would rather make contact with the posterior of Chaing Kai-Sheik than glance at his daughter," she said.

I went downstairs and made some French toast . Twenty minutes into the morning newspaper, the phone rang again.

"You're not going to like this," Feng Feng said.

"Try me," I said.

"I am going with my little sister to take some action on this issue, returning tomorrow."

"You said your sister was more of a wiseacre than you."

"Uh huh," she said.

"Can you trust her?"

"Actually, yes I can. She believes that keeping information away from my parents makes us closer."

"I have enough trouble thinking of you as an adult, much less your 17-year-old sister," I said.

"She was eighteen on Wednesday and people say that she's a genius. I'm afraid, though, that it might not be good for you to be seen with us, because of whatever it is you're involved in.'

"Jack has a place on the water in Santa Barbara. I'll have his house-keeper there buy a lot of groceries and then take the weekend off. Can you or your sister cook?"

"My sister wants to be a physicist but they made her take home economics in high school. The down side is she only cooks American food. She'd probably like the chance to test her recipes on an important Caucasian. Of course, I cook Chinese food."

"Does she know about me?"

"No, but you can tell her you're number two after Clark Gable. She saw your latest movie."

"I mean you and me."

"You've repeatedly told me there is no you and me, so I never bothered to mention it." She seemed to really be enjoying herself.

"I'll pick you up at Hill and Fifth Street in an hour and a half. There are bathing suits at his place and lots of women's clothes from some of Jack's wives and assorted friends, so you won't need to bring casual clothes."

"We'll take the bus up Hill and we'll both be looking very old,' she said.

"I'll be wearing a moustache on my lip and a brown fedora on my head."

"Try not to get that mixed up," she said, hanging up the phone.

If Feng Feng looked like the Good Princess who was going to inherit the throne, then Judy was the Impulsive Princess. You can probably picture her: beautiful, willful, ready to take on anything, disdainful of convention. Quite honestly, she was stunning; with the same pink and white skin as Feng Feng but darker hair. She was 5' 8", with a full bosom and a wasp waist. The total package made her look older than her big sister.

It seemed clear that Feng Feng, hadn't told her what to expect, but she went from disbelief to a studied nonchalance in a heartbeat. She shook my hand and said," My name's Judy, what's yours?"

"Tommy," I said. "How did you get the name Judy'?"

"Cary Grant said 'Judy. Judy, Judy' in some movie, so I decided if it was worth saying three times, It was the name for me."

"Are you comfortable being a Judy?"

"Not really, but it sounded more exciting than You Yung."

I was heading out to the San Fernando Valley through Cahuenga Pass (on a late summer day the temperature could hit 100 in the Valley, but be closer to 75 in Santa Barbara) accompanied by two of the most beautiful women on the planet.

"I remember what your mother looked like and I guess I shouldn't think an apple should fall far from the tree," I said. "It would be nice to see her again."

"No it wouldn't," Judy said. "She'd kill you if she knew you were squiring her beautiful daughters to a political meeting."

"I guess Feng Feng didn't tell you we were actually going to Santa Barbara," I said.

"That beats protesting a war between white men we never met."

I laughed. She was like a Feng Feng on 14 cups of coffee.

"I told you," Feng Feng said. I noticed she wasn't attempting to insert herself into the conversation.

"You were bad enough," I said.

"In China, someone as impolite to great ladies as you are would live in back with the animals and only come out when it was time to slaughter a pig," Judy said.

"Judy, he's not strong enough to deal with you," Feng Feng said.

"What are you like on a date? Boys must run away after the first five minutes," I said.

"I've never been on a date. Women like Feng Feng and I are only dreamed about."

I couldn't help laughing.

"Did anybody ever tell you that you look like that guy in the movies?" she said.

"No. Who would that be?"

"I can't remember his name but he can't decide whether to hit somebody or sing them to sleep. That guy looks okay on screen, but I'm sure he's very old and held together with tape."

"What if that guy decided you weren't worth singing to?" I said, moving into my newest character.

"It wouldn't matter. His singing would probably kill me deader than a doornail," Judy said.

"Stop it," Feng Feng said, "Sit in your seats and face the front. We'll have recess in Santa Barbara."

Jack's beach house had five bedrooms, a steam room, and a patio that ended in the Pacific. The red clay tile roof, the bougainvillea with its red/purple flowers and the sound of gulls, all conspired to create the perfect backdrop for a summer day. The cook had left a pot of chili and a warm dip made from yellow cheese on the front burners, with venison warm in the oven. Limes and lemons laid out on wax paper in the bar had been cut to complement the gin, vodka and tonic. There was Coca Cola and Canada Dry for the kids.

The girls had spent time in their bedrooms trying on suits, while guessing who had worn them. I tried to steer them away from one probably worn by Mae West to protect them from feelings of insignificance, but Judy pulled it out of my hand. They came out and sat on the white wicker couch, their bathing robes covering their suits. The radio was playing *South of the Border*, by Gene Autry.

"Do you go to the beach often?"

"We've never been to the beach before," Feng Feng said.

"Don't you swim?"

"We both have learned how to swim, but we would never go sit in the sun. In China the whiter your skin, the higher your chances are for getting a good man. That's why women who grow up in the Yangtze Delta are so prized," Judy said.

"In Wuxi, where our mother is from, women swallow ground up fresh water pearls to keep their complexions white," Feng Feng said.

"Maybe this wasn't a good idea," I said.

"No," Judy said. "It's good for us to see this world. Maybe, some-day we'll be allowed to live in it. Of course then our skin will get terrible and all the pearl powder in the world won't fix it."

"But if we get a sunburn, mother will get suspicious," Feng Feng said.

"Let's walk down to the water and give you a taste of this lifestyle," I said. "Ginny, I'm bringing a drink down for Feng Feng and me. Do you want a coca cola or ginger ale?"

"Don't you have anything stronger?"

"Your sister is 23 and one drink sends her to Shangri La, with a stop in dreamland."

"Feng Feng, tell this B actor about my abilities," Judy said.

"One day she drank six glasses of Moutai, which is sixty per cent alcohol, and then went to the movies with me. I fell asleep in the second feature and she had to tell me how it ended. I think she has a hollow leg," Feng Feng said.

"I'm bringing two bottles of champagne then," I said, finding a larger silver ice bucket and filling it with ice and two bottles of Dom Perignon.

We sat down at the water's edge, where I popped the cork on one bottle and filled the glasses Feng Feng had carried. They wore straw sombreros so their parents wouldn't smell a rat tomorrow. An afternoon breeze came in off the water and we finished one bottle. We decided to have the second under the awning that hung off the back of the house. When Judy was looking down the beach towards Ventura, Feng Feng touched my hand, but shortly afterward sleep tackled her and drove her out of bounds into dreamland. I picked her up and carried her to the living room couch, where I plumped a pillow and placed it under her head. Back under the awning, Judy had taken off her robe and was moving into the second bottle, seemingly unaffected by the pride of France.

She looked at me and said, "I knew she was in love, although she never would admit it. What's going on?"

"Nothing's happened. We're just friends," I said.

"I know nothing's happened because I know my sister. But I remember when she was crying and was depressed. It was at the same time you got hit on the head in Washington."

"I'm not going to take advantage of her. I suppose she'll marry the doctor your parents have picked out for her and we won't see each other again." When I said that I felt a chill and wondered why the air had gotten colder.

"She already messed up her chance with the doctor. When she said no, he was introduced to Miss Chinese New Year in San Francisco."

"I didn't know that."

I looked at her, and while I was thinking about Feng Feng, noticed that Ginny's legs were perfectly shaped, long and, apparently hairless. Someone once told me Chinese women never needed to shave their legs. This information needed to be kept from American women who would want all of them deported.

"I think you love her," Judy said.

"Maybe I do, but she and I are just friends."

"Please don't hurt her," she said, sounding like a child for a second. She seemed to realize that and added, "She not as tough as I am."

"I don't expect anything from her but friendship. I promise I'll never knowingly hurt her."

"Unknowingly would be wrong too," Judy said.

"Neither way; I promise."

"You're tougher than your song and dance movies and less scary than your most recent film," she said.

"You or your sister will never get to see the scary part, but it's there."

"I am going to have to protect her and the rest of your family by pushing her away."

This comment was met with silence.

"Did you grow up with Joan Blondell too," I said.

"Yeah, but I was five years younger and could incorporate the thinking behind her approach more than Feng Feng. My sister has the patter down straight, but really is a sweet Chinese girl. I look like a Chinese girl, but I'm really like Joan Blondell," she said, bumming a Camel from me.

"We bought a 35mm. projector because mom's family has lots of money and my father wanted to get the American idioms right. Then they set up a screening room. I figured out how to run the camera and played those movies over and over again. I don't think they wanted to change my thought process but that's what happened. I understood, right from the start, what the double entendres and allusions meant, so it gave me a peek into a society with a completely different value system. I don't think Feng Feng got it until we moved here, which is why she's as sweet as she is, behind that witty self protection."

"But you've never had a date."

"Do you really think a Chinese boy could handle me?" she said, laughing.

"Your parents probably watch you like a hawk," I said.

"I wouldn't do anything to embarrass my parents. There is this concept of shao suin that I'll bet Feng Feng told you about. I owe it to my parents to be careful and anyway, men are too easy to figure out. It's like dissecting a frog. Everything you're told is going to be there before you cut them open is what's there. Some guys just put up some smokescreens. In addition, with white guys you always suspect they are thinking about you as someone they can take advantage of, because no one will care."

"That's another reason I'm not touching your sister. The world is a pretty cruel place and she needs someone who will treasure her and protect her."

"Why couldn't you do that?"

"At the moment things are going on that would prevent that from happening," I said. "I also don't see myself getting married. My best friend has tried it too many times without much to show for it."

"My sister cried when she read about the 'Angel' who was taking care of you."

"That whole situation is very hard to explain, anyway, I thought she didn't talk to you about it."

"I'm a woman. I'm going to Berkeley. Do the math," she said.

"Feng Feng says your IQ is 160."

"A Cal Tech test said it was higher. It's just the result of heredity. My mom is even smarter than my father, but she was a Chinese woman and they're just supposed to run the household," she said, in a tone of exasperation. "Feng Feng has a high IQ too. If I hadn't figured out what was happening to her and why, then the tests would be wrong."

"I'm not sure Einstein would have even noticed," I said.

"Yes, but I'm a woman who reads psychology books my father brings home to me from the UCLA library. That's why I want to ask you about your sister," she said.

"You're all over me like a cheap suit. Give your brain a rest," I said.

"You can't get married because you think your sister's perfect and you can't find a carbon copy of her. You two spent so much time together you were a couple, presumably without the sex," she said.

"Holy crap, what did you mean 'presumably?'"

"I guess I hit a sore point. You probably didn't, but who knows what goes on inside the human mind?"

"I think it's good you're going into physics because if you go about talking to people this way, no one will ever lie on your couch unless you're already on it," I said.

"You care about my sister and wouldn't do anything, but you said that because you wished I was under you on a couch," she said. "That was a dead giveaway. I read Freud and that was some kind of verbal slip."

"You're whistling up a drainpipe," I said.

"I'm the most interesting woman you ever met, admit it. My sister is a person most guys want to marry. I know I'd scare most men, but it doesn't bother me. Life should be an adventure, not a process of pouring yourself into a cake pan to fit into its shape, or, God forbid, a muffin pan."

"A muffin pan is a very scary concept," I said.

"You love your sister and she's one of the most beautiful women who ever rolled down the turnpike. She probably also kept you out of trouble and made you tie your shoelaces. You haven't found any-one else who has the looks and the power to organize your life, so you've decided you won't ever get married. You're wrong, though; my sister meets all your criteria. You just don't want to see it because you'd have to let go of part of your sister. I read about something like this the other day."

"You've never had a date and still have to be told to clean your room, so this pint sized analysis isn't worth the paper it's printed on,"

I said. "Anyway Feng Feng has become Ginny's best friend, the only woman she trusts. She wants me to marry Feng Feng."

She just sat there, immobilized by what she'd just heard.

"It's your job to take care of your sister when the break happens. That has nothing to do with psychology, only security," I said, pouring us both another glass of champagne.

"You've got what is called a good 'ego' because this would outrage most men in this world."

"Thanks. By the way, just because you're so smart doesn't mean some guy couldn't knock you for a loop," I said.

"Only if he looks like Clark Gable and can smash an atom."

"Feng Feng may have told you I'm number two, right behind Gable."

"Then you better keep practicing, buster," she said, sounding like Rosalind Russell, with a dash of soy sauce.

We sat out there silently watching the ocean and the gulls. It actually wouldn't be a bad thing to have this girl as a sister-in law; that is if I were the marrying kind.

When Feng Feng awoke she set the table, so we had the venison stew and the cheese dip as we discussed the invasion of Poland, *Gone with the Wind*, my new picture, and Louise Boudreaux.

"I can understand why all the men have replaced questions about my sister with questions about Louise Boudreaux, but why are you two interested in Louise Boudreaux?"

"Didn't you ever watch your own movie?" Judy said.

"Not really," I said. "I frequently watched the dailies, the film they'd shot that day, but I never saw the whole picture. I was always talking to someone or answering questions anytime the whole thing ran."

"The words used were 'burns up the screen,' Feng Feng said, a touch of irritation in her voice.

"She seems like the kind of woman no man could resist," Judy said.

"But of course it was just work for you," Feng Feng said.

"Just business," said Judy.

"Did you have to rehearse a lot?" Feng Feng said.

"Was it hard work?" Judy said.

"She has bad breath and burps a lot. She's actually not very attractive in person," I said.

"Yeah, and I'm a monkey's uncle," Judy said. She looked at Feng Feng and said, "How many times did you make me see that movie?"

"We just went once," Feng Feng said, looking offended.

"I saved the stubs," Judy said. "We went three times. It was the first time I realized you didn't like watching people kiss on screen."

"They have to put Louisa into this girdle that goes from up there to the bottom of her thighs," I said. "It's very unpleasant to be next to."

"Since she was French, did you kiss with your tongue?" Judy asked.

"I don't know how to do that."

"Yes you do," Feng Feng said.

"Being with the two of you is like getting a frontal lobotomy without anesthesia," I said.

Judy and I were drinking vodka with a little tonic and Feng Feng was heavy into the Canada Dry. I suddenly realized I was having one of the best times of my life. Then I remembered that this experience would probably never be repeated and felt cheated.

"Are we making you sad?" Feng Feng said.

"This is the kind of night you want to last forever," I said, "even if you're the punching bag. You're like the Soong sisters crossed with Laurel and Hardy."

"The only Soong sister who looks as good as we do is Ching-ling and she's in her 40s and seems to have a very good cook," said Judy.

"Ginny, that's the cattiest comment I've ever heard," Feng Feng said.

"It's true. Think of how many guys wanted to marry you after they just saw your picture," Judy said. Feng Feng went shy and didn't respond but I know that Judy was sending me a message that her sister wouldn't be on the market forever.

"Let's play blackjack," I said, as I got up for the chips.

"Chinese love to gamble, but no one wants to play with Judy because she counts cards," Feng Feng said.

"We want to meet Joan Blondell. Can you set it up?" Judy asked.

"Sure, I'm friends with her husband, Dick Powell. I'll set it up when we get back to Los Angeles."

"For us it will be like visiting Mount Vernon," Feng Feng said.

"No, more like Lourdes," Judy said, shuffling the deck.

That's the way the evening went until we all shuffled off to our rooms, our bodies dulled by alcohol or the demon grip of ginger ale. I lay there, holding tight to some ethical sense I couldn't escape, until sleep removed the tension and desire from my body.

The next morning we arose early so we could appreciate the place before we drove back to Los Angeles. The trip down Highway One could take forever.

"If we can harness the power of the atom, the world will be a better place," Judy said as we got up from a big breakfast. "Imagine being able to light a city from a plant with boilers that didn't need coal."

"I'll read a book on it and ask you questions about it next time we go to a political meeting," I said.

"Politics is discussed most effectively at the beach," Judy said.

When Judy was around, Feng Feng became the older sister and let Judy make all the wisecracks. She sat back with the detached amusement of a mother with a precocious child. Some guy was going to get a good wife out of Feng Feng. The man who ended up with Judy would learn what it would be like to harness the atom.

"I've had enough coffee and doughnuts," I said. "Should we hit the road?"

The women reluctantly agreed and we headed out for the highway to return them to their cocoon and me to my divided life.

CHAPTER SIXTY

I called Meike at six the next evening, guessing I wouldn't catch a beautiful woman home at nine p.m. I was wrong.

"Liebchen, I was just thinking about you. What are you doing?"

"Thinking about you, of course," I said. "What have you been doing the past few days? I called on Thursday, but couldn't reach you."

"I was with a friend who has shown us a nice present I must tell you about," she said. "I came back late Thursday night."

"Would you describe it as lovely?"

"It's in the same category as the Bayeux Tapestry."

This meant that it was historical and as valuable to the Nazis as the eleventh century tapestry that was the pride of France. It depicted the Norman conquest of England, which I'm sure the French believed was the birth of culture in Great Britain.

"That must be beautiful."

"He lives in a wonderful place. Everyone rides there and you would feel right at home. "You will meet him soon."

She was quiet for a moment and then said, "I just took my nightgown off because it is too hot here. Washington is no place to be in the early Fall, but with the activities overseas, I need to be around to help."

"I understand the Poles invaded Germany, you had to respond, and all of a sudden things became more and more complex." I didn't believe that for a minute, but I figured she just might, so I threw the bone. "You have been very busy, but I imagine you still look quite beautiful right now." That, of course, I truly believed.

"Do you miss me?"

"Would flowers miss the sun?" I said.

"Do I compare favorably with your movie stars?"

"I've honestly never met one more beautiful than you," I said.

"When are you coming to see me?"

"Soon."

"How is that Norwegian woman?"

"She hasn't even arrived on the set, but I understand she's arrived in America. I'll be meeting her soon."

"She's not much to look at, people tell me."

"I can't really say."

"Do you have to kiss her?"

"It's in the script, but I promise I won't enjoy it."

"It is our destiny to be together, remember that when you are close to her."

"I don't want to talk or think about that, but I miss you."

"You had better think about that," she said, her voice going icy.

I hung up the phone. It seemed like the right time for a drink, so I made myself a Cuba Libre and opened the door to sit by the pool, just as the phone rang.

"You hung up on me," Meike said.

"Don't ever threaten me again," I said and hung up for the second time. Let her stew on that overnight.

It had seemed hot when I first planned to sit outside, but when I reached the poolside I felt cold. Even a robe didn't seem to help much, as I pondered "destiny."

CHAPTER SIXTY ONE

We'd been shooting for about three weeks, when I met with Feng Feng.

"You have to promise me something," I said.

"You want me to spread your ashes over Santa Barbara from a seaplane?"

"If you have the chance to do that, feel free, but I think my mom would like to spread them over a Connecticut field," I said.

"Does this have something to do with your blond Nazi, the one who was outside my house?

"Yes. You have to promise that no matter what you think of me, if Ginny or I call you and warn you that you're in danger, you have to take Judy and your parents and clear out of your house," I said. "This is also the last day we're going to be spending together."

"Is there going to be a wedding announcement that says you've been wed during a Blitzkrieg?" She had tried to use a joke to make light of what I was saying, but her heart wasn't in it and she looked as if she was going to cry."

"This is a different kind of lightning war, one in which you make sure no one burns down your own house."

"Does it involve a little apple cheeked girl from the far North?"

I ignored the question and said "And if I ever call you, you get your parents and Judy to my ranch in the Valley. Take a cab there and Fernando will know to drop everything and begin driving you back and forth to school. This is not going to happen for months, if it happens at all, but you have to start preparing for this."

"This sounds pretty serious," she said.

"We can't have any contact from now on. Look, I already admitted I feel something for you, but this is getting crazy and your family is in real danger and things could get worse. I've written down Jack's private numbers at the studio and at home. You must call him directly after you hear from me about any more trouble. Call Ginny and tell her what's going on. You should prepare written instructions for your parents and for Judy. She has to be convinced to follow these instructions. If Meike hadn't shown up that time in front of your house, we wouldn't have to do this, but she did."

"Why?"

"She can put out a squirrel's eye at 100 yards, so you'd better think about Judy and your parents." The word "shao suin" in Chinese involves the importance of filial piety and describes what a child owes to their parents. Confucius had provided me with a means of protecting Feng Feng from her other instincts.

As she got up and walked to the door, I could see the message had registered and it saddened me. The world I lived in had crashed into hers, rattling the teacups and sending a cold wind into the life her parents had created with hard work and intelligence. I had become the white man with the virus that could eliminate an entire tribe.

CHAPTER SIXTY TWO

It was early, and I already had a bottle of Chivas on the table with Ballantine Ale for a "back." The way I figured it, soon I wouldn't have the energy to change any records, so I'd turned the radio to NBC and was listening to broadcasts from Europe. Edward R. Murrow spoke from London on how German magnetic mines had inflicted heavy damage on Allied shipping.

Then William Shirer talked about the how the Nazis were moving towards East Prussia and believed it should be returned to the Fatherland.

Eric Severeid spoke from Paris about the grim mood in a country that had done so much to avoid a confrontation but where many citizens expected the Germans to attack through Belgium. French Generals, however, were confident, said Severeid, that the Maginot Line would make it impossible for the Germans to place their feet on French soil ever again.

The news had been horrible, so I hurried off to bed hoping a dream about peace would send me into a tranquil mood. Then I quickly wished you could bet against anticipated dreams, so I could afford to own another horse.

Just then, the phone rang and I was pulled back into the past. I had known Michael Quinn since his arrival in Hollywood in '33. That was back in my chandelier swinging days when I'd been known to close down bars with Barrymore, Bill Fields and, very occasionally, with him. We'd made Hollywood parties the stuff of legend before I wised up, bought the ranch and gave up the night life for the stable and the smell of orange blossoms. The farther I distanced myself from those boozy nights of oblivion, the less I saw of Michael. Of all the old drinking companions, I missed him the least, so it was surprising to hear his voice on the phone.

"Tommy, it's been a long time since we had some poteen in the shebeen," he said.

"Yes and because of that, my liver daily sings Alleluia."

"I think we should get together tonight or tomorrow," he said.

"We're still shooting, so I don't want to wake up tomorrow and be reassembled through pills whose bottles I'll never be shown, so the director can stay on schedule," I said.

"We have a friend in common," he said.

"We've got a lot of friends in common and some of them are even alive," I said.

"This guy has the same last name as a town," he said.

"Shit," I thought, "von Darmstadt." However, I said, "Have you ever had any Apfelwein?"

"No, but I had a friend destroy his kidneys on Calvados. How about we meet tomorrow night at the 'Minstrel Boy' on Vermont?"

"What time?"

"About ten," he said.

"Just you and me?"

"For now," he said.

The Minstrel Boy was known for its corned beef and cabbage and a generous pour of Jameson's Irish whiskey. I'd once tried to order a Bushmill's, before the bartender flashed me an angry look and explained it was distilled in the British occupied north. I never asked for it again. Tonight I pledged to limit myself to two whiskies, with no beer backs. Michael could compensate for my limitations on his end.

A young man with a high tenor voice was slowly singing *Whisky in the Jar* as my eyes scanned the pub's occupants. As I passed a group of older, working class men, I noticed a younger man passing a hat around the room. Michael was sitting in a large booth with two starlets who seemed to be making him happy in a multitude of ways.

"Tommy Babcock, movie star" he said, gesturing to the girls to leave us alone for awhile. One of them ran her hand down my crotch as I sat down.

"They're passing the hat for the IRA aren't they," I said.

"Of course. Did you think it was for the Ancient Order of Hibernians' Christmas party?"

"Nice girls," I said.

"They're collecting for the Salvation Army," he said, smiling.

"You say we have a friend. Who is it?"

"You wouldn't have put your kidneys in jeopardy if you didn't know who it was," he said, smiling again.

"Where did you see him?

"I was in New York. We met at the place that pushes Berliner Weisse," he said, referring to a beer flavored with fruit syrup.

"If people knew you'd been with him, you wouldn't get many new roles," I said.

"Every one should know I've got nothing against Jews. There are a good lot of them in Dublin," he said. "I hate the British and that's all I care about. They're fighting them, so they are my pals of the moment."

"How's your life going? I hear that wife number two is out on her ass?"

"She didn't like the hours I kept and my companions," he said, smiling.

"Such as the girl scouts I found you with?"

"Correct. She had a very restrictive approach to holy matrimony," he said, knocking back a shot and washing it down with a glass of Schlitz, Milwaukee's finest.

"She's beautiful. I would have thought she was a keeper," I said.

"Pretty is, as pretty does," he said. "I need your help. How about loaning me your ranch for a weekend?"

"Why?"

"I've got some sons of Erin that need to meet with some goose steppers this weekend to iron out some details of a plan," he said.

"If you touch the horses I'll make Irish stew out of you," I said, making it very clear with a look that said I'd kill him if anything went wrong.

"Your tough guy act is carrying over into real life," he said. "You need a Guinness to settle your stomach."

"One," I said.

He sent one of the girls to get it, along with two shots and two beers for him.

"I never picked you for a Nazi," Michael said, brushing back the jet black hair that fell into his face at any opportunity. "I thought you were good buddies with Jack, among others."

"That was just business. You know how careful you have to be in this town," I said, wondering if he had said that to Von Darmstadt.

"I'm sorry I was wrong," he said. "It's one thing to ask the Nazis to help me against the black and tans, but they aren't the kind of people I'd like to live with."

"To each his own," I said, letting the foamy Guinness draft flow down my throat in one long, smooth action. "I wouldn't think a speech about morality was your strong suit."

"Probably not," he said, pulling one of the women close to him. He kissed her and quickly turned his back on me. It seems that even immoral men needed to throw stones at those with less scruples.

CHAPTER SIXTY THREE

Saunders flew out to Los Angeles so he could worry in proximity to my newest problem. I went to his hotel and brought a bottle of Glenlivet with me. I fixed him a scotch and opened a book on archeology I'd recently purchased. It was always better to let Saunders stew in his own juice than start a conversation with him. Therefore, having something to read was essential, because he could take forever.

I hadn't seen the inside of a library since I signed the contract for the second picture. The minute I knew I had that money coming, I went on a massive book buying binge, with advice from Larry Powell at UCLA and Jake Zeitlin, who always tipped me to the best new editions. I was saving all the books for inclusion in my grandfather's library, which my dad would eventually pass to me, unless Meike shot me first.

"Who did you tell him worked at the ranch?" he said.

"I didn't."

"So you could have a Mexican girl who took care of the place?" he said.

"Of course," I said. "But I don't think that's a good idea."

"We could put a woman I call "Rosa" in there. You could say she doesn't know English, but they will be left a few words in translation they can use to have her get them what they need," Saunders said.

And with that Saunders left the room to prepare a plan to infiltrate the wily sons of Erin.

I greeted Michael Quinn with a bottle of Johnny's 12-year-old (and cheapest) Scotch and a box of domestic cigars. He greeted me with a sneer.

"Well if it isn't it my favorite Nazi," he said.

"I'll have to call Goering and tell him you two are washed up."

"We appreciate your letting us use your ranch," he said, grudgingly.

"I always appreciate sentiments from the heart," I said, tiring of judgments from debauchery's number one box office star.

"God you repulse me," he said, just before I put him in a choke hold and kidney punched him, letting him fall to the floor.

"You ought to stay sober for one day so you could get in some exercise," I said. I pulled a Smith and Wesson from my jacket and walked backwards away from him into the kitchen. Watching him carefully, I indicated to the agent I knew only as Rosa that she should come into the living room.

"She doesn't speak English. Fernando always communicates with her in Spanish, but she will bring you beer and sandwiches, as well as ice for your drinks," I said. "I assume you'll be drinking my liquor."

Quinn started telling Rosa in Spanish just how beautiful she was.

"If you or anyone else touches her, I will kill you," I said. I had the feeling Quinn believed me. He'd grown up doing jobs that included castrating sheep by biting their balls off in New Zealand. He spent a couple of years as a bouncer in New York speakeasies owned by Irish mobsters affiliated with Joe Kennedy. His second language was violence and nothing scares someone like Quinn more than a man who doesn't think about long term consequences when he gets angry. At that point, I wanted him to do something so I could end his life and bury him under the barn. With him gone it would be a better world. His wife would get any money he had left, the girls would find someone new and more women would walk down the aisle with their hymens intact.

"I've put together a list in Spanish and English. When you want something brought to you, just point to it," I said.

I walked out the front door just as a car pulled into the driveway. It was filled with hard looking men trying to look casual, but broadcasting they were men who enjoyed hurting people no matter who occupied Belfast. They should thank Churchill and his whole social class for providing them with a political justification for their savagery and brutality.

CHAPTER SIXTY FOUR

Saunders had been called back to Washington because the "phony war" was confusing Washington. Roosevelt needed some assurances on British strength and resolve, so Saunders, as Winston's direct report, was to brief the President. Chamberlain had become a joke as Prime Minister. In fact, Sam Bernstein, of Apollo Pictures, had put his arm around a starlet he was screwing and said she was so good at what she did; she was the Piece in Our Time. Churchill was becoming an emblem of English fortitude to American eyes and Saunders could convey Churchill's resolve better than anyone in Washington. After all, he had been leaking information to Churchill when the Great Man was in the wilderness. Saunders had foreseen what Hitler would do and knew who could lead the British out of their isolation and the fright induced denial that held them like a deer in the headlights.

Saunders had ordered me to stay as far away from the ranch as possible. I gave that order five seconds of reflection and parked my car among the orange trees where it wasn't visible.

I'd grown up hunting and practiced with the Springfield before the war ended, so my skills with a rifle were better than that of most Americans. Six months ago, I'd obtained the relatively new Garand rifle that had excited the army. Joey Colesantro, who was a technical consultant on both of my recent pictures, had taken me to a range in Glendale and showed me how to get the best out of my acquisition. I pulled it out of the trunk, buckled on an ammo belt with a .45 on it and set off to a position I'd constructed near the house. Fernando, who as usual hadn't asked any questions, had helped me arrange limbs from a sycamore hit by lightning last week into a setting of dirt and fertilizer close to the house. I figured the fertilizer would decrease any visitors' interest in my Nazi blind.

I hadn't been noticed and laid down in an odiferous hideout that would have driven Jesse James and the Clantons to the nearest jail to surrender. When I was young, Nicholas, one of the hired men, would let me ride on the back of a makeshift manure spreader pulled by the Bay mare on which I'd first learned to ride. The horse, Tobey, was slow but gentle, with a consistent temperament, even in estrus. I don't know how a female got the name Tobey, maybe from someone who didn't have the sense to check out her private parts. Days riding on the manure spreader and afternoons loitering in the barn got me accustomed to the smell of shit, in all of its manifestations. Maybe that's why I was comfortable in Hollywood.

As it grew dark I could hear the sound of conversation, but couldn't make out the words. Every once in awhile, someone would tell a joke that would make the men laugh. I'd lain there three hours when I heard Rosa scream and saw her running across the lawn and into the fruit trees. A man followed her, yelling at her to stop, slowly closing the distance between them. I dropped the rifle and followed. Because I knew the landscape and how the trees had been laid out, I could maneuver quickly in the dark. I found her among the Valencia oranges, with the man holding Rosa down and pressing a knife against her neck. I grabbed the long hunting knife I'd brought back from Germany and drove it into the man's back where I figured his heart should be. I pulled the blade out and he fell over. I grabbed his hair and pulled the blade across his throat from his left side to his right as he looked back at me, apparently still partially alive. I hoped my face stayed with Michael Quinn as he descended into hell.

"You smell like caca. Please take a shower," Rosa said. I left the hotel room, scoured my body and washed my hair three times. I liberally sprinkled bay rum on my exterior. I then returned to the living room of the suite. Rosa needed to disappear and quickly.

She had been quiet during the drive over the Sepulveda pass and along Sunset into Hollywood. Her comment on what I'd done to her olfactory senses was the only one she'd made.

"What is this I'm drinking?" she asked.

"It's called a French 75. I suppose it's named after the big guns the French used in the Great War," I said. "It's concocted with Champagne and gin."

"Are you planning to get me drunk so I'll forget tonight?" she said.

"I know you won't forget it, but I thought the immediacy of it might recede a little," I said.

"You probably want to know what happened."

"The story can wait, if you don't want to tell it right now," I said.

"No," she said. "I just might as well get through it."

She was quiet for what seemed an eternity. "It started out fine. They ate and drank as if the world was running out of provisions. They had the card, so they would ask for things by pointing to the English word on the sheet. Quinn tried to catch me up a couple of times by speaking in English, but I let my mind go back to Barcelona, where I only spoke Spanish.

"There was one Irishman called 'goose' who had lived for awhile in America in some place called the Finger Rivers, or something like that. He made the sound a doe makes when you cut its throat. They all thought that was funny. Then Quinn said he would give them a break by raping the "Mexican" in front of them. He said both sides could have me afterwards, in order to show unity of purpose.

"I immediately headed out the back door, making sure I made no noise. It was only a minute later that he must have discovered I wasn't in the kitchen. He yelled at me and told me to come back, so I started to run. He came after me, but I took off into the trees. "If I hadn't tripped, he never would have caught me. He was not in good shape and I could have outrun him. You know the rest," she said.

"I'm glad I hid."

"You weren't supposed to be near the ranch," she said.

"No."

"You could have destroyed everything you have been working on if you had been caught," she said.

"I know," I said.

"Saunders will be very angry and he should be," she said.

I didn't say anything.

"If it comes down to it, you're going to have to shoot your Nazi sweetheart, because she works with the same kind of men who tried to destroy my life tonight," she said.

"I imagine it will come to that," I said.

Rosa called Saunders and told him about today's events.

"You shouldn't have been anywhere near the ranch, you know that," he said after she put me on the phone.

"Yes."

He had been waiting for an argument and had prepared his response only to be thrown off cadence. The line was silent on both ends.

"I'm not condoning what you did, but I want to thank you for saving Rosa. It sounds as if she would have died if you hadn't disobeyed instructions," he said.

"Thanks," I said.

"Don't ever think about recruiting another movie star, even if he's Goering's best friend. I don't need any other prima donnas," he said.

I didn't say anything.

"On another matter; what do you know about Klaus Feuerbach?" said Saunders.

"His last name means "brook of fire," I said. "I've never heard of him before. What do you know about him?"

"His father emigrated from Germany in the 1880s and founded 'Feuerbach Brewing,' which makes 'Fire Brook Beer.'"

"I tasted one right before Prohibition and I remember it tasted good, better than most," I said.

"Now it tastes like the urine from a draught horse, but Prohibition ruined the taste buds of Americans, so no one notices how bad their beer is," Saunders said. "Well Klaus, who is about 50, is one of the best hosts in Washington. All the people who want to be seen as powerful head out to his horse farm in Northern Virginia where his French chef supervises a cadre of kitchen help in preparing delicacies for congressmen and others whose normal fare is sausage and gravy or grits and squirrel," Saunders said.

"I can hear in your voice some censure of the culinary tastes of my fellow bumpkins." I said.

"Winston talks about being American on his mother's side, but never asked for grits when I've eaten with him," he said. "New York is a world city, but your nation's capitol is a testament to America's belief that everything European smacks of debauchery."

"I always considered that to be quite prescient," I said. "After all, Adolf isn't from Alabama, although he could have been, I suppose."

"Your friend, Meike, has stayed over at his home a couple of times," he said.

"Adolf's?"

"Of course, but I'm talking this time about Feuerbach's."

"Stop, stop, you're breaking my heart," I said, sarcastically.

"I hope it doesn't bother you because that would be a bad turn for us," he said. "By the way, one of my men took ill at the last moment and I got to see Meike for the first time."

"What did you think?"

"She's much more attractive than any woman in the British Isles, except for my wife, and that is only because I am forced by my upbringing to make Mrs. Saunders the lone exception," he said, reluctantly.

"I don't think you can get my job," I said, "you sound too much like Neville."

"Now you should always wonder 'If I find myself in trouble will Saunders help me out of it?' That had the same insensitivity as accusing a man of becoming too friendly with his sheep."

"Why do you think she was there?"

"I was hoping you could answer that for me. He has never voiced any political predilections whatsoever. In fact, no one has ever understood why he has continued to have his parties now that Prohibition has been removed from your constitution."

"Hitler came to power after the Volstead Act was repealed, so maybe he picked up a new political interest," I said. "Maybe his father learned to brew beer in Alsace after 1870 and he couldn't stomach the idea of the French brewing Fischer beer in Strasbourg."

"These insights remind me of our Prime Minister's over the past two years. They sound very interesting, but they are indicative of a man who doesn't connect to the world around him," he said. "Perhaps you should plan to come back here and see if you can find out what is going on."

"On some days, I am more frightened of Meike than I am of Himmler."

"Men are on the streets of Berlin looking for morsels of information and you are afraid to come to your own nation's capitol?" Saunders said.

"All right," I said. "I will catch a plane tomorrow. I'll stay at the Hay-Adams again and will call you to keep in touch. If I have to meet you, we'll get together at the bar we mentioned before. I'll make sure I take two cabs before I meet you."

I hung up and looked at Rosa who apparently was supremely displeased. "Oh, I'm as frightened of Meike as I am of Hitler. Please don't make me come to Washington and have sex with her," she said in a high pitched voice.

CHAPTER SIXTY FIVE

I had to fly into La Guardia and take the train down to Washington, so Meike met me in Union Station. If anything, her figure looked even better, and the late winter cold brought out the pink in her cheeks, as if unconsciously certifying Aryan perfection.

She threw her arms around me and I felt the conflicting emotions that threatened to turn the pressure in my skull into a gusher. She looked like an angel. As lust overpowered revulsion, I felt like a rat.

Both male and female travelers looked us over. I was glad the moustache was attached very tightly, while the wire rimmed glasses proved strong enough to withstand the intensity of her affection.

"We need to get out of here and into a taxi," I said. "You're too beautiful and I've been in too many movies to give us much more time before we're recognized."

"I have a taxi waiting," she said, grabbing one of my bags.

We made it outside unrecognized. The cabbie took my bags and we settled into the taxi's back seat.

"When England gives up, we won't have to hide. Everyone can know of our love," she whispered in my ear. "That fool Lippmann is touring France's ridiculous Maginot Line, although his idea of its uselessness is very perceptive. Why would any country put fortifications on only part of their border? The French should make wine and love and let us run their country. The same goes for Toskana, a place Germans' love, but is so chaotic and unorganized."

"I would imagine that chaos and disorganization are part of Tuscany's appeal. A Florence run with rigidity might never have allowed Bernini to produce his artistic triumphs," I said.

"That is one of the reasons I love you; you are a romantic."

I kept myself from shivering and let her press against me. She insisted we go to her apartment before the Hay-Adams; the way she was moving against me I wondered if we'd even make it there.

When we emerged from the taxi, the cabbie grabbed the bags and she had him take them up to her room and put them in the corner. The moment he left, she locked the door behind her and pulled a Luger out of her purse. I looked at the gun and stood there, waiting for a flash from the muzzle and the impact of lead hitting my chest. There was no way a marksman of her caliber would miss a vital organ at this distance. It seemed like an eternity as I stood silently next to the bed.

I figured the less I said before she shot me the better. Giving the Nazis any information would be stupid, so I decided to shut up. For some reason, my mind focused on what my kids would look like if I married Feng Feng. Their hair would be black, of course....

Time seemed to go by slowly, as if she was intentionally making me wait so I would anticipate my death.

All of a sudden, Meike began to laugh. "You should see your face. You thought I pulled this out to shoot you?"

I looked at her, not understanding the joke.

"This is to protect you, you foolish man, not kill you," she said, the concept making her eyes fill with tears of laughter.

"I'm glad to hear that," I said, still wary. Her humor seemed out of proportion to the situation at hand.

"When I realized you thought you were going to die, I just had to make it last a little longer. It was so funny." She was almost doubled over from the concept.

"I can't believe you're having this kind of fun at my expense," I said, really getting angry.

"I'm sorry." She kissed me and held me and tried to make up. I thought of many reasons I could end up gut shot in an alley.

"Don't worry, Baby. England will not last past next September and we can be married without worrying your country will ever fight mine. When England is invaded, everyone will give up the idea there is something noble about that funny looking Churchill and realize Germany is the future, just as Lindbergh does."

"I think we may have to wait until Hollywood is convinced you're not anti-Semitic for us to walk down the aisle," I said, grimly.

"You know I'm not," she said, indignantly.

"Yes, but everyone knows your boss with the funny moustache is, so they may not warm to the concept right off, especially when he begins to kill all the Jews he comes across."

"He will never do that," she protested.

"Look, if he does, it doesn't matter to me. I'm thinking of my career," I said.

"It should matter to your," she said, disappointed. "I trust the Fuehrer, but you don't seem to care about the Jews. I had a woman who took care of me when I was young. She was wonderful.

I could never understand this disconnect, but knew it was nothing I could ever use to turn her. She was too complex to place in a box, but her patriotism drove her as strongly as her emotions. Would she stop the Nazis from taking this woman away? I didn't have the answer.

"So you have the gun to protect me?"

"Last time you were here they attacked you. They would still like to kill you," she said. "While you're here I'll be with you. They know no one is better with a gun than I am."

"Von Darmstadt would be able to stop them."

"I hope that is true, but I'm taking no chances," she said. "You'd better not go after someone again that way unless you are ready to kill them. I can't believe you were that foolish."

I knew she was right, but it wasn't the first time I'd impulsively lost control. She pulled me on the bed and undressed me, using every part of her body when she made love, writhing and licking me so everything from the waist down had electric current passing through it. The feeling was so intense, I wanted it to end because my nerve endings couldn't take it, but my body wouldn't let it go.

After we were satisfied and exhausted, we fell asleep. As I went under after Meike's appetites had taken my body to the limit, I found a quiet place, temporarily free from carrying an imperfectly spinning mechanism somewhere within me.

At around nine I awoke as she entered carrying a tray with German style meats and cheeses, pumpernickel bread and duck pate. On the dresser there were already bottles of ginger ale and a couple of glasses with ice.

"Danke," I said. "There wasn't much coal left in the boiler."

"I'll provide the fuel if you remember I'm the conductor."

"Who am I to disagree with railroad management," I said. "If I'm not moving, what use is my cowcatcher?"

"Trains never had cowcatchers in Germany because we take care of our cattle," she said.

"Why do I think you like things the American way?" I said, pulling her towards me.

"In two weeks I want you to be my escort to a dinner party in Virginia."

"Sure. Who's holding the party?"

"A friend of mine named Klaus Feuerbach."

"How good a friend is he?"

"Don't be jealous. You know I only love you," she said.

"Okay," I said.

"You'll see," she said, earnestly. "He is a friend of the Fatherland who shares many of our dreams."

"I don't share all your dreams."

"But you want the German people to be treated fairly and this is his goal."

"I want that, of course. My German blood is what has enabled me to achieve what I have."

"You will have a fine time at the event," she said, mounting me once again.

CHAPTER SIXTY SIX

Because I wanted to see the horse country of Virginia, we drove out in the middle of the afternoon and took our time on the roads bracketed by white painted fences and large pastures in which horses trotted or stood in the luxury of Spring.

I could see thoroughbred/warm bloods bred for jumping, Tennessee Walking Horses bred for pleasure and Hackneys bred for edginess and trotting ability in front of a sulky. Meike looked like she was bred for everything else most men wanted.

While the trees were bare, the temperature was in the high 50s and the air told you the trees would soon flower. For a moment, I wished I hadn't moved from Connecticut to California so I could once again appreciate the feeling such a day used to bring. Days like this take away memories of winter the same way a new girlfriend helps you forget a woman you believed you couldn't live without.

Meike wore a long mink coat I bought her in Washington yesterday morning, a gift that gave her face the wattage to light up a stage. I'd never even read a script about a character as rotten as the guy I was playing today. Would I garrote her during sex after she told me

Hitler was really named Susie Goldberg? Or would I stab her in the chapel after she's decided to take a nun's vows to atone for those she's killed in the Fuhrer's name? Perhaps I should enjoy the days with her because they might end with my farewell to this Saturday serial by taking three perfectly shaped bullets whose holes would be covered by coins with Adolf's kisser on them.

Her natural blond hair was down on her shoulders and, as always, she wore only lipstick and mascara, emphasizing her perfect Teutonic complexion.

This road we'd entered reminded me of France with its Lombardy Poplars giving grandeur to an otherwise uneventful stretch of black-top. Soon we turned onto another marked by a split rail fence that seemed to have no beginning or end.

We finally entered a larger highway where we spotted an outbuilding and a sign reading Brierly Farms.

German is a cold language especially when the word you is said with "Sie." However, the use of "du" slightly humanizes its inherent distance. I always told Feng Feng, and myself, that my relationship with Meike was one of expedience, but sometimes that was a lie. In the vicinity of her ripeness and vitality I could feel I was tethered to her by an unseen cable of passion and desire unless I caught myself. So I thought of Feng Feng and remembered Meike was crazy.

"So, what's this guy's story?" I said.

"Klaus is a very nice man who has the interests of the Third Reich at heart. He recently acquired some papers we might find useful," she said.

"What kind of papers?"

"They aren't governmental. Let's just say, they provide us a sword," she said. "Von Darmstadt won't let me talk to anyone about this. Only he and I know of their existence. Canaris, of course, understands their importance."

"Well my interest isn't in papers, so I will leave the two of you to those secrets, while I mingle and ponder whether dinner will be accompanied by beer or wine," I said. "I don't suppose my favorite beverage will be on the table."

"Only you and the men who repair the roads' in Hessen drink Apfelwein." She made one of her half-comic facial expressions which always accompanied allusions to Germany's unique fermentation of Johnny Appleseed's finest. I had, by this time, forgotten exactly what it tasted like, but enjoyed the pained looks of Germany's ubermensch when I brought it up.

"I wouldn't mention it in front of Klaus; he will immediately think less of you."

She had a sense of humor, but I never quite knew how to take her dismay. I would find out, I suppose, if I ever ignored her strict instructions. We soon pulled up a long private road that ended in a circular driveway fronting something resembling a plantation home.

I actually thought it looked a lot like Jack's place. (I decided Jack should marry Vivien Leigh because homes such as these should really have a Scarlet O'Hara)

A Negro man in tails opened the front door. Meike called the butler, "James," and greeted him warmly. He gave her the kind of smile that says; "I would give you a warmer welcome, but this is the South and I'd better be careful." A circular staircase that led to the second floor began behind the entranceway, but we moved to the right into a large room clearly designed for entertaining. There were prints of famous horses and an air of Southern gentility that didn't seem to go with the name Klaus, but the man who kissed Meike's cheek didn't fit any Aryan stereotype either. He was short, maybe 5' 6" in elevator shoes, and was thin in a way that didn't say "fitness," but instead said debilitating illness. However, he was handsome, with a face that belied the condition of his body.

"It's quite an honor to meet you," he said, in a manner that fit someone who had learned manners to cover up a less than perfect life and had learned to smile, no matter how crappy he felt. "Meike says you ride."

"If I hadn't learned to dance, I would have never dismounted," I said.

"A man after my own heart," he said. "My horses brought me back from a very dark place and they are my wife, children and friends all wrapped up together. I don't like traveling, except to go to horse shows, although I occasionally go to Georgetown."

A fiftyish blond woman came over, excused herself to us and whispered in his ear. He immediately apologized for the interruption and went off to solve the problem.

"When did he get polio?" I said, watching him pull his right leg along as he crossed the room.

"He was thirteen and was the top rider and jumper in his age group. They say he couldn't get back on a horse for another thirteen years, not until many operations," Meike said, clearly in awe of his will.

"Is he the man I read about who gave so much money to Roosevelt's rehabilitation center in Warm Springs?" I said.

"Yes, but I don't think he cares for Roosevelt any more than we do," she said.

"Perhaps his philanthropy in this case stems more from an interest in the afflicted than it does warmth toward our nation's leader."

"I assume that's true because he is a friend of Germany and Roosevelt is not," she said.

We spent a pleasant evening talking with congressmen and with gentlemen farmers, with whom I discussed horses. After the other guests had departed, Feuerbach asked us to join him in his library.

The library itself was an impressive, if small, creation. Three sides were covered with built in mahogany bookshelves. The large stained glass chandeliers had been designed by a young Frank Lloyd Wright and came from the estate of the bankrupt founder of a brokerage firm in Rochester, New York.

Feuerbach pulled out the War and Peace volume of the Harvard Classics Shelf of Fiction and opened an accordion letter file of brown heavy paper that had been secreted behind it. He pulled out a sheet of writing paper and read from it aloud: "My dear Lucy, It has been a month since we were together. I miss the touch of your hand on my face and the way you always look so splendid. I apologize for the fact that I love doing what I do so much. I have always said to you that I felt it was my duty to serve my country, but you've always known I enjoyed this 'calling.' Unfortunately, of course, this continues to prevent the union for which we both devoutly wish. We are like two birds of some special species who find a glass door separating them. At least, occasionally, the door opens and we unite, only to once again find ourselves behind the glass, where we anxiously await the next opportunity."

Feuerbach closed his reading of this written admission of love, an admission that would probably ruin any marriage, while handing its author the short stick in any divorce settlement.

He showed the letter to Meike whose eyes widened. She got up and went to Feuerbach and gave him a long kiss on the cheek.

"I've pulled a very rare port out of my cellar, if you would care to join me," he said, ringing a silver bell.

We sat and talked of Goethe and Schiller and sipped the port. Every once in awhile, Klaus would look slightly too long at Meike as she recited Goethe, but it was probably the only real enjoyment he'd had in a long time. There were certainly fortune hunters who would marry him, but he seemed to be the kind of man who would know why they were interested. His pride would be too strong to make such a bargain. The worst thing a man like Klaus could probably imagine would be finding the woman he'd married in the hay with a groom. He would want the real thing or he'd take nothing.

CHAPTER SIXTY SEVEN

I watched the events in Europe unfold as the presidential campaign took off in earnest. Taft and Dewey were expected to fight it out until the convention in Philadelphia, while Democrats waited for the word from on high. There were some people who thought Roosevelt might not run, but I figured these individuals didn't have any blood in their veins, or hadn't been in a street fight, or begun to understand the lust for power that filled the breasts of most politicians.

On the same evening that the Germans invaded Norway, my choice to lead America appeared on the "Information Please" quiz show, answering questions in his uniquely casual manner that ingratiated him with his radio audience. I knew what Wendell could do for the country and I could see other Americans coming around to my point of view. Without having to tie himself to a policy of isolation, as Taft and Dewey had, Willkie picked up support from Styles Bridges in New Hampshire and Sinclair Weeks in Massachusetts. Many on Wall Street had expressed support for him, while citizens in the West appeared to like what they heard. I wasn't a Republican, but if I would walk a mile for a Camel, I would walk twenty miles to vote for him.

During the weeks I spent in Washington, I'd begun to notice that Meike seemed to be ascending higher in Rudi's organization. She seemed to get the special assignments that would take her away for two or three days. Meike would come back exhausted, but with a look of achievement I'd only seen on Oscar winners and championship jockeys. It seemed to me that she needed those highs and I wondered if all the assignments were like the one in San Juan Capistrano. There was always a Walther PP around the apartment, but I couldn't find where she hid the rifles, if there were any. Maybe with her looks, every assassination could be completed within three feet of the victim. She had always appeared proud, but now the pride seemed to imply mastery, as if she had been summoned to Valhalla, or at least, Cooperstown. She had always wanted ownership of me, but now Meike acted as if she had finally taken possession. She seemed to think there was no line where she ended and I began, much as a baby seems to see no separation between her and the world into which she's been delivered. Did all the things she would say really tell me how she thought? I'd read those lectures that Freud had given a long time ago in Worcester, a town only people from New England know how to pronounce, but it was all pretty hazy. In other words, all the stuff I was hearing wasn't going in one ear and out the other exactly, but she sounded like somebody who was killing people and I had to be the person to stop her or my soul was going to burn in hell. Pretty simple, huh?

"You seem to be very contented these days," I said to her in early June.

"When I was discarded at nineteen, I thought my life would end. There is no way I could imagine becoming what I am," she said. She was wearing just the right kind of red lipstick, bright, but substantial. Her eyes had seemed bluer than I had remembered, and there was a force that emanated from her as powerful as the Ark of the Covenant.

"Describe to me how you feel," I said.

"Sometimes I feel that I can bring life or extinguish it," she said. "When men look at me I can tell they want to possess me. Women are afraid of me; as if I could take everything they have and walk away with it."

"That must feel pretty powerful," I said. "Is it growing stronger?"

"Yes," she said. "Some days it seems as if you are the only tether I have to this earth."

"Do you need the mooring line or do you want to cut it so you can soar?"

"I would be afraid to cut the rope because I don't know where I would fly to, although I feel it would be someplace full of power and excitement," she said.

"Soon you may not need the anchor?"

"No, Baby, I don't want to be without you," she said. "If anyone ever tried to take you away from me, I would kill them."

"What if I wanted to walk away from you?"

"You never would want that. You know we are meant to be. There is something important that occurs when we're together," she said.

"I don't feel comfortable with how you look at this. People are drawn to each other, but one person never owns another or really falls apart when a romance ends. Some people go off the deep end, but that implies something about who they were before the romance began."

"Are you calling me crazy?"

Her anger was exploding and I needed to put it back in its hiding place. "What I'm trying to say is, if a woman's husband leaves her it may seem catastrophic, but she will eventually find a way to cope with it. Eventually, because the woman is beautiful, another man walks in and her life gets back to normal."

"I have left men, but only one man ever left me."

"He was evil and treated you badly. I understand why you wanted revenge," I said.

"If someone left me it would be the cruelest thing I could imagine," she said, her jaw tightening and eyes blazing with the light of a religious zealot charging Satan.

I decided I should change the subject of this conversation, so I sat back and waited for her anger to subside. It was like watching a pot cool. Although the steam had disappeared, putting your hand in the water too soon might ruin your tennis game for awhile.

CHAPTER SIXTY EIGHT

Every day I'd see a different Meike.

"I don't see why you can't be around more," she said.

"I have my own life. This is why I hate getting involved. Just when you think you've met somebody who can put themselves in your shoes you find out you're wrong," I said.

"And just as you're disappointed, I realize you care so much more about yourself than you do me," she said. "Don't you miss me when I'm not there? Don't you roll over in the middle of the night and wish I was lying next you? I do those things and want someone who will miss me and feel a tear in his heart."

"Have you always needed this much? I think this is just a little bit crazy," I said.

All at once she threw a vase to the floor while her face turned crimson, the way a child's does when a tantrum erupts. Thank God she thought she loved me because she was capable of killing me there on the spot. The word "Crazy" always seems to blow a fuse in fruitcakes who already wonder if they've got bats in their belfries.

"You pig, who are you to say those things to me? Many men would do anything to have me. You are lucky I even let you touch me," she said. "If I told you that you could never see me again, you wouldn't be able to take it. You have me in your blood. Other men have tried to forget me and they haven't been able to do it." She acted like a queen who controlled the most important item, access to her.

"I'm not like those other guys. I truly can walk away from you in a second. Keep an eye on the closing door."

"Come back here," she shouted, which really angered me. I let the door close behind me and began to walk back to the Hay Adams. I could hear the sound of someone running behind me. Then I felt Meike fall to my feet, grab my pant leg and pull on it. I looked down into the eyes of a frightened child who'd had her dog taken away. The transformation frightened me. I lifted her up under her arms and brought her to her feet. We walked back to the apartment while she held onto my arm and softly cried.

I felt trapped, and the walls were closing in.

When you get involved with someone mentally unstable, you know her appeal exceeds what you can get from a woman who has a ground for their sexual electricity. If there is no ground and there are no boundaries, the current moves quickly through your body. Once you've experienced it, you know it's available nowhere else. I'd often wondered at friends who'd let some crazy starlet use them until they're empty shells with empty wallets. They reminded me of guys addicted to cocaine or opium who would drive down Central Avenue, or into Chinatown, frequently in a panic, to get a drug to stop the pain. After being involved with Meike I could understand how somebody's brain couldn't generate enough pleasure with another woman to avoid a devastating withdrawal. Luckily for me, fear would have been enough of a stimulus to make me run like hell.

I was lying next to her, completely spent, unable to even entertain the idea of another coupling. Meike, however, seemed to have as much energy as when she began.

"There is a document that shows what America has planned for the Fatherland and for Japan. Roosevelt demanded it and an officer named Wedermyer is in charge of pulling it together," she said.

"Are you sure?"

"I'm sure," she said.

I rolled over and looked at her blonde hair and perfect body as I took in the information.

"There is someone who can obtain it for us," she said.

"Who is that?"

"Rudi said I can't tell anyone. He isn't telling Canaris or anyone else," she said.

"That's best," I said.

"I don't like keeping anything from you," she said.

"I keep information from you," I said. "It's all right."

"What do you keep from me?" she said.

"I was just trying to explain that people don't have to tell their lover everything," I said. "I don't want to know everything."

"Do you love me?"

"Of course I do," I said.

"Then you should never keep anything from me," she said. "I will leave my job and come marry you, if you want that. I will tell you everything."

"Our jobs are too important for us to think about that now. There are many things that have to be taken care of," I said.

"Do you believe what I just said?"

"Of course," I said, although I didn't.

"If I let men fall in love with me, it is only because it is part of my job," she said.

"What does if feel like to take someone's life from them?" I said.

"As if you are an angel bringing justice to those who wish to keep Germany weak, as weak as we were after the war. It is my job to make sure I stop them before they hurt The Fatherland?"

"Does it ever seem like the wrong thing to do?"

"There was a boy in his 20s in Pennsylvania who had a puppy dog way of looking at me," she said. "He seemed so pure, almost as if he talked to God. When I pushed the knife into his heart it seemed very wrong. He looked like he loved me, even after he felt it going in," she said, her mind apparently attempting to wish it away.

"Do you think about it often?"

"I had to take sleeping draughts for a few weeks afterwards, or I would lie there all night seeing his face." She experienced an involuntary shudder.

"Can you see his face now?"

"I won't allow myself to see it. It was starting to make me crazy."

"Don't think about it now," I said.

"I wish men didn't think they loved me. It makes it very hard to kill them."

"I understand."

"It would be impossible for me to kill you. If they tried to kill you, I would stop a bullet meant for you," she said, tears coming to her eyes.

My arms closed around her and I pulled her close. All of a sudden she seemed very young. Now her face looked like that of an angel. Unfortunately, I was sure she hadn't recently talked with God.

CHAPTER SIXTY NINE

"The Nazis believe Roosevelt has ordered plans drawn in the event we have to fight both Japan and Germany," I said to Saunders, before swallowing some Ballantine Ale. "Does this taste like carrots to you?"

"Ballantine Ale always tastes like carrots. Don't you like it?" he said.

"You're the first guy who ever agreed with me about carrots," I said.

"And I'm English, also. You must feel twice blessed, my son."

"Have you heard anything about this plan?" I said.

"Our chaps have been meeting with the Americans for almost a year now to coordinate strategy. We believe there is a master plan for a two-front war," he said, as if it were of little importance.

"Meike is the person who's been ordered to get hold of it. I heard about it last night while she was talking to Rudi."

"You have such fine names for your friends, Tommy. Did you all attend the same school? Did your parents grow up together?" he said. "Damn it, can't you remember these are the people who kill women and children, and want to wipe out my country."

"Whoa, big fella. Let's relax a minute. England isn't even my country, and you're telling me how I can talk about these people I have to keep a relationship with," I said, getting up to walk away.

"Come back," he said, grabbing my arm. "Things are a bit difficult. Winston is making my life a living hell. He can never quite grasp what Roosevelt really means. That's hard for him. He isn't in charge of his country's future and that makes him irritable."

"Roosevelt has told people he doesn't let his left hand know what the right is doing, so you can tell him he's not alone."

"Winston is staking everything on bringing your countrymen into this war. To him, it is a simple thing. Hitler is the Antichrist and anyone who can't grasp that is a fool," Saunders said, looking strained. "It is hard for me to explain that Americans are against getting involved because they helped us out in the Great War. He doesn't understand anti-colonial sentiment. The unfairness of the Versailles Treaty is something he once acknowledged, but feels is irrelevant now. I've told him this country is bitter about the last time they sent men to Europe."

"And for good reason. The justification for that adventure wasn't there. Your country and France never paid your debts. Only Finland honored its obligations. In fact, you hear comments such as 'Brave Little Finland.' Now there's a country we might support," I said.

"That's quite enough. I didn't ask you to provide me with more examples. My comments could have been followed by, 'you've got a sticky wicket' or something of that order," he said, visibly perturbed.

"Any guy who said 'sticky wicket' would get beaten up in Brooklyn. Let me say I understand your difficult situation," I said.

"I very much appreciate that," he said, sarcastically.

"What about the war plans?"

"They exist. That goes without saying," he said. "If plans weren't being made and if they weren't talking to us, it would be dereliction of duty. Any world leader has to know what he's able to do if things turn out to be as bad as possible."

"The Nazis want those plans and Meike can obtain anything," I said.

"You are overestimating her power."

"I have known or gone out with some of the most beautiful women in Hollywood. They don't have what she has," I said. "If she goes looking, some man will give the plans to her."

"You talk about her as if she was a Typhoon or Hurricane. No woman comes close to that standard," he said, looking exasperated.

"Remember, I warned you." I shook his hand and left the small restaurant, wondering if only I felt this way about her. I dismissed that concept out of hand.

Saunders told me that in 1934, Hitler placed Rear Admiral Wilhelm Canaris in charge of the Abwehr, the Army's intelligence organization. It was modeled on the British Intelligence Service and targeted the United States from the beginning. Everyone knew America's vast industrial capacity could decide the outcome of any future conflict, as it had in the Great War. Even if America didn't actually enter a war on one side, the countries it supplied with planes and ships would come out on top.

Except for the efforts of Wilhelm Lonkowski, who had been running a spy ring in America for Germany since 1927, Von Darmstadt was given responsibility for all espionage in America. His agents would obtain industrial and military secrets and deliver them to Forschers, Abwehr employees who had been placed on German transatlantic liners as couriers for Canaris.

Von Darmstadt had a great deal of autonomy and Canaris had picked a man without the distorted outlook of a doctrinaire Nazi, who shared a love of the Fatherland, with a distrust of Hitler's values and attitudes towards race. The more I knew about his operation, the more impressed I was at von Darmstadt's skills at organizing and balancing conflicting interests. Meike said von Darmstadt was the most respected man in Section I, the overseas intelligence arm of the Abwehr. He, in turn, looked on Meike as his right hand, and if he saw the dark underside of her talent, he chose to ignore it.

Meike had once told me no man could hold out on her very long, so she obtained much of the important information transferred to the Forschers. There were days I wondered what Meike had to do to get that information.

CHAPTER SEVENTY

Wendell hadn't announced his candidacy, but he was making speeches around the country and there were more political commentators who saw him as the fresh new face who could gain the White House for the Republicans. Only in a script by Frank Capra or Walt Disney could Willkie win the nomination at this late date, but I'd been in enough musicals to believe it possible. Hell, in the movie version I could be Secretary of State, with a couple of good songs about Foggy Bottom. When I wasn't busy creating problems to be solved in the general election, I went to a pistol range owned by a friend of Saunders, making sure I called ahead to make sure I'd be able to enter and exit virtually unseen.

I had lost some weight which also helped change my appearance. People always looked heavier on the screen, so people were always surprised how screen actors appeared in public. Some female stars were almost cadaverous in person, in ways that were downright unattractive.

However, I had a problem. Someone was following me; I was sure of it. It was either that or my night job had knocked a screw loose. I voted for sanity and used the tactics Saunders taught me. I went into a nearby hotel, crossed the lobby, and quickly turned into a long hallway, sprinting almost to the end. I stepped into a room being cleaned, startling the maid. After I took off my glasses and hat, she recognized me. I put my finger to my lip and she was silent. I grabbed her hand, which she didn't seem to mind. I had a view of the corridor and waited until Hans passed, heading for the exit door at the end of the hallway. It was possible to hear his hand turning the knob and exiting the building. Shortly afterwards I went over and closed the door to the room.

"Besides being good looking, you're also Tommy Babcock, aren't you," she said. She had blond hair and was what a man would call "pleasingly plump," at an age when that could still be a positive thing. Her round full face was Rubenesque. I could see in her beauty the corn fields and state fairs of the Midwest.

"Guilty, as charged," I said.

"Why were you wearing that ugly hat and bad looking glasses," she said a smile on her face.

"Why do you look like every Iowans idea of perfection?" I said.

"I'm from Waterloo, Iowa, but I asked the first question?" Her face was impish, like the homecoming queen would look when approached by a second string football player.

"I don't always want to look like Tommy Babcock. As you could see, I'm trying to avoid a reporter."

"Do all reporters in Washington look like criminals?" she said.

"To tell the truth more than half of them are."

"How come you're doing this in Washington?" I asked, still wondering why the Nazis were looking for me.

"My mom died and my Dad wanted me to fill in for her, so I packed my suitcase, grabbed the money I'd made babysitting and hopped on a train to Chicago. I had just enough money to buy a ticket to Washington. I hadn't finished high school, so here I am doing hospital corners."

I put four twenty dollar bills in her hand and said," buy some clothes for those times when you aren't making beds. You're a knock-out and ought to show yourself to the men of our nation's capital."

"That's wonderful, she said holding more money in her hand than she'd ever had at one time. "Could I have a kiss to go with it, so I could tell girls that I'd kissed you?"

"How old are you?" I said.

"I'm 18, want to see?" She went to a purse that had seen better days, opened a wallet and handed me a driving license.

"Is Waterloo, Iowa a good place to live?"

"Everybody's really nice. I've got a lot of friends there, but I've been afraid to write because my father might find out where I am," she said, her face darkening, and then, as if from pure instinct, her puckish look reappeared.

"If you want a kiss, then I consider myself a lucky man."

She put her arms around my neck and gave me one of the best kisses I'd ever had. Her hair smelled clean and her skin gave off a natural scent a man can't describe in words, but rejoices when he finds it. She clearly was an endurance athlete who believed a person should use their entire body in this exercise. I broke loose in as polite way as possible.

"You didn't like it? Every boy before has appreciated it." She looked hurt and petulant.

"If I wasn't involved with somebody else, I'd ship you on a train back to Santa Monica, California, so I'd have a reason to hurry home."

"So you liked it?"

"Very much," I said.

"Then how about one for the road?"

"Only if it's shorter than the last one."

As you might have guessed, it wasn't.

Six minutes later, I emerged from the room and headed to the lobby to check out the situation, remembering to don my glasses and fedora. Not being Tommy Babcock was very time consuming. I knew that if Hans was looking for me, I was in trouble and I was sure his efforts were sanctioned. He wouldn't have gone off the reservation again, because this time Von Darmstadt would have had him eliminated as a threat to his American operation.

Hans didn't seem to be anywhere in sight. I was pretty sure they discovered the engine was a dud. I walked down the street to a department store and used the payphone in the lobby to call Saunders.

"Hans is trying to find me, so I think our little engine is a bust."

"You certainly have a way with Germans of all stripes, don't you," he said, half laughing.

"I think I might laugh myself out of this spy business," I said, angrier than I had a right to be.

"Touchy. Did he try to shoot you or attach a bomb to your posterior?"

"In a very short time something will be placed up your posterior, right before I get on the Sunset Limited, never to return." I hung up.

I quickly checked into a different hotel. That evening I turned the radio to CBS and heard surprising news.

"There is momentum building within the Republican convention for the newest entrant into the presidential race, Wendell Willkie.

"Politicians have told me they've never seen anyone's candidacy move as quickly as Willkie's.

"A few weeks ago, everyone had written off the Presidential chances of this Hoosier-turned-Wall Street lawyer.

"With a lock of hair always somewhere near his eye, he was an unlikely hero in a field populated with the likes of dapper Tom Dewey and the reserved and dignified Robert Taft. Taft is known as 'Mr. Republican' but on this evening one hears more and more about an Indiana man named Wendell.

"A few months ago, people were unsure whether he was even a Republican. Tonight he is sounding like the man to lead the GOP out of the wilderness. It is truly astounding.

"Perhaps Republicans have decided that America has changed. Franklin Roosevelt, of course, figured that out eight years ago. If the GOP has had its antennae out, then this spokesman for independent utilities and property rights has a chance.

"Supporters say you can't buttonhole Willkie and that he's never forgotten where he came from. He says too many folks are still waiting for their hopes and dreams to be realized."

I figure that reporter had the pulse of my country.

Meike hadn't been at her apartment for a couple of days and hadn't called, so I began thinking about what might be going on in Philadelphia. For the Nazis, Willkie was a nightmare. If Roosevelt ran for a third term, and if Wendell ran against him, there was no way Germany had a chance. Either man would act to take steps to support democracy around the world. American neutrality would be in name only.

It was necessary for me to move quickly, so I went into the bathroom and shaved my moustache. Since Hans was already following me, there was no reason to wear a hat. I wanted every ticket agent and cabbie to give me every break, so I had to trade on my fame. Most American men weren't interested in making a nuisance out of themselves, and most women could be brushed off. If that ever changed, I doubt that anyone would ever want stardom.

I put Meike's spare Walther PP in my pocket. It was time to catch the next train for the City of Brotherly Love. I figured the Baltimore and Ohio was the best route, so I went down and hailed a cab for Union Station.

The cabbie, a Pole from Pennsylvania, didn't recognize me. However, my arrival at the B and O ticket counter was testament to the power of King Gillette. I stood in line under the station's 90 ft., barrel vaulted roof while a woman from Scarsdale, N.Y., asked me every question known to man. I autographed her train schedule, happy to hear she wasn't traveling to Philadelphia. When she reached the ticket counter, she proceeded to tell the brown haired girl with freckles who I was.

"Can you believe I've been standing right next to Fred Astaire?"

"I'm sorry, ma'am but that man behind you is Tommy Babcock," she said, a broad smile crossing her face.

"The man who used to be famous before his sister went out on her own?" The disappointment in her voice was tangible.

The girl laughed and sold her a ticket. I hoped it was to Buffalo. It would serve her right.

"Mr. Astaire, can you sign my autograph book?" said the girl behind the ticket counter.

I signed it "Fred Astaire"

"Okay, Okay, I meant Tommy Babcock," she said, worried she'd tried to be too cute. "I loved your movie with Louise Boudreaux. I liked your second picture as a private eye, but I didn't like that Finnish lady. She wasn't exciting enough for you."

"Norwegian, and you're right, she wasn't," I said, crossing out Fred's name and adding my own. "Can I get a private sleeper to Philly?"

"I was supposed to save one for a Pennsylvania congressman, but I'll give it to you," she said.

"That might get you fired if he's in a position to vote on railroad issues."

"Tomorrow's my last day. My family's moving to Los Angeles," she said, laughing.

"Call the Magellan Studio and tell them to put you through to me. I'll arrange a tour for you and your parents," I said, happy to get the sleeper, even though I wouldn't be closing my eyes.

The "Royal Blue" train was one of the most comfortable trains in the country. The air conditioned cars on the Blue Line promised a refuge from the world while I planned my next moves. I closeted myself in the sitting compartment and made sure once again the Walther had all seven bullets.

Then I went over the Philadelphia map I'd purchased in Union Station before opening a pint of JTS Brown and pouring some into a glass. They say there are scotch drinkers and bourbon drinkers and never the twain shall meet. I was a restrained drinker who was willing to give corn, grain, potato or rice liquor a place at my table. The ingredients used to make the booze that I drank in the 20s were best unexamined and forgotten. Just knowing what was used would probably kill me. I experienced the finger of good bourbon slipping down my throat, and then felt it hit my bloodstream. The first time a guy takes a drink, he shows the world that involuntary shudder the body makes when it hits his system. First, he learns to hide it in front of other men and then if he gets too used to the stuff it seems like nothing special. This would be the only tipple I was having before I found Wendell and made sure he was protected. Once I found Wendell, it was important to make sure I only had one for every three of his, because he was a Hoosier who had looked demon rum in the face and said, "Come in and make yourself comfortable. We've got a lot of places to go together."

About a half hour into the train ride, there was a knock on the door.

"Who is it?" I said.

"Conductor," said the voice. That one word told me the individual's native language was German. Even in this melting pot of the world, the chances the conductor had a German accent on this run, this night, were slim.

"One moment, please," I said. I picked up the Walther and positioned myself. The door opened outward and the hinges were on the left side, so he would be standing to the right of the door. I turned the knob to the left and came out with the Walther at shoulder level, which was right in the middle of Hans's forehead. His breath smelled like cheap brandy, cigarettes and limburger cheese. I closed the compartment door with my right foot while keeping my gun on him. I had him turn around and march down the hall toward the dining car, my pistol pressed into his spinal cord.

"You thought we wouldn't figure out the engine was no good," Hans said. "You forgot that Germany has the best engineers and scientists in the world."

As we reached the end of the car, I told him to open the door in front of him. He grabbed for the gun, so I held on tight, spun him around, and pushed him into the wall, slamming him with my left hand.

He broke loose and hit me in the gut. I thought for a moment, he was going to take me down, but I put a left into his nose that slowed him down and put me in the driver's seat. I was no longer in control of what was happening; the inner engine had taken over.

I kept hitting him in the face, over and over again, unrelentingly, turning his face into the spitting image of a deformed squash. Hans was experiencing every year of training since I was in third grade. I was drawing on every push up and every time I had hit the heavy bag, until he fell to the ground. I kicked him over and over again, until I stepped back and forced myself to stop. Something in me felt very ashamed. I could see my grandfather standing there and I wouldn't look at his face. But I didn't have time for that. I picked up Hans's body and carried it through to the space between the cars, opened the door and sent his body hurtling off into the dark Maryland night. I admitted to myself I enjoyed turning Hans into mincemeat. I could lie to myself and say I thought only of the people he'd tortured and of Karl and Liesel and the other Jews who'd suffered, before I turned him into pulp. But let's be honest; for a few minutes on June 27, 1940, I'd become Hans.

CHAPTER SEVENTY ONE

I descended from the train, walked out of the station and entered a city whose mood was half State Fair and half Fifth Avenue, as if the Davenport Rotary Club and the New York Stock Exchange had scheduled breakfast together. Americans got up early, because many of their families were not very far removed from farms or the frontier. The Rotary Ann's, of course, were out having pancakes and bacon with the other appendages as they waited for the department stores to open. Their husbands were drinking coffee and wolfing down scrambled eggs with other delegates to build up strength before striking deals in smoke filled rooms. There were elephant caricatures everywhere, because the Grand Old Party had hit this town like a freight train and a store or building without an American flag was owned by a man who was, firstly, very out of touch, and secondly, demonstrably unpatriotic. I imagined a Shriner's convention in the Los Angeles Coliseum.

As I headed into the Warwick Hotel, where Wendell was staying, I saw an old friend, Rollie Marvin, the mayor of Syracuse.

"Marvin, how are you," I said. "It's Tommy Babcock."

"You don't say? I just saw your most recent picture at the State Theatre. You scared the hell out of me."

I did a Jimmy Cagney imitation that cracked him up. "We enjoyed ourselves when I played in the Salt City. The barber in the Taft Hotel is the best I've ever seen. I need him in Hollywood."

"As long as I'm mayor, Sal can't leave town," he said, breaking into a wide smile. Marvin was a dynamic force. "I backed Willkie and now that he's our nominee that man in the white house is in for it."

"I'm going up to see him now. Wendell is a great man," I said.

"So are you. The food is still good at the Century Club, so come and visit," he said, before he was approached by a couple of other delegates. Back during Prohibition everybody was looking for booze and Syracuse wasn't far from Oswego on Lake Ontario where Johnnie Walker and Gordon's Tower Guard liked to come ashore. Syracuse was a great place to play in the old days, and it never ran out of hooch. The people were good and the audiences there appreciated every one of our musicals, but its two weeks of summer looked surprisingly like fall.

Wendell had been nominated for President. I'd wondered how many ballots that had taken. American politics was less predictable than I'd expected.

CHAPTER SEVENTY TWO

Wendell Willkie was happy to see me. He always treated me like a best friend from grade school in Indiana. Wendell developed a rapport with everyone, but everyone thought their relationship with him was special. Hell, I did.

He told me all about how he came to end up with the nomination and then he focused on me.

"I thought you were going to bring a fiancée to meet me the next time we got together?"

"What I remember is that you ordered me to do that, and then I came to and realized it was a helluva long time ago that I enlisted and that war had ended," I said.

"A lot of people in America think I know what we should do, so don't you think you're throwing away insights from the Oracle of Delphi?"

"We don't have time for this," I said, in a hurry to sit him down and explain my concerns. I began to outline my worries.

I'd only spent ten minutes with Willkie when it happened. As the Germans threw open the door, a look of shock came across Meike's face. I quickly put a bullet through her partner's forehead and pointed the Walther at Meike's heart. She seemed to be immobilized by my presence, so I turned off my feelings and plugged her in the chest before she could get off a shot, knowing she would kill Willkie.

Her gun fell to the floor as she began to slump over and I rushed to catch her just as she hit the floor.

"You shot me," she said in German. "I loved you. How could you shoot me?" The look on her face combined shock and sadness.

"Wendell is one of two people who could be my next President and he's the better human being of the two."

"You should have tried to convince me to marry you and give up what I was doing. I never really loved anyone before you." She was having trouble catching her breath and her strength was ebbing. "The man in Germany was a young girl's obsession. I was a cold person, empty person before we met."

It was true that she loved me. It was true that I never gave her the chance. It wasn't just the warnings I constantly received from Saunders, or the thought of Dachau. Meike was the most frightening person I had ever met and the thought of marrying her ranked right up there with being circumcised on a moving John Deere tractor. The day I'd heard she followed Feng Feng home from the studio was the day she went from an adventure to a threat to everything I cared about.

I tried to think of something to say as I stroked her hair. Her breath came in gasps, until she closed her eyes.

"I'm calling an ambulance," Wendell said. I could hear him turning the dial to each letter and number, then hearing the dial return to 0 for the last time and resting.

I held my arms tightly around her, knowing the ambulance was already too late.

"When I was over there in 1918, I would hear the stories of the men who would see the face of the German soldier they were about to kill and freeze up. It would be the last decision they ever made," Wendell said.

As the police pushed the door open, he said, "Thanks for saying I'm a better man than that bastard in the White House."

At any other time, I would have laughed.

"Tell the cops to keep this quiet, because I have some loose ends to tie up."

"You're not kidding?"

"This is a very big project with other dimensions."

"It sounds like there's a movie in this. I'm trying to think of an actor old enough to play you," he said.

I reached Saunders from Wendell's phone and told him what had happened.

"Was it very hard for you to pull the trigger on Meike?" he said.

"Unfortunately, it wasn't hard. She said she would've come over to us if it could have been her and me," I said.

"So, let me understand this. Did you want to marry her and make her the mother of your children?"

"Of course not, but I didn't want her to die," I said. "Killing someone you've spent a lot of nights with isn't the easiest thing. She may have been crazy, but she loved me. She may have been an assassin, but she never would have shot me."

Saunders apparently didn't want to deal with this or couldn't. "By the way, one of the first things that Winston did when he went to the Admiralty was to make you a commander in the Royal Navy, so when you decide to fight alongside us, you'll probably receive the Victoria Cross."

"I'm an American and can't receive a British medal," I said.

"You will be able to accept it if we become allies," he said. "Get a hotel room in Philadelphia or hire a car to New York. Sleep for a day and then we'll explore this subject further," he said.

"Saunders. How do Limeys tell other Limeys they feel like shit?"

CHAPTER SEVENTY THREE

The sky was too blue and the weather too warm for a day in which I'd murdered someone who loved me. Such a death should occur in early November when the leaves have left the trees and the sky is the color of an old blackboard, with only crows around as witnesses. Wendell had arranged to have a car waiting for me when my train reached Washington, so I was driving into Virginia horse country, cursing the sun and praying for darkness where the outside world might match what was left of my insides.

The CBS six p.m. newscast broke the news I'd killed the assassins after Willkie. Up until that moment, Wendell and his colleagues had been able to hold back information about my involvement. Now I knew it would be impossible to keep newspaper reporters from uncovering the whole story.

I quickly reached Brierly Farms. Some grooms were bridling their horses and taking them back to the barn for the evening as dusk settled on the south. I turned the Lincoln's lights on and slowed down, unwilling to arrive too early to Feuerbach's. It seemed clear to me that whatever lay hidden behind the Harvard Classics held great importance for the Germans.

Meike's image came back. I pulled over next to a hayfield to find unbidden tears flowing. Look, it wasn't like a girl cries. It was something guys don't do, but it sometimes happens. I knew the only way to keep going was to make the pain an integral part of me and use it. "I loved you. How could you shoot me?" Those words weren't going to leave me anytime soon. The picture of her lying there on the floor of Wendell's hotel room was flashing in my mind like a neon sign on the fritz. She had hesitated and let me shoot her.

Waves of guilt rolled over me like heavy surf from a Nor'easter. I wished my car was a coffin in which the pain and the memories could die. Could my grandfather have killed a Confederate spy who loved him? I doubted he could have, or that he would have been in a situation where that choice was necessary. I hit the windshield with such force I cracked it. I hated Hitler for using the German psyche after Versailles and turning latent anti-Semitism into a noble crusade. At least Meike had been free of that. But she had equated a victory for the Nazis as ordained. Of course I walked in on the last act and I'm the one who killed her. I snuffed her life out the way you turn off a light switch. I remembered why I was here and drove on to another rendezvous with Hitler's henchmen.

CHAPTER SEVENTY FOUR

After leaving my car on the service road behind the main house, I walked around and figured out the house's floor plan. The library was an addition to what had once probably been a back parlor. The helps' entrance was close by, so I carefully opened the screen door and entered a side kitchen, probably only used when large groups were entertained. This was a time when dancing came in handy as I traveled soundlessly down the hall on the balls of my feet. When I reached the library, I flipped the light switch, partially illuminating the room. Stepping in the direction of the Harvard Classics, I heard Klaus's voice.

"They say on the news that you killed her. How could you do that?"

"She was there to kill Willkie, and she would have? She loved me and treated me well, but I'm an American."

"She was sweet and kind to me, but she loved you. Couldn't you have talked to her into quitting, or living with you in California?"

"You're not a Nazi, just some guy who loves Germany. There is a difference. She killed other guys who weren't Nazis, but cared about the Fatherland. Do you think I wanted to be in this situation?"

Just then Gerhard emerged from a corner not penetrated by the lamp's glow. "You will be heading in the other direction from Meike," he said. "A pig like you, though, deserves to die slowly. You will beg me to kill you before this night is over."

"Why aren't you over there fighting on the Russian front, Gerhard? Are you afraid to stand up like a real man or do you only kill people when there are crowds around to cover your tracks?" I said, although it probably would have better if I'd swallowed those words. That's the way things break for me sometimes.

"If I wasn't going to enjoy torturing you so much, you would be killed for those comments alone," he said, veins bulging in his neck.

Feuerbach said, "You are not going to kill anyone, Hans. I'm sure a lot of people know where he was going tonight. I would immediately be suspected. In addition, I made it clear I was obtaining this document, not joining some kind of Nazi underground. I paid for the letters because of Meike, as much as for Deutschland. She is gone. I want you to take your gun off Mr. Babcock."

Gerhard responded by hitting Klaus over the head with a granite ashtray, while never taking his gun off me. Klaus was heading for the land I lived in not so long ago. I was ready to go for the .45 in my pocket just as a shot hit Hans in the chest and threw him to the ground. When he tried to get up, I finished him off with a shot to the head. I instinctively grabbed the War and Peace volume and extracted the letters, stuffing them in the pocket recently vacated by my gun. I then put the volume back where it came from. I walked over to the phone on the magnificent cherry wood desk and dialed 0 and asked the operator to connect me with an ambulance company or hospital. As I waited on the line, the old butler came in.

"Mr. Babcock, I didn't know you were here," he said, before seeing Feuerbach slumped over in the chair.

"James, we need to get him to a hospital. He's a good man who shouldn't die," I said.

"Yes sir, Mr. Feuerbach treats me like a human being worth something," he said, bending over him. "We heard on the radio that you saved Mr. Willkie's life. Negroes know that he believes we should be treated better, like Mr. Feuerbach does. Mr. Feuerbach never talked down to us or treated us bad. God will make sure he lives." The old butler was practically in tears, but had been in service too long to let us see any drops fall.

Just then, Saunders walked in.

"You have to stop acting like the Lone Ranger," he said. "When they told me you were picking up a car near Union Station, I knew where I needed to be."

"Nice shot through the window," I said. "I wouldn't have had the time to pull the gun out before he shot me." I looked at him and said," You know your moustache is looking good."

"I'll accept that as a 'thank you,'" he said, as he examined Klaus. "His heartbeat is strong and steady. I think he may have a good chance."

"He deserves one. There's nothing treasonous about getting hold of some letters that aren't government documents. He wasn't going to join some Nazi cell. He loved his days at Heidelberg and Meike. That's what his motivation consisted of," I said. "And Meike really cared about him."

Saunders was looking at me, knowing to keep any comments he might have stitched down tightly. Surprisingly, the comment came from behind him.

"She really cared about me?" was the question that emanated from somewhere in Feuerbach. The butler reached over and grabbed both of Klaus's hands and held on.

"She really did," I said.

Feuerbach smiled and then went back to the land he came from.

"I'd say that was a hopeful sign."

Saunders smiled and said, "I would think so." He pulled at his moustache and said, "While we're waiting for the ambulance and the police, let's take a look at those letters."

He opened one, while I looked at another. Mine read; "Dearest Lucy, the White House is quiet tonight. I was thinking of the last time we were together in Warm Springs. It was a jolly time. You always make me feel so alive.

"Years ago, giving in to my mother's ultimatum that led to our parting was a mistake. I have spent so many nights thinking of you. My feelings haven't changed."

I continued reading until the bottom of the second page, which was signed, "Franklin."

That signature made this letter more than the record of an illicit love. It could be a sword in the hands of a GOP that had been outfoxed at every turn and which was fated to remain the minority member of a national legislature. It could become the pin to prick what some saw as the ego-filled balloon of a class traitor who had turned on his Harvard classmates and neighbors in Hyde Park, New York.

These letters would destroy the possibility of a third presidential term. If the Republican Party had chosen Taft, Dewey, or in a moment of madness, Lindbergh, the Germans would not have had to worry about our coming to England's defense. None of his opponents, other than Willkie, would support intervention, and a majority of the American people would be happy.

"I'm going to hold on to these letters. You can tell the president, if you want to, that you helped me find them," I said. "Of course, at this point, no matter who wins the Presidency, America will be ready to fight. You may want to keep yourself out of this in order not to piss FDR off. Churchill has what he's after. Willkie is on your side. By tomorrow night, if I don't hear from you, I'm going to call Ickes and tell him what I have here and that if the Democrats don't make a stink about Irita van Doren these letters will never see the light of day."

"I hope all your faith in Willkie is not misplaced," he said. "I pray you are right. You aren't going to tell me where these letters are going, are you?"

"With all the publicity, from now one, I'm someone who loves England, but is just an American."

"Of course, just like Clark Gable," he said, with a wink.

CHAPTER SEVENTY FIVE

I walked into Union Station 15 minutes before the time set for the rendezvous. Approaching the news stand, I leaned back against the staircase. I was as anonymous as a Hollywood star could be among the potted plants that gave a sense of style to this passenger rail hub. As I loitered there, a young officer took his seat at the metal, glass topped, tables that gave the area the feel of a French sidewalk café, without the German officers. A German had planned to come, but....

The man who'd kept the appointment was an army second lieutenant with a face as callow as could be, seemingly fresh from four years at West Point. There was probably a folder in the courier bag at his feet. I waited a few minutes while I picked the FBI agents out of the crowd, then went up the stairs and came up behind one of them posted at the rail overlooking the café area.

"I already killed her. She won't be showing," I said.

"So she's the one you killed, Mr. Babcock. You must feel pleased with yourself," he said, turning around and smiling.

I wanted to say "fuck you," but, for some reason, I held back. I instantly regretted it.

"She would never have gotten the document. He reported it to us soon after she approached him," he said.

"Before you got to her, and after she realized she'd been tricked, Meike would have opened him up like a surgeon carving a Thanksgiving turkey. Then she would have killed a couple of you," I said.

"We're a lot better than that," he said, giving me a condescending look.

"Then why did a movie star have to save Willkie," I said, turning around and heading towards the New York trains.

CHAPTER SEVENTY SIX

I was in a suite atop New York's Pierre Hotel.

I called the ranch and Judy answered.

"Judy, can I speak to your sister?

"And hello to you too," she said. "Why would I let that happen?"

"Because you're in my house and I care about her," I said.

"You caused her enough trouble for a lifetime. I don't want her to talk to you," she said. I could hear a struggle and voices arguing in Chinese, before Feng Feng picked up.

"I received the call yesterday from your friend Jack. He said you'd called him and wanted us picked up and taken to the ranch He told us to be ready. He also spilled the beans that at first you wanted to leave me a wedding present from the sale of the ranch if you died, but that later you told him that you'd made a will leaving me the ranch. He said he thought you were crazy." She took a minute to catch her breath because the sentences had been fired off like bursts emerging from a machine gun. "That means a lot to me, although I don't want you to die so I can learn to yodel."

"Somebody else wants to get on the phone." she said.

"Guess who's helping me take care of Tom today?" Ginny asked.

"I give up, who?"

"Her name is Liesel."

"Isn't she beautiful?" I asked.

"Yes, and she awaits your return," Ginny said. "She wants to say something to you."

"Onkel Tommy, Ich liebe dich," Liesel said, quickly getting off the phone.

"You have to stop this international heartbreaking cartel from doing more damage," Ginny said, laughing. "Since it seems to be your duty to disrupt the female population, I'll put Feng Feng back on."

"Feng Feng, I want the four of you to stay at the ranch. I'll call Wendell and have him call the Governor of California to ask him to send law enforcement people to guard the place."

"They'd be willing to guard Chinese people?"

"I just heard today that I'm a national hero as well as right behind Clark Gable at the box office. These days everyone wants to be nice to me," I said. "Please stay there. If anyone else dies I'll wrap my mouth around a twelve gauge shotgun, and I'm not kidding about that."

"Okay, we'll stay. Judy never said anything about you, so my parents think you're just a great hero who wants to help Chinese people. I'll make sure she keeps her mouth shut and I'll make up a story. When are you coming back?"

"I don't know. Killing Meike made me realize what a rotten person I am. I don't want to be around anyone."

"You saved the Republican nominee for President from assassination.'

"I killed someone who loved me."

"You had to do it." She paused for a moment, "Do you love me?"

"Yes, but I'm not very good for anybody."

I hung up the phone and opened a window to get some cross ventilation. How should I behave now that I'd told Feng Feng I loved her? David Niven, a man I respected, had already left Hollywood for the Royal Air Force. Churchill wanted to give me a medal. Now that I know how to kill, maybe killing was my destiny.

I took my bathrobe off and began to do sit ups. Before I knew it, I had completed 100 and my pajamas were wet from exertion.

It was going to be a long night.

CHAPTER SEVENTY SEVEN

The next morning I called the ranch and spoke to Fernando.

"Is the whole family there?"

"Yes they are and they all seem to be comfortable," he said. I was shocked by his upbeat voice and the perfect English.

"That's great," I said.

"There are two Highway Patrolmen at the gate and two behind the house," he said. "I know you want your friends to eat well, so I will be going into Los Angeles with Mrs. Chung so she can buy a lot of ingredients for cooking," he said.

"That's great," I said, wondering if he was going to surprise me by singing the *Ave Maria*, or something by Cole Porter.

"Say," he said, "Miss Feng Feng is your girlfriend, right? She talks like it," he said.

"Yes. Why do you ask?"

"I was just wondering," he said. "I'll put Miss Feng Feng on the phone."

"Holy smokes," I said to Feng Feng. "Did you put some strange herb in Fernando's tea?"

"He's been wonderful," she said. "He's very well spoken and quite handsome."

"Fernando?"

"This morning he gave us a tour of the ranch and he put on a suit to show respect," she said.

I didn't know what to say.

She then whispered, "Judy owns him."

"So love comes to Andy Hardy," I said.

"That sounded like Mongolian to me," she said.

"Just a show business joke," I said. "So Fernando, the tower of strength, now has a ring through his nose. Does Judy like him?"

"He's nice, but does he understand relativity? The poor man will end up disappointed. He already told my mom that Indians are descended from the Chinese and that some bridge closed and they couldn't get back home," she said.

"The Chinese on the Mayflower went back with the ship because they didn't like the looks of Plymouth Rock," I said.

"Killing her made you very upset, I can tell. I feel very bad for you. Your jokes don't sound right and your conversation sounds like you're just trying to keep up your end and that's all," she said.

"I feel guilty about telling you this. She was beautiful and treated me great, but she was nuttier than a fruitcake. It was like being near one of those tornadoes that pick people up and throw them across villages. When the neighbors clean up, they always find bodies, not live people.

"I'm surprised at how easy it was to pull the trigger. It seems to have changed me and that's driving me nuts."

"We could have used a couple of people like you after Chaing fled and the Japanese surrounded Nanjing," she said. "You had to kill those people; you didn't set out to do it."

"Thanks for trying to make me feel better but it may be a while before I get over this. This isn't the first person I'd killed since I began doing this, but she certainly was the person I knew the best," I said.

"Relax on the ranch. You and your sister haven't lived in a big place in a long time. Your family ought to stay there for awhile. By the way, I'm willing to make an honest woman of you," I said.

"Really?"

"What will your parents do?"

"Turn you into wonton soup," said a voice on the phone.

Feng Feng was silent for a moment. "That makes me feel wonderful. I feel really wonderful." There was joy in her voice.

"If Judy got off the line, tell her she can stay as long as she wants and if she wants to marry Fernando, I'll vouch for the fact his mom ran a Chinese restaurant in Juarez."

"You are such a sap," said Judy.

"Shen jing bing!" Feng Feng responded.

I had an idea. "Since you're living on a ranch you ought to learn to ride my quarter horse. See if Fernando can find a guy named Jimmy Williams and have him give you lessons."

"Okay, Pardner," Feng Feng said. "I'll start making baked beans Sichuan style when I see your wagon train at the top of Sepulveda Pass."

I let that image go, but let her voice stay in my mind until the ceaseless activity of midnight Manhattan carried me off to sleep.